# saVage

## CHRONICLES *of* NICK:
### SHADOWS OF FIRE

## SHERRILYN KENYON

OLIVER**HEBER**BOOKS

# PROLOGUE

"His father doesn't want him."

Azura froze as she heard the last words she wanted to hear. "What?"

"Lord Jaden said that he has no use for anything that'll tie him to you. He told us to take it from his sight and drown it."

Fury boiled up within her with such ferocity that she slung her arm out and obliterated the demon beside her with her powers. That made the imbecile in front of her, clutching the infant, step backward out of fear.

He should be afraid. Normally, she'd have already disemboweled him for delivering news she didn't want to hear, as that was what she always did.

"Now, repeat what you just said to me."

The demon gulped audibly as he shifted the baby in his arms.

"He said that he had no use for a child, and for you to drown it."

Using her telekinesis, she ripped her worthless son from the arms of the demon before she splintered said demon against the far wall.

The baby hovered in the air before her, squalling. Red in the face and weak beyond her tolerance. Pathetic, disgusting waste of breath and time.

Another useless brat. Why had she bothered?

She had no use for it, either. The sole purpose of conceiving the hideous thing had been to tie Jaden to her. She should have known he'd be smarter than that.

Still, Jaden was a god of light. As such, she'd expected him to at least want to see his own child cared for. To raise it. To not just ignore it.

But if he didn't want that...

She waved her hand and banished the whiny, smelly thing to whatever demon desired a baby. She had no time to change diapers or feed something so worthless.

If she was lucky, it'd be dead within hours and she'd never have to look at it again...unlike that other thing she hated more than anything.

"What happened?"

She turned at the sound of her brother's voice. Darker than the sin he'd invented, Noir stood head and shoulders over her. He was ruggedly handsome and so cocksure that she wanted to slap him for it.

The only thing that kept her from it was the knowledge that he didn't slap back.

He punched.

She'd like to say that she was meaner, but she knew better. Noir was the most corrupt and dangerous being ever spawned, and she had no desire to test him.

"You were right about the beast." Those words absolutely galled her, and she was surprised she didn't choke while saying them.

He tsked at her. "Of course I was. Nothing controls Jaden, and you know it. He's an entity unto himself. I told you not to waste your time."

"Shut up."

Instead, he moved closer to her. "So what's to become of that brat now?"

"Who cares?"

He arched a brow at her. "*You* should."

"Why?"

Laughing bitterly, he shook his head. "You really have no idea what you've created, do you?"

Of course she did. "I had a baby." It wasn't as if it'd been her first.

"No, sister. You had a *god*. One born with an equal share of light and dark. This one isn't like your other halfling, the useless son born of that pathetic Naṣāru you crawled into bed with, or our precious daughter."

A sick feeling began in the pit of her stomach as she considered a fact she'd missed before.

"Yeah," he said, cruelly. "Just like with Mastema, he could turn on you. You have delivered something into this world that could easily have the same powers as you *and* Jaden. More, even. You never know how such powers will merge, any more than you know which side such a beast will choose to serve. His father's...or ours. And the powers of his children could be even stronger, depending on who their mother is."

"Then why did Jaden refuse it?"

"He's an idiot. Always has been. He acts with no thought and all emotion. He never sees the future. Failure to think ahead. Normally, you have more sense."

Yes, she did. But she'd been so focused on controlling one of their greatest enemies that she'd lost sight of the means by which she'd chosen to leash him.

An unpredictable child. As her brother had noted, she'd already had one turn against her.

"How do we guarantee the brat will side with us?"

Noir laughed bitterly. "We don't. No one can predict what a child will do. They're vicious that way. You have to beat them into shape and pray that you've beaten them down enough that they don't dare try to defy you."

That tended to be true. Sadly, everyone she knew had a child that had turned on them no matter how much they'd controlled them.

Everyone. Including her. She'd done her best with her eldest son. Beaten him until he couldn't stand. Until he was unconscious. It'd done her no good whatsoever. Little brat had refused to obey even the simplest request.

*Kill it...*

Now, before he grew older and so powerful that she wasn't able to end his life. That would be the best and safest thing to do.

It was the only thing to do, really. Why chance another son turning on her?

Determined to set this right, she left Noir and headed to the demonic realm where she'd banished her bastard.

Azmodea. She hated it here. Dreary and dark, it was populated by demons and other bottom feeders she didn't want to deal with. Why was this even a place?

Created by the Source, it was said to be the realm where all hope went to die. Where misery was born and all evil flourished. Personally, she just thought it was depressing. Why demons wanted to congregate here, she couldn't imagine.

In fact, there was nothing more wretched to her than being forced to live here.

"And it smells like hell's farts! Ugh! Why does it stink like this?" she shouted in frustration and fury as she stamped her foot.

Snapping her fingers, she willed herself to the place she'd banished her brat.

Azura found herself inside a building made of drab gray walls that echoed with something that sounded like a dull, buzzing waterfall. Not melodic or soothing. Irritating.

"What is making that noise?"

No one answered.

Even more agitated, she turned around slowly to see more nothing. Just ick. Everywhere. Drab, boring ick. "Where's my baby?"

"Why do you want a child?"

The voice came out of thin air.

That would be disturbing in its own right, but the fact that she couldn't sense anyone or anything...

It actually sent a shiver up her spine.

"Who are you?"

The buzzing waterfall grew louder and seemed to move closer. What the hell?

"I am Darkness. The shadows are my friends."

Azura smirked. "Don't play with me. I'm not in the mood. I need my child."

"The one you threw away?"

"None of your business. Hand him over. Now!"

The disembodied voice tsked. "How thoughtless of you to misplace a child."

"I didn't misplace the beast. I banished it."

"For being born?"

Azura growled in her throat. "For being an annoyance. Should I banish you, too?"

"Only if you can find me." The voice trailed off.

Azura wanted blood. But there was no trace of her child or the creature taunting her. None of her powers detected either of them.

Had that little bastard died? That would be a blessing.

Sadly, her luck wasn't that good. Which meant she'd need to send her soldiers out to find him.

"If it's the last thing I do, I'll see you dead, brat! And you too, annoying voice! Run if you like, but I will find you."

MICHI DIDN'T SPEAK or move until she was certain the angry goddess was gone. Clutching the naked baby boy in her arms, she felt terrible for him. "Do you even have a name, little one? Did she bother to give you one?"

He blinked at her, then yawned and snuggled against her shoulder.

Poor, poor thing. No one wanted him. His mother—not that she wanted to call that beast of a goddess a mother—had thrown him away to this realm with no regard for such a precious treasure.

Who could do such a thing?

Had Michi not been napping in this area, there was no telling what would have happened to the child. There were many here who would have eaten him. Or done even more unspeakable things to the innocent babe.

Now...

"What do I know of being a mother?" She wasn't much more than a kit herself.

More than that, she hated being in a human body more than anything. Normally, she was a white fox. She'd been a fox when the boy had appeared next to her on the cold floor. Squalling, he'd rudely awakened her from her nap.

Her first instinct had been to kill him just to get him to stop crying.

But he was a baby. A tiny, harmless little thing, reaching out to her for comfort.

And she'd been unable to deny him what he sought. So she'd changed into a human body and picked him up to soothe him. He'd quieted down instantly.

"You are cute." His blue eyes glistened in the dim light

while he sucked on his fist and cooed ever so sweetly. Dark hair covered his small head.

So trusting. She couldn't remember a time in her life when she'd trusted anyone. Not for anything.

No. Something like this should never be harmed. Life would strip his innocence from him all too soon. There was no reason for her to turn him over to his monster of a mother so that she could make him a monster in her image.

He needed someone to protect him and show him a better way to live. At least for a while.

"You'll be my little kit," Michi whispered. "I'll take care of you, precious. Just remember when you're older who your enemies are and who protected you from them."

**1**

---

FOUR YEARS LATER

"Mama?"

Michi smiled at the tender little voice that never failed to warm her. "Yes, Xevikan?"

"Why can't I go out and play?"

"You know why."

He sighed heavily at the answer she gave him almost every day. "It's been years, Mama. Maybe the evil goddess forgot me."

She laughed. Years...While it was the whole of his young life, it was only a blink to the ones who were looking for him. Immortals didn't measure time the way others did.

And Azura had not forgotten. Her demons searched constantly for any sign of this child. They were still desperate to reunite him with a mother who had no real use for him. Michi's worse fear was what they'd do to her baby. The stories they heard of what happened to those in Azura's court...

Stuff of nightmares.

"How about we play together in our den?"

Xev made an adorable face at her. "I don't want to play the hiding game. I want to explore what's outside our home."

If only they could. It made her heart ache that she couldn't give him what he wanted most. "It's too dangerous, love. You have to stay here so that I can love you."

Pressing his lips together, he sat down heavily at her feet. "Fine. We can play the hiding game. No one will see me."

He vanished.

She'd be afraid, but he sat on her foot so she knew he was still there. "You're a good boy, Xev."

He reappeared and lay back with a heavy sigh. "Can you at least teach me to turn into a fox?"

"I don't know if you can."

"Can we try?"

Michi considered it. She really didn't know what powers he possessed. Other than the ability to simultaneously annoy and charm her. He was amazing in that capacity.

Turning into a fox, she licked his cheek. "Of course we can."

He giggled and wrapped his sweet little arms around her neck while he buried his face in her fur. "I love when you're a fox, Mama."

"I love you." She nuzzled his cheek. "Now close your eyes and imagine being a fox."

He did.

Nothing happened.

Just as she was about to tell him that she didn't think he could, he changed forms.

Into a cat.

"Did I do it?" His voice was so excited as he held up an orange paw.

"Sort of. Would you like some milk?"

"What?" He cocked his head.

"You're a cat, sweetie. Not a fox."

He made a sound of supreme annoyance. "A cat?" He shook his head, then returned to his toddler form. "A cat?" he asked again in an adorable, sad tone.

"It's not always easy to change, little Xev. Sometimes, it takes great effort."

He sneezed and turned into a fox.

She laughed at the shocked expression on his perfect face. "There you go. That wasn't so hard, was it?"

"Didn't mean to do it."

"That's the way it goes. Sometimes things happen when we mean for them to, and other times...they just happen when we least expect it and aren't looking for it to happen."

"Can I turn back?"

Such a simple question. "Sometimes."

"Sometimes?" His eyes widened in panic.

She nodded. "Some days you want to turn back and

other days you need to just trudge forward. No matter what. No matter how much you want to stop."

He frowned at her words. She was giving him advice he was far too young to understand.

But the day would come, sadly, when he would know exactly what she meant. Even if they were immortal, time would pass, and no matter how much she wished it, she wouldn't always be here to protect him. His mother continued to hunt for him, and her demons were relentless. Every part of Michi said that the day would come when Azura would separate them.

Or something else would.

All Michi could do was try her best to hone his powers and teach him what she knew about hiding and shifting. About life and living. To give him as many skills as she could before his enemies came for him and forced them apart.

He crawled into her arms.

She turned human so that she could hold him close. "I might not have birthed you, little one. But you're my baby just the same."

"Love you, Mama."

Burying her hand in his soft, dark hair, she cherished those words. How weird that she'd never wanted a child. Or anyone to take care of, for that matter. Life was too harsh for that. It was hard enough just to watch out for herself.

Yet this precious baby she loved so much had fallen straight into her lap. Now, she couldn't imagine not having him with her. The thought of his loss filled her with such terror and pain that she couldn't even contemplate it.

"Michi!"

She winced at the goddess's angry call. Inari was the one person she couldn't ignore, and she couldn't imagine why her goddess had such a tone with her. What could she have possibly done to incur her goddess's anger?

Kissing Xev's head, she nudged him toward her bed. "Stay here until my return."

"I know. Talk to no one. Don't let anyone know I'm here. Never be seen or heard."

"Exactly." Michi pulled away from him, and then carefully concealed the small hole that led to their den so that no one would know either of them had ever been there.

Spreading her hand wide, she touched it as love and fear swelled inside her. She hated to leave him alone even for a moment.

If only she had a choice.

With a deep breath to steady her nerves, she left him and went to the goddess she served.

Alone in her private garden, Inari stood before the mirrored wall that showed her millions of scattered images of the human world. Michi had never understood how her goddess could follow them all, but Inari never seemed to have any trouble discerning one from another.

Or hearing the pleas of the many. Perhaps that was what made her a goddess while Michi was nothing more than a poor demonic servant.

Tall and lithe, with long black hair that fell to her ankles, Inari was the most beautiful woman Michi had ever seen. No one could match her for grace or wit. Even water envied her for calm dignity.

"You summoned me, my lady?"

Inari's dark brown eyes held sorrow inside them. Her entire demeanor bespoke of some deep sadness that had the goddess wrapped tighter than the blood-red cloak she clutched. "Do you remember whom you serve?"

"You, my goddess."

"That's right. But I've seen in my mirror that you have loyalty to someone else."

"Never!" Michi took her human form so that Inari could see the sincerity. "Why would you doubt me?"

Inari held her hand up to show a gust of smoke that solidified into figures moving about.

Michi gasped as she saw herself taking care of Xev in their hidden den.

Inari's gaze flared with fury. "Is that not another god you care for?"

She didn't see Xev like that. "He's a child, my lady. Just a baby."

"A god, nonetheless."

Technically. "He has no power. He's as helpless as…" She struggled to find an example, but only one thing came to mind. "Well, a babe."

The figures fell and faded to nothing while Inari stared at her. "He won't always be such. All too soon, he'll grow into an enemy."

"No, great lady. His heart is pure. He's a wonderful baby. He'd never cause harm, especially not to you."

That angered the ancient goddess even more. "Are you arguing with me?"

"No, lady." Only an absolute fool would do that.

"Then kill him."

Those words tore through her with barbed edges that left her soul bleeding. Her breathing intensified.

"Did you hear me?" Inari said through clenched teeth.

"I did." But Michi couldn't believe Inari would be so callous or cruel.

"I want his heart brought to me. You have one hour."

One hour. How could she make such a demand? It was unreasonable.

Michi wanted to scream. How could she kill the very infant she'd suckled and cared for?

*Turn him over to his mother.*

Her soul screamed even louder at the thought. Surely, death would be kinder for the child.

But the thought of that...

No. She could never kill her baby.

Michi bowed low before her goddess and then returned to the den where she'd left her most beloved son. The only one she'd ever loved.

"Mama?"

That single word made her heart soar and shattered it into pieces. "I'm here, love."

Xev crawled toward her. "Are you all right?"

She pulled him into her arms and held him close. Tears choked her, but she didn't dare let them fall. "No. Not really." She would never be right again. Not if she did this.

He hugged her close. "Don't be sad, Mama. Smile and it'll make everything okay."

That succeeded in causing her tears to flow. It was something she'd said to him many times whenever he was hurting.

Now...

There was no help for them. No way to make it better.

She was going to have to give him up, and it would destroy her.

Xev placed his tiny hand to her cheek. "Why are you crying, Mama?"

"Because I love you."

"That should make you happy."

It did and it didn't.

*Damn you, Inari!*

Damn the mother that had birthed him!

Most of all, she damned herself. How could she let go of the one and only person who meant anything to her?

"You're hurting me." Xev squirmed against her, making her realize just how tightly she held him against her body.

"I'm so sorry, kit."

"It's okay. I'm not running away. I told you I'd never leave you or our home."

Her worst fear for him outside of his mother finding them. If only it was still her worst fear.

"Xev, if I do something, will you forgive me?"

"Always. You're my mama."

That only made more tears blind her. "I will always be your mother, love. Always. No matter what happens or where I am. But I have to return you to the one who birthed you."

"No!" His face blanched. "You said she'd hurt me."

"I know. But if I don't, another goddess will kill you."

He scowled. "Mama, I don't understand. Why would anyone want to kill me?"

She placed her cheek against his and sobbed. "I have no choice, baby. I have to do this." Even if it meant her life. She couldn't let him die.

He was worth her life. He was worth everything because he was everything to her. "Just promise that you won't forget me."

"You're my mama. How could I ever forget you?"

But deep inside, she knew he was too young. He'd never recall her when he was older, or if he did, he'd curse her for this betrayal. And who could blame him? This was an unforgivable act.

It didn't matter. He was her life. She'd spent the last handful of years protecting him, knowing she'd be killed if Azura found them.

Her hand shook as she cradled him.

Dying inside, she stood up and transported them to the court of the bitch who'd forced them into hiding.

Azura sat on her throne, laughing with her brother, who terrified Michi. Her skin was an icy blue that matched the coldness of her white hair and eyes. Everyone claimed this goddess had no heart. No soul.

She took mercy on no one and was incapable of love.

Michi wanted to run. But while she had the powers to

hide from Azura, she didn't have the ability to deceive Inari. Inari would always know the truth.

And she'd kill them both out of spite. No one defied Inari's orders.

*I have to do this.*

The moment the goddess saw her and the boy she carried, Azura's countenance turned to stone. She stood up slowly.

So did Noir.

"What do you have, fox?"

"No, Mama. Please," Xev whispered.

For the first time ever, Michi denied his wishes. "I have to," she said under her breath, for both of their benefits.

Walking on legs that threatened to buckle, she headed toward the Queen of All Shadows. "I have your son, my goddess." She knelt before her and prayed that this was the right thing to do.

Azura plucked Xev from her arms and held him up by the scruff of his shirt. "What a puny thing you are." Sneering, she raked a glare over Michi. "Is it housebroken?"

Her stomach sank with such force that she feared she'd vomit. "He's potty trained, lady."

Xev bit his lip as he saw his birth mother for the first time. The look of fear in those beautiful blue eyes seared Michi's soul with pain.

Azura tossed him at her brother, who didn't even try to catch the boy. Instead, he let Xev fall to the floor, where he lay unmoving.

Shattered by that sight, Michi started forward, but Azura cut her off.

"What do I owe you for your service?"

"Can you protect me from Inari?"

Azura scowled. "What?"

"The goddess Inari. She ordered me to kill your son. I brought him to you instead. I know you've been looking for him."

Laughing, Azura exchanged a look with her brother that Michi didn't understand. "You want me to save you from the wrath of a goddess you serve?"

"I do."

"Very well." Azura snapped her fingers.

Michi's throat closed until she could no longer draw breath. Her ears began to ring. Choking, she fell over and did her best to gasp.

Azura was killing her.

Of course she was. Why would she expect mercy from a goddess known for vengeance?

But at least her final sight would be her son...He pushed himself up and started to run for her.

He never made it.

# 2

## FOUR YEARS LATER

"Daraxerxes!"

Xev sighed heavily at the name he hated almost as much as the woman who'd given it to him. Rising from the dice game he'd been playing by himself, he turned to watch her appear in his dismal little room that had about as much personality as the shadow demons who usually spied on him at his mother's behest.

"What are you doing?" Azura demanded.

"Avoiding you," he answered honestly as he put his dice bag into his pocket.

As expected, those words caused her to backhand him. He ignored the pain of the blow. He was too used to them to feel it anymore. It was, after all, her standard greeting.

The first thing he'd learned when his mother died was that this bitch had no mercy or use for him, or anyone else.

Their hatred was a mutual thing, as the mere thought of Azura could wreck even his best mood. Though, to be honest, he expected that his was a little stronger than hers, given the fact she fueled his hatred every single day.

Licking the blood from his lips, he gave her an insolent stare. "Is that what you wanted?" To knock him around for no reason.

She hissed at him. "Watch your tongue!"

"I would if I had eyes in my mouth. Sadly, that task is impossible."

She drew back to strike him again.

Xev vanished before she had the chance.

"Come back here, brat!"

He reappeared in the corner, where he floated above the floor with his black wings gently flapping, out of her reach. "Rather not."

"You can't hide from me!"

Willing to test that theory, he flew out the window and left her to rail at his fleeing shadow. There was no telling why she'd sought him, and honestly, he didn't care. Her rages were legendary. The only good thing about them was that they didn't usually last long. They were too violent. Not even such a crazy goddess could sustain them for long.

Skimming the sky, he looked down at the world where men and women lived. A world Azura was hellbent on destroying, for reasons only she knew. Though he suspected it was because she couldn't stand for anyone to be happy.

For anyone to have peace.

He didn't understand it. His aunt, Lilit, had tried to explain it to him many times.

"It's not her fault, dear. We were born as we are. Three made of darkness and three of light."

That had only confused him more as he stared at his golden-haired, golden-eyed aunt. "You're not."

"Like you, child, I'm both. Torn between the two. A foot in two graves, always."

Xev was only now beginning to understand that last bit. While he had the same urge as his mother to lash out and destroy everything around him, especially whenever he was angry, he didn't like watching others suffer.

Such as the little girl in the field below. She was crying over something, and that made him ache for her. Why was she so upset?

Curious, Xev flew closer.

No older than he was, she wore a plain, baggy dress that was far too large for her skinny limbs. Tears streaked her rosy cheeks.

"Mama!" Her scream ricocheted through the trees.

There was no mother to be found.

Had her mother died, like Michi had?

Wanting to help the unknown girl, Xev lowered himself to the human world and then tucked his wings into his skin so that they wouldn't frighten her. He'd learned long ago that people didn't like things that were different.

And his black, feathered wings were definitely different from their human bodies.

She ran past where he was hidden behind a tree.

"Are you all right?"

She turned toward him and screamed. Until she saw that he was a boy and not something scary.

If only she knew the truth…He could be scary if he wanted to. But he didn't want to frighten her.

She paused in the midst of her screaming. "What are you doing here?"

"Standing."

Unlike Azura, who hated whenever he stated the obvious, the girl laughed. "So you are."

He took a step closer to her. "Why are calling for your mother?"

"I lost her."

That explained it. "Did you forget where you put her?"

That made her laugh even harder. "No. I wandered off to chase a bunny. When I tried to find my way back to the stream where she was washing our clothes, I couldn't find it."

Oh. He'd never had that problem. Michi had refused to allow him out of his sight. And he'd tried to lose Azura, many times. Sadly, she always found him.

Xev held his hand out to the girl. "I can help."

"Can you?"

He nodded. Finding people wasn't very hard. But then, he wasn't human. For some reason, he just knew where they were whenever he wanted someone.

She placed her hand in his and held tightly. That sensation was odd to him. He'd never touched a human before.

For an instant, he felt his mother's powers rising inside

him. They wanted to lash out and see her scream. To break the delicate bones in her hand and feel them burst in his palm.

But it was just a fleeting impulse. One he pushed down furiously. He would not be the monster who'd birthed him. He didn't like seeing others suffer.

He wanted to be like Michi. Kind and generous. Someone who protected those who didn't try to harm him.

So, he used his powers to search the wind and aether that surrounded them always. Michi had called it the voice of the universe. If one listened, one could find everything in it.

And he immediately saw her worried mother. Like her daughter, she was crying and calling out as she searched frantically in the forest. "Your name is Chani?"

"How did you know?"

Xev offered her a glib smile. "Your mother's calling for you."

"You can hear her?"

Nodding, he let go of her hand. "Follow me." He started in the opposite direction of where the girl had been heading.

She refused to follow. "Are you sure this is right?" she asked, her voice trembling in fear.

"Positive. You can trust me, Chani. I'll take you to your mother."

Still, she hesitated before she decided to follow after him. "Are you from the village?"

"No."

That seemed to confuse her. "Then where do you live?"

He started to answer, then stopped himself. They weren't supposed to interact with humans. While he didn't know what the punishment was, he knew Azura would gleefully mete it out to him. One thing he'd learned long ago was not to give his birth mother any reason to reach for a whip.

"Does it matter where I live?"

Chani screwed her face up. "Guess not."

Now that he was with her, she no longer cried, and actually appeared happy.

Weird.

No one was ever happy when he was around.

*That's not true.* Michi had always been happy whenever he was near.

Xev winced at the memory of his beloved mother. He did his best to never think of her. It hurt too much. Yet he couldn't seem to stop himself.

Even now, he could see her beautiful face. Feel the warmth of her hugs. It was the only happiness he'd ever known. Probably the only happiness he'd ever have in his life. Maybe that was why he clung to it.

Although he was enjoying Chani's company. Even if they didn't speak, she was still comforting, and he had no idea why. Was this normal? The gods knew he never enjoyed the company of his mother's demons or the other gods. They were a nasty lot he did his best to avoid at all costs.

Chani began to hum and sing.

After a few minutes, she stopped and eyed him. "Do you have name, boy?"

"Xev."

"I've never heard that name before."

He shrugged. "I've never heard Chani before, either."

She laughed as she skipped beside him. "Then we're both unique."

Maybe. He wasn't sure what would make a god unique. Humans either, for that matter. All he'd ever heard about them was that they were animals, incapable of rational thought. Though, to be honest, she seemed to be as smart as any god or demon he knew.

Smarter than many, actually.

She was definitely kinder and more fun. Unlike the others he knew, she wasn't trying to hurt him. She seemed happy enough just to exist.

That was unfathomable to him.

And all too soon, they found her mother and a group of men who were searching the woods for her.

Xev paused as he watched Chani run into her mother's arms. Weeping, the woman scooped her up and cradled her the way Michi used to hold him.

Sadness filled him as he watched them. *I miss you, Mama.* More than he could express. She'd been so kind and gentle.

Most of all, he missed having someone who worried about him. Someone who didn't hit for no reason.

The girl's mother rained kisses over Chani's face until she saw him at the edge of their field. "Who is that?"

Chani smiled. "He's my friend, Xev. He helped me find my way back to you."

Her mother clutched Chani to her side as she walked toward Xev, while the men walked away and returned to wherever they'd come from. "I can't thank you enough."

He felt like he should say something, but he didn't know what. He wasn't used to gratitude. Only insults.

Biting his lip, he became nervous.

"Where do you live? I'd love to tell your parents what a wonderful boy you are."

He couldn't tell her where he lived. She'd never believe him, any more than Azura would believe he was a wonderful boy. Besides, Azura would probably hurt her for being human.

"I don't have parents." That was the truth, as neither his mother nor his father wanted much of anything to do with him. He might as well be an orphan. He'd have been better off as such.

She gasped at his words. "None?"

"My mama died." Also true. He had never considered Azura his mother. Just a massive pain he'd rather avoid.

"What of your father?"

"Never met him." Mostly because Michi had impressed upon him that meeting his father would be a very bad idea.

Azura hadn't softened that opinion. *He hates you and everything to do with you. He told me to kill you when you were born, and I should have. Why didn't I listen to him? We all would have been better off!*

Since Jaden had never made any attempt to see him,

Xev had no choice other than to believe Azura and Michi that his father hated him and wanted him even deader than his birth mother did most days.

Chani's mother gave him a sad expression. "I'm so sorry. You poor thing."

How strange. He'd never felt particularly poor. In fact, he had everything he could need. Food. Clothes. Plenty of demons who envied him. Although that last bit had never made any sense. He'd gladly trade his life for one of theirs just so he wouldn't have to deal with Azura.

No one had ever called him poor before. He wasn't even sure what made someone poor.

The demons were right. Humans were peculiar.

With a smile, Chani's mother held her hand out to him. "Would you like to come to our home? Least I could do is feed you for your kindness."

Chani's face lit up. "Oh, do come, Xev! My mother is the best cook in all the world!"

He scowled at her opinion. "Have you sampled all the food in the world?"

Chani looked confused, while her mother laughed.

"Come on, sweetling."

Since he had nothing else to do and really didn't want to go to his home, Xev trotted along after them.

"You really were lost," he said as he noted how far Chani had traveled as she sought her mother.

"Right? I have no idea how I walked so far by accident."

"Did you not realize it?"

Chani shrugged. "I kept thinking if I kept walking, I'd

find something familiar." She held her hand up to her lips so that she could speak to him behind her cupped fingers. "I didn't find anything, until you. Had you not been there, I'd have been lost forever."

Her mother shook her head. "How many times have I told you not to run off on your own?"

"I know, Mama. I'm sorry. I won't ever do it again. I promise."

Shaking her head, her mom sighed heavily. "You have no idea what could have happened to you! I'm so glad Xev found you and not someone a lot scarier."

Chani rolled her eyes as if she didn't believe her mother.

"Your mom's right, Chani. There are a lot of evil things that live only to make others cry. They're bigger than you are and faster. When they catch you..." He broke off at memories he wished he didn't have. "You should always stay with your mother. Stay close to home." Like Michi used to tell him to do.

She'd been right about that, too.

Her mom stopped, then knelt down by his side. "Has someone hurt you, Xev?"

"Many times."

She drew him into a hug like the ones Michi used to give him. "I'm so sorry."

He didn't understand why she was sorry. But he liked the hug. He'd missed them so much. There was nothing better he could imagine than the sensation of someone holding him close.

Kissing his cheek, the woman pulled away and ruffled

his dark hair. She took his and Chani's hands and walked them back to her small cottage.

A weird pain that he didn't understand hit him hard in the center of his chest. "I'm sorry that I made you sad."

Chani's mother smiled down at him. "You don't make me sad, Xev. The world does. It should never be hurtful to a child your age." She lifted his hand up and gently kissed it.

Xev slowed as he saw their tiny home. It reminded him of his den with Michi. Except they'd never had furniture inside theirs. And that was okay. He hadn't needed any. Michi's fur had been the best bed imaginable.

Chani ran to the small table and sat in a chair.

Xev frowned as he saw the four other chairs around the table. "Do you have more people in your family?"

Chani laughed at his question. "My father. He's away from home, selling our crops and some of Mama's bread." She reached for a bowl in the center of the table that had a cloth over it. Pulling back a corner, she showed him what it contained.

Xev sat down beside her as she handed him a piece of the loaf. He was expecting it to taste like the loaves they had at his mother's palace.

But this was sweet and wonderful. "You're right. Your mom is the best cook in all the world!"

Her mother laughed as she set down two glasses of milk for them. "I'm glad you like it, Lord Xev."

"I *love* it!"

He spent the next hour sampling everything the

woman put in front of him. He couldn't remember a time in his life when he'd eaten so much.

Indeed, his stomach felt as if it would burst. At the moment, he probably weighed so much that his wings wouldn't be able to lift him from the ground. That was okay. He didn't want to fly home.

He envied Chani for being able to eat like this all the time.

Her mother smiled at him. "I'm glad you like my food."

"I do! It's wonderful." Xev reached for his glass and burped loudly. Heat scalded his cheeks. "I'm so sorry!"

Laughing, she patted him on the back. "Best compliment you could give me."

Chani giggled. "Is there any cake, Mama?"

Xev smiled at his favorite word in the world. "Cake? You have cake, too?"

Chani's mom laughed again. "Where are you two putting all this food? Are you sure you don't have hollow legs?"

"I had a hollow belly, but it's almost full now." Xev screwed his face up as he thought about it. "But I'm sure there's just enough room left inside it for some cake."

Shaking her head, she walked to a small cabinet and opened it so that he could see the honey cake it had concealed.

Eyes wide, Xev exchanged an eager look with Chani.

"You'll love it."

"I know I will." Rubbing his hands together, he could

barely wait for her mom to cut him a slice. He dug in the moment she set it on the table in front of him.

It was just as good as Chani had predicted. Maybe better.

Her mother laughed at his eagerness. "Don't lick the plate, dear. I have plenty more where that came from."

Xev pulled away with a bashful grin. "It was so good that I couldn't stop myself. I wanted to make sure I got every last bit."

With that beautiful smile, she kissed his head...then brought him another slice.

Xev dug in.

*Where are you, brat?*

He flinched at the sound of Azura's shrewish voice in his head. It was as if she always knew whenever he was happy, and she sought to destroy it. Could he not have one day where she didn't storm in and ruin everything?

*Don't answer.* It never ended well when he answered, and he was having too much fun to be bothered with her.

So he ignored her summons.

They spent another hour laughing and having fun. Xev never wanted it to end.

But just when he was getting up from the table, the door burst open. Xev couldn't breathe as he recognized the six demons who were under Azura's control.

Chani and her mother screamed and tried to run, but the demons surrounded them. Clutching one another, the pair cried and begged for mercy.

He shoved the demon closest to him. "Leave them alone!"

"Xev, don't. Just do what they say." Tears streaked Chani's mother's beautiful face. "He's just a boy. Don't hurt him!"

Keramon turned on Xev with a hiss. "You should have answered when you were called."

The demon turned toward Chani.

Xev screamed, then blasted the demon with a fire bolt. Normally when he did such, a white light shot out of his hands and knocked his target away.

This time…

Keramon exploded.

Eyes wide, Xev stared at his hands, unable to believe he'd done that. What was *that*?

The other demons shrank back from him.

Like he was his mother. That caused a sick lump in his stomach. He never wanted anyone or anything to recoil at his presence.

Not even a demon he hated.

His birth monster appeared instantly, as if Keramon's death had summoned her. "What is going on here?"

He winced. The wrath on her face was legendary. He'd never seen her any angrier.

"Answer me!" she demanded.

"He's protecting humans, lady."

She arched a white eyebrow at that. "Pardon?"

The demon on his left gestured at Chani and her mother.

Terror whipped through Xev. There was no telling what she might do to them.

Without thinking, he ran and put himself between them and Azura.

"What. Are. You. Doing?" Each word was punctuated and spat between her clenched teeth.

He met his mother's gaze without flinching. "Please don't hurt them. They're my friends."

That only angered her more. She grabbed him and pulled him to stand in front of her. "Don't worry. I'm not the one who's going to kill them. You are."

Xev's stomach sank. "What? No!"

She twisted his arm so badly that it felt as if she'd wrench it from his shoulder. "Do it!"

Snarling, he shook his head. "Kill *me*!"

That caught her off guard. He saw the shock on her face. She wasn't used to anyone ever refusing her orders. But he wasn't anyone. He was her mistake, and they both knew it.

"Xev?"

The panic in Chani's voice made him want to retch.

"You won't harm them, you snake! I won't let you."

With a furious shriek, Azura threw him to her demons. "Take that home and watch that worthless slug until I get there!"

Xev tried to fight them, but Azura had done something so that he couldn't. His powers wouldn't work at all. He couldn't even free his wings. He was utterly helpless.

Utterly pissed.

"Don't you dare touch them!" Those were the last words he said before the demons hauled him home.

Fear and grief mixed inside him as he looked at the

gilded throne room and the demons who were stationed around him to keep him from leaving. Growling, he felt his powers surging. He had to go help Chani and her mother. He owed them that much.

Xev tried to leave.

A demon caught him and knocked him back.

Xev hissed as pain exploded across his cheek.

Laughing, another demon stepped forward to hit him.

In that moment, something inside him snapped. He'd been hit one time too many. Tortured more than anyone should be. He was done with it.

*I'm not an animal.*

He was a god...

His wings sprang from his back at the same time he felt a massive electrical surge through his entire body. A sonic boom radiated from within him, throwing the demons back. The windows around him shattered...

Along with his mother's throne.

Xev had never felt anything like this. Throwing his head back, he roared with the ferocity of emotions he couldn't even begin to explain.

It broke whatever spell his mother had placed on him and allowed him to return to the small cottage where he'd known the first real peace he'd experienced since Michi died.

Flames lit the darkness as they licked against the wood and thatch of Chani's little cottage. There was no sound other than the crackling fire.

Not until he heard Azura's shriek.

"Who let you out!" Not a question. A shrill demand.

Xev snarled at her. "Where are they?"

She gestured at the fire.

Pain slammed into him as he realized that she'd killed them both. Not that he hadn't already guessed what their fate would be at her hands. But the confirmation tore him apart. "They were innocent!"

She laughed bitterly. "No one's innocent. Grow up."

Of course she thought that. She was rotten to the core of her immortal soul.

Furious and in bitter need of retribution, he blasted her before he could think better of it.

Azura gasped at the sensation of his blast that sent her rolling backward.

Sadly, not as far as he'd hoped. She caught herself, then rose slowly to her feet. Time stood still as she stood yards away from him and glared with a hatred he could feel all that way to his blackened soul.

"How dare you!" She returned his blast.

Xev used his powers to put a shield between them. It didn't work. Her powers tore through his as if his didn't exist at all. The blast felt as if a thousand knives slashed at his body. It, too, sent him careening.

He tried to use his powers to catch himself, but they weren't there.

Just as he thought he'd never stop rolling and spinning, he was jerked in the opposite direction by another thunderous blast.

He finally stopped tumbling at the feet of Azura.

She moved to stand on his wings, right where they were attached to his back. He couldn't move. Couldn't even twitch his wings. She had him completely pinned. "You better remember, little bug, that I make my happiness from ripping the guts out of vermin like you. Just because I birthed you doesn't mean I won't rip these wings from your spine and laugh at your pain."

Azura ground her foot against him until he cried out in agony. "Never, ever use your powers against me, or next time, it'll be you that I burn into oblivion. Do you understand?"

"Yes."

With one fierce kick to his head, she left him there and vanished.

Xev sobbed at the agony in his soul. Pain for the friends he'd made who had died because of him. This was all his fault. It was so unfair. Their kindness hadn't deserved this level of cruelty.

They should have been cherished for eternity.

And he wept for the fact that he knew Azura would never allow him any form of happiness. She was too cruel for that. No matter how little he experienced, she loved to ruin it. Took a sick pleasure denying him everything.

Even a friend.

"Why didn't you just kill me?" he breathed. "Why am I here?"

He didn't want this life. Didn't want to breathe another breath. He was so tired of it all, and he was just a kid. How much worse would it be when he was grown?

How was this his fate?

"I'm so sorry, Chani!" She'd been happy. She and her

mother had shared a wonderful life with a love he'd never know.

And they were dead because he'd returned her home.

It was all his fault. He *was* a monster. Worse than the demons his mother enslaved. They had no choice. They looked like the monsters they were.

Him...

He'd made himself look human, and he had killed a girl he just wanted to be friends with. He should never have talked to her. Never gone home with them. How could he not know better?

*I'll never make friends again.* It was too dangerous. He refused to be responsible for another death. While Azura might relish her cruelty, he did not.

Whatever he did, he'd stay out of sight. As far away from Azura and Noir as possible.

It was the only way he'd ever survive.

## 3

TWO YEARS LATER

Xev sank into the shadows as deeply as he could. More than anything, he wished that he could vanish into them and become nothing more than a vague, distant memory.

"No, you don't."

He froze at the sound of an unexpected male voice beside him.

Before he could move, the darkness there formed into the image of a boy somewhere around his age...probably older. His hazel-gray eyes were the strangest color Xev had ever seen. As was his hair. Neither light nor dark, he had strands of both that blended together to make those strands form a peculiar shade of brown.

There was something about him that seemed familiar. Xev felt as if he should know this boy, yet he'd never seen him before. That much, he was certain about.

"Who are you?"

"I'm hatred. Persecution." A sly smile curved one half of the boy's mouth. Not a smirk...something else entirely. "Hostility. But you can call me Shadow."

"Shadow? That's a weird name."

"It's fitting." He raked a curious stare over Xev's body. "Why have you invaded my domain?"

Xev scowled. "What domain?"

"Skatos...the shadows. This is my home. You don't belong here."

Rolling his eyes, he scoffed at the boy. "You don't own the shadows."

"You're right. They own me. Why are you here?"

"I'm trying not to be seen." He jerked his chin at Azura. "I hate her."

Shadow snorted. "We all hate her. But what has she done to you personally?"

"She birthed me."

"Ah."

Xev arched a brow at that. "You're not surprised?"

"Not really. You're not her first kid. Doubt you'll be her last."

That news floored him. He'd always thought that he was an only child. "I have siblings?"

Shadow nodded.

"Where are they?"

"Avoiding her. Like you."

That made sense. But it didn't answer his question. "Seriously, do you know where they are?"

Shadow let out a tired sigh. "Anat is usually not far away from her side. They share genetic cruelty, and Anat revels in it. Because of that, Azura tolerates her more than any of the rest."

Xev knew that snotty toad. With long black hair and cruel eyes, she was almost as nasty as Azura. "I've met her." He just never realized they were related. "Who's her father?"

"Noir."

Ah. That made even more sense. "No wonder Azura pets her."

"Not really. Azura isn't much of a mother. Noir, however, adores his daughter and dotes on her endlessly."

"I didn't think he could feel anything."

Shadow passed a snide smirk toward him. "You're not a girl. And you're not his."

"I don't want to be either one." Especially not if it drew Noir's attention. "Are there any others?"

"Probably. Hard to keep up with the kids they spawn." There was a note in Shadow's voice. One that said there was a lot more to this story.

Then Xev saw it...

Shadow was his brother. At least half. He shared Azura's sharp features. They were beautiful on her.

On Shadow...

It gave him a strange, masculine beauty. Not pretty. He was too rugged for that. But they were similar enough that it was unmistakable.

Yet Xev didn't understand why Shadow kept that knowledge from him. He must have his reasons. Then again, Xev didn't trust easily. Being a child of the Queen of All Darkness tended to do that to people. No doubt, Shadow was every bit as jaded and suspicious of others as he was.

"Where do you live?" Xev asked, thinking it might give him clues about the brother he'd never met before.

"You're standing in my home."

Xev picked his feet up and frowned. "The sidewalk?"

"The shadows. I claimed them a long time ago."

Weird place to claim, but who was he to judge? "Aren't you lonely here by yourself?"

"Better lonely than abused. Besides, the silence soothes me."

That made sense. And like Shadow, he found it soothing himself. Xev liked being able to walk in the shadows where others couldn't see him, but he could see them. It was a nebulous realm that he'd just discovered. "Can I stay here? I can be quiet."

"You sure? 'Cause I haven't seen that side of you."

Xev felt heat rush over his face. He was being chattier than usual, and he wasn't sure why. Normally, he didn't say five words in a week. Not even to himself. "Aren't the shadows big enough for more than one person?"

Shadow gave him a droll stare. "Trust me. We won't be alone. I should warn you that a lot of unsavory things call this place home, too." Taking his arm, Shadow pulled Xev deeper into the darkness that expanded into a whole new world. One with its own landscape.

There were even buildings here.

Xev's jaw dropped. How had he never known this

existed? Obviously, he hadn't gone far enough into the darkness to find all this. "Where are we?"

"I told you. Skatos. The land in between."

"Between what?"

"Realms. From here, you can access any world or realm you wish."

Xev gaped as the possibilities ran through his mind. "Really?"

Shadow nodded. "You just have to make sure not to get caught coming or going."

"Caught by what?"

"Pretty much everyone. Gods. Men. Demons. None of them like it when you step out from this realm into theirs. Tends to freak them out."

That made sense. Xev would be pretty pissed off to find someone stepping out of the shadows into his room. "You do that a lot?"

A smile slowly spread over Shadow's face. "I love to shock others. Fighting and frightening's in my blood."

There was something insidious in the way he said that. It made Xev wonder how much of Azura ran in Shadow's DNA. "Can you show me how this all works?"

Shadow grinned again. "Sure. Follow."

Xev had to use his wings to keep up. He'd never seen anyone move so fast in this life, especially without wings. It was obvious Shadow had been born for this realm. Here, he was home. He knew every twist and turn as he led Xev through the shadowed landscape and towns to pop out in different places.

When Shadow finally stopped, Xev found himself staring out at a metal waterfall. "Where are we?"

"Another universe."

Xev scowled at him. "What do you mean?"

Shadow jerked his chin to the left.

Xev looked through the thin, shimmery veil that separated them from the world. Like a lightweight curtain.

A man and woman were on the other side, laughing.

"Can they see us?"

Shadow shook his head. "Only if we breach the barrier."

Xev watched as the couple began to kiss. "Isn't this creepy?"

"Very much so. Just think of all the times you've been alone and thought you were being watched." Shadow wagged his brows at him. "You probably were."

Xev didn't like the sound of that. At all. "Have you ever watched me?"

Shadow showed no remorse. "I watch everyone."

Xev pulled back. "You perv!"

Shadow laughed. "Doesn't change the fact of what we can do." He moved a few feet over. With a wry grin, he walked through the veil, then stuck his head back in. "Care to join me?"

A part of Xev wanted nothing to do with this. But he was curious.

Surely, Shadow hadn't jumped into the room where the couple had been kissing.

Had he?

Moving cautiously, lest he find out his brother wasn't right, Xev stepped through the veil.

He saw nothing. No couple. No Shadow.

This was even more disconcerting.

Had his brother left?

Even more curious about the realm and where Shadow had vanished, Xev kept walking. Green and blue lights danced off in the distance in front of him. Never in his life had he seen anything like it. The lights appeared to dance.

Shadow laughed in his ear. "Those are neon lights."

Xev didn't understand the word. "Neon?"

"Yeah. There are all kinds of things here you can't imagine." Shadow beckoned him closer toward the edge of a cliff. Down below, it appeared as if stars had fallen from the sky. Thousands of lights twinkled on the ground. It was unlike anything Xev had ever seen before.

"What are those?" he asked.

"City lights."

"City lights? You mean torches?"

Shadow smiled. "No. Tuck your wings in, then follow me. There are things here you can't imagine."

Xev tucked his wings, even though he wasn't too sure about what they were doing. He followed Shadow through more darkness to emerge from shadows on what he thought was a street. But it was unlike any he'd ever beheld before.

Instead of dirt, the ground was solid and wet. Puddles were everywhere. Fog covered the...

They were definitely walls, but these weren't the walls he was used to.

"They're cement."

Again, Xev didn't understand the words Shadow was using.

This time, he didn't have to ask. Shadow explained it without his asking. "Mixture of clay and...other things. It's a building."

Xev had never seen a building like this. "It's exceptionally tall."

"Yeah, they build them that way here."

Incredulous, Xev looked up at the top that reached like a mountain toward the sky. That was impressive. Even more impressive? Some kind of metal bird flew overhead with a roar that would shame thunder. "What is this place?"

"The Ichidian universe."

Xev gaped again as he turned in a circle, trying to take everything in. "I don't understand."

Shadow winked at him. "There are so many worlds in existence. You only know one." He held his hands out and gestured toward the sky. "Expand your horizons, kid. We can go anywhere we want to."

Xev didn't speak as he saw a group of people leaving a building and walking down the street. They had on clothes unlike anything he'd ever beheld or worn. Materials that defied description. "Can we live here?"

"Sure. Until Azura summons you. And yes, she can reach you here. Just like us, they can come through the shadows."

And she would. He knew that. She'd never let him have any peace. "Do you visit here often?"

Shadow shook his head. "There are some things here that are spectacular. But it's not my world. For better or worse, I prefer what I know."

Xev understood what he was saying, but it would be nice to be someone else for a while. Some days, he'd rather be anyone else than himself. "How did you find this place?"

"I've spent years exploring them all."

That was what he wanted to do. "And how can you find your way back and forth?"

"Listen to the aether. Find a shadow and you can go anywhere."

His heart sped up at the prospect. Maybe he could escape his mother, in spite of what Shadow said. Or at least make it harder for her to find him. "Can I time travel?"

Shadow snorted derisively. "Only a very special few have that ability, and even they rarely use it. It's just not something you want to tamper with. Imagine the insanity if beings could time travel at will and change the future."

Xev's mother would probably go back in time to make sure he'd never been born. "That makes sense." He peeked around the corner at all the metallic...*things* he'd never seen before. There were horseless chariots. Iron cans. Blinking lights that had no fire...Endless items he had no names for.

"Is this the same time as we live?"

"That is hard to explain. Time works differently in

different places. A year to us can be more or less to others. But as you can see, they're a lot more advanced on this world. That's the one fun thing about visiting other realms. Some are more advanced and some less so."

"Why don't *you* live here?"

"I like the food. But as I said, it's not home. Crappy as home is, it's what I know and prefer."

"I still don't understand why you wouldn't prefer it here."

Shadow shrugged. "Home isn't a place, little brother. It's a feeling. Like lying in a field on a summer day. It's warm and welcoming. The one place you want to be when shit goes wrong."

Xev considered those words. It was what he'd had with Michi. But that was a long time ago. "Then I don't have a home."

"That's the worst part of life. Not everyone does. But sometimes, you can make one, even with your enemies."

That didn't make sense to him. "How?"

Shadow pulled him back into the darkness. They ended up in Xev's realm. Something he knew because they were watching his aunt, Lilit.

The sight of her made him smile—until she stepped aside, and then his blood ran cold.

She was with his father. Their features were close enough that there was no mistaking them. Jaden had the same coal-black hair. But unlike Xev, his cheeks were dusted with the remnants of a beard he was either growing out or one he hadn't shaved for a few days.

Like Shadow, he would have been beautiful had he

not held an air of rugged authority. That and he had the most peculiar eyes. One was a dark, deep brown and the other a vibrant green. It was both captivating and off-putting at the same time.

Xev had never seen eyes like that. But he recognized the vexed sneer on his father's face.

"Don't you have someone else to annoy?" Jaden asked Lilit.

She gave him a droll stare. "No. Besides, I like annoying you most of all."

"Why?"

"Everyone else is afraid of you, brother. You need nettling so that you know you're not perfect."

Jaden snorted. "I know I'm not perfect. If I was, I'd have a better sister."

Rolling her eyes, she sighed irritably. "You're so mean. Is that why you pushed me from the egg?"

"Noir pushed you. I was the one who tried to catch you before you fell."

"Oh...that's right."

"Too bad you're not," Jaden said under his breath. He let out a tired sigh of his own.

This was the first time in his life that Xev had actually seen his father. He only knew who Jaden was because of those mismatched eyes everyone commented on.

No one looked like Jaden.

Xev was so close to him right now that he could reach out and touch him.

Or punch him.

The latter was definitely what he really wanted to do.

This was the bastard who had ruined his life. Had Jaden just kept it in his pants, Xev would never had been born.

*That's not what ruined your life.*

The fact that Jaden had refused to acknowledge him was what had ruined him. Had he just taken one second to admit he had a son...

Michi might still be alive.

"You okay?" Shadow asked.

No. How selfish could someone be? He was his son. And Jaden would most likely attack him if Xev dared let the god know that he was in the same room as him.

His heart pounding, he turned to his half-brother. "Do you have a father?"

Shadow went pale. "Ah, God, I'm so sorry, Xev. I wasn't thinking. I wanted to show you that people could live with their enemies. Jaden hates Lilit, and yet here they are."

Jaden turned around and looked straight at the shadows where they were standing as if he could hear them.

See them.

Shadow grabbed Xev's hand and pulled him back into the Skatos that connected everything.

"Did he see us?" Xev asked.

Shadow shook his head. "He doesn't have the same powers you do."

"Good." Xev didn't really mean that. Honestly, he wanted to zap his father where he stood. But that would only get him hurt. While he might have different powers, he wasn't stupid enough to think he could win a fight against his father. He was still too young and too new to what he could do.

But one day...

One day, Jaden would pay for what he'd done.

Xev turned to his brother, desperate to change his life. "Will you let me live in the shadows with you?"

"The Skatos is vast. I couldn't really stop you even if I wanted to."

"Good." Xev was relieved to know that this could be an option for him.

Shadow started away.

"Who's your father?"

He stopped instantly. "What?"

Xev's common sense told him to stay silent, but he couldn't. He wanted to know why Shadow was doing all this. "I know you're my brother. You look too much like our mother. Which makes me wonder who fathered you. It's not Jaden, too, is it?"

Shadow let out a bitter laugh. "No. I'm part Naşāru."

They were divine protectors of humans. The absolute enemies of Azura and Noir. Always had been.

"How is that even possible?"

"I'm told that Azura and my father once loved each other. Desperately. Until our aunt, Lil, seduced him in the guise of our mother to get back at both of them. Even though it was a trick Lilit used, Azura refused to forgive my father for it. She's hated him ever since, and Lilit, too."

"And you?"

Shadow nodded. "Nothing more than a bitter

reminder to my parents of what they once shared. I'm best left to shadows. Out of sight. Out of mind."

"I'm sorry."

"It's all right. I don't mind being the bane of their existence."

Shadow might say that, but Xev heard the bitterness in his voice. He knew the pain in his own heart. No matter how much you denied it, there was always that part that wanted the love of a mother and father. It was an innate need. A hunger that nothing really filled.

"You can always call me brother."

Suspicion clouded Shadow's eyes. "I appreciate what you're saying. But time has taught me not to trust intentions, no matter how pure they may seem."

"You can trust me."

"Famous last words. If you learn nothing else from me, little brother, it's to never trust anyone. And I do mean *anyone*."

Xev wished he could make his brother believe in him. Unlike the others, he would prove himself. Everyone needed family. Michi had taught him that.

And he would teach it to Shadow.

Shadow gave him a dark, sinister stare. "Let me give you one more piece of advice, Xev. Learn to embrace your pain. Let it feed your need to survive. Your need to prove the world wrong. You're not what they think you are. Be more than anyone expects. Most of all, you be you."

"What do you mean?"

"We're born of two worlds and belong to neither. Castoffs. Hated nothings. No one expects anything of us.

So defy them all. I'm only a demigod, but you, Xev...you're a full-blooded god. Learn your powers, pick a side, and let no one tell you who you are or what to believe. Be defiant."

Be defiant. How easy Shadow made it sound. But Xev had no idea who he was.

*You will.*

He blinked at the sound of Shadow's voice in his head.

With a smile, Shadow clapped him on the back. "I believe in you, kid. And until you betray me, I'll be here for you. And after you betray me, I'll kill you."

**4**

---

TEN YEARS LATER

Xev watched his mother's pet as Anat rode her army against a group of humans. While he had no great love of humans, he had even less for his sister.

What an overstatement that was.

Ambivalent to humans, he truly detested his sister. He'd like to say it was strictly jealousy, as a part of him did begrudge her all the affection she hogged, but really, he didn't want any attention from Noir or Azura.

His hatred of her went much deeper than that. Anat Laguerre was just mean. Hateful and hate-filled. No one could stand her. She was the worst part of her parents, mixed with an obnoxious ego that somehow managed to surpass Noir's.

So Xev did what he did best...caused chaos. He sent a bolt straight to her chariot and flipped her over, while taking care not to harm the horses that pulled her.

Exceptionally childish, he knew. But fun nonetheless.

He even laughed like the villain he was as he heard her profanity over the noise of her army. She wasn't used to anyone challenging her. Most wet themselves in her presence.

Not her little brother. His job was to torment her, and he took it seriously. It was one of his more favored pastimes.

"I feel as though I should admonish you for that. But rather, I admire it."

Xev froze at the sound of the last voice he'd ever expected to hear.

The last voice he wanted to hear.

"Go screw yourself, Father." He started to fly away, but Jaden caught him with his powers and held Xev by his side. It was even more infuriating that whenever his mother slammed him into something or backhanded him.

"I'd like a word with you."

Xev scoffed. "You wanted nothing to do with me, remember? No. Wait...You wanted me dead. Right? 'Take him and drown him'?"

"Yet you live."

"No thanks to you." Xev raked him with a sneer. But what he hated most was how much he favored this asshole. If he could, he'd scar himself just to keep from seeing Jaden's face reflected in his mirror.

"You have no idea how much I hate your mother."

Xev curled his lip at what had to be the dumbest comment in the history of...everything. "Really? You should try having her as a mother. Thanks for that, too, by the way. And I promise you, whatever you think *you* feel for her pales in comparison to my feelings of adoration."

"I know."

"No, Jaden. You don't." He tried to pull away.

"Daraxerxes, listen—"

"I don't use the name she gave me. And you know nothing about me. So go." He gestured off toward the horizon. "Leave. Don't let my wings hit you in the ass on your way out."

Jaden sighed heavily. "Careful of the powers you carry, boy. I've spent my entire existence trying to keep those around me from stealing them or finding another way to control me so that they could lay claim to them. You have no idea what you are and what burns inside you."

"Well, had my father ever been around when I was a kid, maybe he could have taught me something other than hatred for the fact he threw me away."

"It's not that simple."

Xev curled his lip. "I would *never* walk away from my child. You're a god and a piece of shit!"

"Be careful how you judge others, boy. The brush you use to label them often paints a hellish landscape for you to call home."

"What's that supposed to mean?"

"Pray you never find out. But I want you to know this. As bad as you think your life has been, had I claimed you, it would have been far worse...for both of us. Hate me all you want. But what I did, I did in an effort to save you the pain I knew you'd have." With that, Jaden released him and vanished.

Xev stood there, confused and pissed.

Could there be any truth to that statement? He wanted to deny it, and yet...

Azura was complicated. Most of all, she was crazy.

*Your father's selfish, through and through.*

Yeah. He couldn't believe him any more than he could believe his mother. Jaden never did anything unless he benefited from it. They were horrible people.

*I'm better off alone.*

An orphan even though both of his parents were still alive. The real reason he hated Laguerre. She had their mother's love more than anyone else. And he hated that he was jealous of it. Really, he shouldn't be. Azura's love wasn't something to be coveted. He should shun it as much as he did Jaden's attention.

It just galled him that Azura would be so harsh to him and Shadow while she gave everything to Laguerre.

His fury unfurling, he looked back to where Laguerre was mounting her chariot. As soon as she took off, he blasted her again.

Definitely childish. But it saved some poor human's life and made him happy to no uncertain end.

*You're such a brat.*

He could hear Shadow's voice in his head. His brother wasn't wrong.

"I really need to find something more productive to do with my time."

Taking potshots at his sister was getting a bit old. Even for him. There had to be something more to life than dodging his mother, insulting his father, and tormenting his sister for something she couldn't help.

Shadow made do by hiding away from the world.

While he'd spent a lot of time exploring other realms, Xev finally learned what Shadow had meant about home. The other places were nice to visit.

They weren't home.

Though why he liked it here, he wasn't sure. He was treated much better in other realms where they had no idea who and what he was. So why did he have this sick, incessant need to return to this realm for more abuse?

"Why are you moping like a human?"

Xev let out a tired sigh at the sound of Paimon's voice behind him. Fire rippled across his orange skin as his wings fluttered. He might be a giant demon overlord, but Xev had no use for him, and unlike others, he wasn't afraid of the wretched beast.

He turned slightly, as it never paid to let the demon at your back. "Why are you here?"

If it was to summon him to Azura, he'd send the demon back in pieces.

"Admiring your aim."

He didn't believe that for a heartbeat. "Thought you'd be licking Noir's backside. Rare to see your tongue not attached to—"

"Don't even." Paimon curled his lip as he moved to stand next to Xev. "Do you know where Laguerre's going?"

War, most likely. Hence her name. "Don't know. Don't care."

"You should. There's a war brewing."

*Ooh.* Xev was less than impressed by Paimon's dire tone. "There's always a war."

"This one is going to be between the gods eventually."

He didn't believe that for a moment. They weren't that stupid. But he was curious. "Why do you think that?"

"I hear things, and I'm surprised you don't, given your proclivity for shadow hopping..."

Xev didn't miss the double entendre. Normally, he'd have put Paimon through a wall over it. Lucky for the demon, Xev didn't care to expend enough energy to send him into the nearest mountainside. "I don't spend time with lesser beings."

That brought the desired fury to Paimon's face, as the demon hated the fact that he held no god blood inside him. He considered himself their equal but knew the truth.

His powers were nothing compared to the rest of them. Even Shadow was stronger.

Long ago, Paimon had even tried to lead a rebellion against the gods.

It hadn't gone well for him.

Now, the demon was little more than an errand boy for the gods he'd wanted to replace. No matter how much the demons might hate it, they were no match in power for Xev and his kind.

So, it was little wonder Paimon was looking for another war where he no doubt hoped the gods would kill each other off and leave him standing.

"You shouldn't dismiss us so readily. Like it or not, the gods depend on my kind."

"*Depend* is a bit much," Xev replied. "And not all gods have any use for you at all."

Paimon's nostrils flared with a statement they both knew was absolutely true.

"Be careful who you insult, boy. We're not all as weak as you think, and never forget that some of us have the blood of gods in us, too."

There was an ominous note in his voice. Something that sent a shiver down Xev's spine.

"What do you mean?"

Paimon quirked a brow. "I think you know what I mean. What's the term? The gods like to *slum*?" And with that said, he vanished.

Stunned, Xev stood there. Though why he was surprised, he had no idea. Made sense, actually. Noir and Azura had no scruples when it came to sleeping with anyone who caught their eye.

Lilit either.

His own father had crawled into bed with Azura. Though, to be fair, he'd been told that Jaden was drunk and that his mother had been in disguise.

Still...

How drunk would you have to be to not realize you were in bed with the Queen of All Evil? Even if she were disguised. Granted, he considered his father an idiot, but surely not even Jaden could get so intoxicated that he wouldn't be able to feel her powers, regardless of her exterior appearance.

It'd never made sense to Xev.

Whatever.

It wasn't any of his business what the others did. But it was a shame that they couldn't see the future more clearly.

Or could they?

Xev fell back into the shadows. There was one person who seemed to have the ability to know how things would play out. Eerily so at times.

"Shadow?"

"Busy."

He rolled his eyes at the answer that meant his brother was chasing after a playmate. "Can you put it in your pants for a second and talk to me?"

"Rather not."

"Please."

"You're not that cute, Xev, and you're not my type."

"That's not what you told me last night. You said you'd never look at anyone else again. I can't believe you'd hurt me this way. You're so heartless and mean!"

Xev heard an angry female shriek that was quickly followed by Shadow's curse.

A heartbeat later, his brother appeared in front of him half-dressed. "Really?"

Xev grinned at his brother. "I can't believe it worked."

Pulling on his tunic, Shadow glared at him. "Do it again, and I swear I'll hand-feed your trachea to you... after I rip it out of your body and beat you with it."

That wasn't an idle threat. Xev had little doubt his brother would gleefully assault him. Still...

For one second, he'd gotten the better of Shadow. And that made him proud. Happy, even. Few could lay claim to besting his older brother. "Calm down. Not like you won't find another demon with low standards."

Shadow nodded. "True. They do seem to be in an endless supply, and that makes me deliriously happy." He straightened the rest of his clothes. "So what was of such magnitude that you had to risk your life to annoy me?"

"Paimon just visited me."

He looked less than impressed by Xev's words. "Yeah. Okay. Why?"

"That's what I want to know. He was being cryptic."

"Yeah...and?"

Shadow was right. Paimon lived to appear for no other reason than to hint at something and vanish. He knew it would make you crazy until you figured it out. It was part of his evil and why no one wanted him around.

"He said that there were demons with the blood of gods. Any idea what he was yammering about?"

Shadow ran his hands through his long hair to smooth it down as he appeared to consider it. "He's not wrong. There are several, and you do have another half-brother in those ranks...by your father and not your mother."

Xev's eyes widened at something he'd never been told. "Since when?"

"He's not much younger than you. His mother bartered with Jaden, and out of their deal, Malphas was born."

Those words went over him like an ice bath. "What?"

A tic started in Shadow's jaw, as if he suddenly realized what he'd just said and to whom. "Uh...don't take that to heart."

How could he not? His father refused him and then decided to screw a demon to create another son? Was there any correct way to take that?

It was beyond insulting.

"Where is he?" Xev asked.

"Why?"

"He's my brother. I'd like to meet him."

Shadow eyed him suspiciously. "Are you planning to do something stupid?"

"All the time."

Shadow rolled his eyes. "I don't know about this, Xev. I actually like Malphas."

That angered Xev even more. "You know him?"

At least Shadow had the decency to look sheepish. "I basically know everyone. One way or another."

Xev wanted to slap him so badly that it was hard to resist that urge. "I hate you so much right now."

"No. You don't." He clapped Xev on the back and smiled. "I'm all the family you've got...and Malphas can be, too. If you don't kill him."

"Why would I kill him?"

Shadow let out a long sigh then crooked his finger for Xev to follow him.

This couldn't be good.

A little trepidatious, Xev trailed, wondering what was going on. Why was Shadow being cryptic. That wasn't normally his style. Unlike the others he knew, Shadow didn't play games. Which was what Xev liked most about him.

He had his answer once he realized they were heading to Jaden's domain. He felt his wings spring out of his back, as if in protest of being here.

Before they even reached the palace Jaden called home, he had a bad feeling in the pit of his stomach.

When they neared the shadows of a large, elegant room, that feeling worsened as he realized that his brother was living with their father.

"He's demonborn?"

Shadow hesitated. "That's what I told you."

And his father had accepted this child. Why?

"Don't get that look, Xev. It's not Malphas's fault."

"Was it mine?"

"Your mother is a threat to Jaden. She's a powerful goddess in her own right who wouldn't hesitate to enslave or kill Jaden if she had a chance."

It wasn't making him feel any better.

The only comfort he could take from it was that Malphas was shorter than he was. Granted, it was exceptionally petty, but still...

It was something.

"His mother was a minor demon. No threat to anyone."

"Why did my father barter with her?"

"I don't know. No one does. Other than your father and"—he jerked his chin toward Malphas—"his mother, who's now dead."

Malphas rose from his bed and turned toward the shadows where they stood. With eyes so brown they appeared black, he peered at them. "Who are you?"

"He can see us?"

"And hear you, too." Malphas approached them slowly. "Who did you bring with you, Shadow?"

Shadow looked at Xev expectantly. *What do you want me to tell him?*

"I'm your brother." Xev wasn't sure why he admitted that, given the jealousy that was begging him to put his brother through a wall.

Malphas took the news better than Xev had. "And?"

Xev's temper flared even more. "Really? That's all you have to say?"

"I have siblings all over."

Shadow folded his arms across his chest. "Not from your father, you don't."

Now, appreciation darkened Malphas's gaze. "You're a demigod, too?"

"Full god." Xev took more pride than he should at correcting him.

Malphas flashed from human form into that of a daeve demon. Red skin. Orange hair and wings similar to Xev's. But as soon as that form flashed, he returned to the body of a human. Obviously, Xev had plucked a nerve when he'd explained the power dynamic between them.

"Problem?" Xev asked.

"Curious."

So was he. Why had his father kept this...lesser demonkyn, and not him?

Malphas blinked slowly. "That's simple. He controlled the demon who birthed me. He feared your mother gaining control over him by way of you."

"You can hear my thoughts?"

"One of my gifts. But I normally avoid it. It's only when I meet someone for the first time that I bother. I want to know what I'm dealing with and if they're lying to me."

That would be a handy skill.

Malphas held his arms out and turned around slowly. "Do I meet your approval, brother?"

"I didn't come to approve you. Only wanted to see what made you so special."

"Nothing. Truly. Most of the time, our father doesn't even like me. No idea why he had me or keeps me here."

"Ooh! I got this one!" Shadow danced around in an irritating manner. "Jaden wants an in with the demons. He's trying to befriend them before Azura, Braith, and Noir enslave all of them."

They both turned to stare at him.

He stopped his idiotic dance and shrugged. "I hear things. A lot."

Malphas shook his head. "He sleeps with a ton of demons," he said to Xev. "I can't tell if he's trying to create his own army...or a harem. You should watch them."

Shadow scoffed. "No, thank you. I don't want the trauma or drama that comes with that. We pass time, and they talk. Can't help it if I'm a good listener."

Xev really wanted to hate Malphas, but Shadow was right. He seemed like a decent demon. Wasn't his fault Jaden was an ass.

He looked around the room that still irritated him because it was in his father's palace. "Why don't we go get a drink? Somewhere less annoying?"

Malphas nodded. "Sounds good. Where are we going?"

This time, Xev led them through the shadows to his favorite spot in all the worlds. A small dive on a backwater planet.

Malphas was confused. "Where are we?"

"A place called Trisa. They make the best drinks you've ever had."

"I don't know about that." Malphas scratched at his ear as he looked around sheepishly.

"Hold that thought." Xev led them into the pub that was normally crowded. For once, it only had a few patrons. The last time he'd been here, a massive fight broke out. He still had no idea what it'd been about.

Not that he cared in the slightest.

But he was grateful it was a quiet night. Holding his hand up as they neared his usual table, he let the bartender know to bring his favorite bottle with three glasses.

"Interesting place." Malphas grimaced in distaste.

Shadow took a seat with his back to the wall. He folded his arms across his chest as he glanced around the dark room. "Want to play a game?"

Xev screwed his face up. "I don't like games."

"That's because you usually get screwed when your mom plays them. Trust me, this one has no consequences for you. Just an exercise in powers."

"I'm with Xev, I don't want to play a game where someone gets hurt, even if it's not one of us."

"Again, has nothing to do with your mother, either, sugar bear."

Xev shook his head as the waitress came over with his order and set it down in front of them. He tipped her well, as was his custom, and poured them each a drink. "To screwed-up childhoods."

They clinked glasses and knocked back their drinks.

Malphas coughed and nodded. "Yeah...that is the best I've ever had." Pouring another round, he looked at Shadow. "So what's this game?"

"Who can guess the future."

Xev snorted. "I know I can't. I definitely lack those powers."

Malphas let out an evil laugh. "All I can think of is what a weird joke this is."

"How so?"

"A demigod, demon, and a god walk into a bar—"

A dark shadow fell across their table, causing Malphas to break off mid-sentence. "What are you wearing?"

Shadow quirked an evil grin. "Clothing."

"Never seen nothing like it."

"Could say the same about you, my friend. What hobo did you roll for your accouterments?"

"My what?"

Shadow cleared his throat. "Field dressing. Given the firearm, I'd think you're law enforcement or military. But you don't have the demeanor of a man used to kicking someone else's ass or subduing them."

"What would you know?"

"Shadow..." Xev gave a steely stare to warn his brother to stand down. Last thing they wanted was to draw undue attention to them. This wasn't their world. Definitely wasn't their fight.

Shadow held his hands up in surrender.

Sadly, the human didn't have any sense of self-preservation. "You run your mouth like someone who wants to lose their tongue."

Xev placed a coin on the table and pushed it toward the hapless man in front of them. "Next round's on me."

"Don't take money from strangers. Where are your papers?"

Malphas held his hand up and splayed his fingers out. "You're here for a cold drink and to rest. Go to the bar and be glad you're alive."

The man blinked slowly.

At first, Xev thought he was about to continue the fight. Instead, he turned around and did just what Malphas had told him to do.

He even had a smile on his face.

"What the hell was that?" Xev asked.

"Silkspeech. One of the better demon powers I came with. It enables me to influence others." Malphas winked at him. "Don't worry, it won't work on you."

Shadow poured more drink. "Yeah. It's only for humans, demons, and morons."

Xev was more impressed than he wanted to be. "I suddenly feel shafted in the power department."

"Don't." Malphas jerked his chin toward the man at

the bar. "I can influence his thoughts and memories. You can alter him. Make him a cockroach or whatever else suits your mood."

That was true. Still, the ability to alter someone's thoughts was interesting to consider.

Which brought Xev back to another matter. "How many siblings do we have, anyway?"

Shadow drew a circle in the air with his glass. "With the exception of our sister, all of yours are at this table."

Xev arched a brow. "Really?"

Shadow nodded. "Malphas has a ton of demonkyn brethren, thanks to his mother's inability to show restraint or good sense."

Xev was suddenly glad his parents weren't *that* bad. "What about you?"

"I have you, Laguerre, and a half-brother named Max."

That was interesting. Xev set his glass down. "Demon, demi, or god?"

"Demi."

"Decent?" he asked.

"Don't really know. He keeps to himself and doesn't really like to interact with others. I respect that and leave him alone."

Xev considered that. If Max was related to Shadow and not him, that meant Max had to share Shadow's father. "Who's his mother?"

Shadow indicated their small group. "Our least favorite aunt."

Xev frowned. The only aunt it couldn't be was Cam. As

a goddess of justice, she didn't waste time with such things.

That left two who were awful. "Lilit or Braith?"

Shadow chuckled. "Braith has no patience for children. She wants nothing to do with them. They're parasites in her swirling silver eyes."

Lilit, then. Dangerous and unpredictable. In some ways, she was worse than Azura. She was supposed to provide levity between the three dark gods and the three light ones.

Instead, she caused chaos, and Xev should know. That was his best department.

Shadow motioned the waitress over to order another bottle. Once she was gone, he returned his attention to Malphas and Xev. "Now then, back to our original topic. I want predictions from both of you."

Xev scowled. "Why?"

"Let's call it fun. I want to know what you think our parents and others will get into."

Malphas shrugged. "I think they're going to catch Rezar wearing one of Cam's wigs, while pretending to be Braith."

Xev laughed so hard, he thought he might hurt himself. "Rezar, huh?" Out of all of the gods, he was the one least likely to do such. In fact, Xev didn't think Rezar could even smile. For a "light" god, he was remarkably stern and dark.

Then again, like him, Rezar was a god of chaos. Very similar in powers to Xev.

Shadow sobered. "What do you think?" he asked Xev.

"I don't know. I try hard not to think about the future. Hate the present enough not to care. You?"

"I think Paimon's right. War's coming. We will have to pick sides."

Malphas sat back. "Honestly, I think that's why Jaden wanted me close. He wants me to lead the demons for him."

Xev arched a brow at that bold statement. "They won't all follow Jaden."

"I know. But I command three legions of them."

So did Xev.

And Paimon.

"What side will you fight for?" Xev asked Shadow.

"My own. The gods won't care who we are or who we're related to. They have no loyalty to us, and I have no loyalty to them."

Those words sent a chill down Xev's spine. "So never trust you. Thanks for the warning."

"Not the same, little brother. You've never betrayed me. My parents...selfish from beginning to end. Why would I be loyal to those who've already betrayed me?"

"I can concur with that." Malphas lifted his glass in salute.

While Xev could also concur, he didn't like the thought of the gods at war. They were a brutal lot. And there was no telling what would happen to them.

As Shadow said, love wasn't exactly in their genetic makeup. "Then let's make a brotherly vow to stay out of this."

Malphas nodded. "Sounds good to me."

"To neutrality." Shadow held up his glass so that they could clink theirs against it.

"No war."

They repeated the promise.

Yet even as they agreed to stay out of it, Xev wondered if they'd be able to manage it.

Or if something much worse would come for them.

**5**

———

FOUR YEARS LATER

"I'm done!"

Xev scowled as Malphas appeared in his room. "Don't you knock?"

A knock sounded on the ceiling.

Rolling his eyes, Xev let out a long, tired sigh as he propped himself up in his bed. "You're lucky I'm alone."

"Sorry. Wasn't thinking about your nightly routine. I'm just furious."

"Why?"

"I hate Jaden."

"Finally, common ground." Xev drew the covers up higher over his body, then brushed his hand through his dark hair. "But I'm sorry Dad let you down...again." Xev motioned for Malphas to have a seat on the foot of his bed. "What happened?"

Malphas didn't sit, and he didn't speak for a few

minutes. Rather, he paced Xev's room. "You were right. There's no trust. I'm nothing to him."

How was that a surprise?

"I heard that, Xev. You asshole."

"Sorry. I forget sometimes...and why are you in my head, anyway? It's such a mess most of the time, *I* don't want to be there. I can't imagine being on the outside, wanting in. What is wrong with you?"

"That is a long and winding list that begins with that thing we call a father and ends with why I'm here!"

"Which is what?" Xev was beginning to lose patience. He'd never liked to be awakened from his sleep, and this was becoming a tedious rant. Malphas either needed to answer his question or become way more entertaining in his fury.

"I heard Jaden speaking with Cam."

Xev felt his own stomach shrink in dread. Nothing good ever came when those two got together. Mostly because Cam was a self-important blowhard who spouted off all manner of stupidity. Which she often won their father over to. He'd never understood her ability to do that. It was almost as if she had an unnatural power over him.

"And?"

Malphas paused again. "Braith's pregnant."

Xev's eyes widened at the thought. The goddess of destruction? She who hated *all* creation? Braith had never voiced any positive words to his knowledge, about anything. And especially about children. She was an angry, vengeful shrew who made his mother look like a kitten in comparison. The fact that both Noir and Azura avoided her said it all about her fury and power. "Who would dare touch her?"

Malphas pinned him with a hard stare. "Glad you're lying down...her Sephiroth guard."

"Kissare?"

He nodded.

"Oof." Xev's breath left his lungs with an audible sound that echoed. Sephirii were a nasty bunch of...

He really didn't know. No one did. They'd been created by the Primals as their attack dogs and servants. Each one winged, as he was, they were strictly off-limits to demons. No one was allowed to approach them or even speak to them. Not even the Naṣāru, who were the official army of the gods.

Even Xev kept his distance from them. They were a snotty bunch who saw themselves as better than all other life forms because they directly served the Source gods.

While he was sure his father had probably trifled with some of them, he could only imagine how angry they'd be that one of their "dogs" had fraternized with Braith.

With the exception of Azura, the Primal goddesses were expected to be very circumspect with whom they consorted.

But to be honest, he was stunned anyone would dare to trifle with Braith in such a manner.

Props to Kissare for that amount of courage.

Still, he was confused by one thing. "How is Braith being pregnant a betrayal to you?"

"Jaden wants to use me to spy on them."

"Spy how?"

Malphas glared at him. "You can't tell anyone who the father is."

"Pardon?"

"I'm not supposed to know. Jaden doesn't know. No one other than Braith and Kissare know, and they have no idea that I know he's the father."

"Crap. Your powers..." That made sense.

Malphas saluted him. "That's why Jaden wants me to hang out with Auntie for a bit."

"You'd rather not do that."

"No kidding. I like my anatomy in all its current places. No wish for her to redesign me because I was dumb enough to help my father betray her." Malphas shivered.

"How did you find out?"

"Ran into Kissare by accident...not long after Braith told him. It was all he was thinking about. That and the fact that Braith is now showing, and that everyone would soon know and start asking questions."

Which would be how Jaden knew she was percolating a baby in that venomous womb.

Xev chuckled. "Bet Kissare was wetting his diaper."

That succeeded in lightening Malphas's mood. He laughed, too. "Indeed. Kissare knows what's waiting for him when the others find out he's the father."

"Yeah. I don't need Shadow for that prophecy." Kissare's days were numbered. In truth, Xev felt sorry for the Sephiroth. While they were no friends of his, he wouldn't want to be on that side of the Primals.

Normally, the seven of them couldn't agree on anything. Not even the color of the sky. But when it came to their creations knowing their places...

They would unite to punish the Sephiroth.

Damn. Just damn.

"What are you going to do?" he asked Malphas.

"Lie. I know nothing. Hear nothing. See nothing... Nothing."

Xev arched a brow. "Seriously?"

"Why not? Jaden's just keeping me around to run his errands for things such as this. He doesn't care about me. And I'm not about to cross Braith for a father who barely speaks to me. How stupid would I be?"

Pretty dumb. Forgiveness wasn't in her vocabulary. Torture, however, was her favorite pastime. Second only to a good degutting. "He is sending you into harm."

"With a smile on his face. You think for one second I'd be able to do that to my child?"

Xev shrugged. "I don't know. You *are* a demon."

Malphas's nostrils flared. "*Half.*"

"I thought daeve ate their young."

"What is wrong with you?"

Xev yawned. "I was asleep when my brother came storming into my room and woke me up. Would really like to go back to it. Unless you wish to continue your diatribe."

"Why do I talk to you?"

"No idea."

Malphas growled at him. "I hate you so much."

"Hate you, too."

Malphas used his powers to extinguish the light in the room. "Get some sleep, asshole."

Xev rolled over to his side. "Calm down, Mal. Just tell him you don't know or give him the name of someone you hate. For that matter, tell him Noir's the father. That should strike fear in everyone's heart."

That made Malphas's eyes turn bright red in the darkness. It also caused a deep, evil laugh to bubble out of him. "I should do that. It would make him shit."

"Yeah. Can you imagine? Those are two powers that never need to spawn."

"Definitely. Enjoy your nightmare, brother. I have my own to go face."

Xev felt Malphas leave, which should have made him happy. Instead, the absence left a lingering emptiness inside him. Xev scowled. It wasn't like him to get lonely.

That was what it felt like, though. Horrible loneliness.

*What is wrong with me?*

Several minutes went by before he realized something. It wasn't loneliness.

It was dread. A horrible premonition of what was to come. This child would change everything. He didn't know how he knew that, but he did.

All their fates were going to be tied to this one birth. Forget war. This was going to be so much worse.

## 6

Xev knew he shouldn't be anywhere near the Sephirii. They were...

Good. Just being near them made his skin crawl.

But his curiosity was more than he could handle. He wanted to see the one who'd dare to impregnate the goddess who terrified everyone.

Even his father.

Who would be that courageous?

That stupid?

While he knew Kissare's name and reputation, he'd never seen him. At least not that he knew of. So he was desperate to get a look at what had to be the biggest moron ever born.

Sticking to the shadows so that no one would see him, he went room to room of their gilded hall, searching and listening to some of the most boring conversations he'd ever heard.

Ugh. They were so polite it was sickening.

If he heard one more compliment, he'd vomit. There was nothing interesting about them. They were just so... so...

*Nice.*

Ick! Being around them made him want to go find his sister and blast her just to balance out their sugary sweetness. Anything to get this out of his system. How could anyone live like this and tolerate it? Maybe he did have more of Azura's blood in him than he wanted to admit, because he was really grateful he wasn't one of these poor, pathetic creatures.

He was just about to leave when he heard the sounds of war. Furious and powerful. There was no mistaking the sound of sword striking steel. That sounded much more promising.

Who was fighting? Why?

While it could be a practice, it didn't sound like one. This was the kind of entertainment he craved.

He headed through the shadows out of their temple and into a courtyard in the center of the buildings.

Xev slowed down and scowled as he saw the two combatants. Sadly, it wasn't a battle. Before him stood two Sephirii. One was a large male with white-blond hair he had braided down his back. By the gilded armor he wore that was marked by Braith's sun emblem, Xev knew he was Kissare, the Sephiroth he'd come to spy on. Kissare wasn't just Braith's personal guard—he was also the leader of the Sephirii.

The other...

Xev couldn't breathe as he saw her. With hair so black it reflected the light, she had vibrant blue eyes and a pair of beautiful gold wings that matched her iridescent skin. And she met every sword strike that was leveled against her with a speed, agility, and power that reverberated through him.

Never had he seen her equal in beauty or grace.

Her macabre dance mesmerized him as she sparred with the much larger Sephiroth and held her own like a mighty warrior. She was incredible.

Watching her, he knew there were tricks he could teach her to help her defeat her opponent. While she fought just like all the Sephirii as she'd been taught by them, there were other ways to fight that would make her an even greater, more lethal soldier.

"Halt!"

She froze at Kissare's command. Her sword hovered barely a finger's breadth from the male in front of her.

Kissare smiled. "Impressive, Myone. Keep this up and one day, you might prove to be our commander."

She shook her head respectfully. "I could never replace you, *kyri*. Nor would I want to." She lowered the sword and bowed to him. "It's simply my honor to be tutored by you. Your skill is an inspiration to all of us."

"My honor to train *you*."

Xev rolled his eyes as they began that shite again, and his stomach heaved. Did they really believe this tripe? He couldn't imagine being so polite all the time. He'd break out in hives if he even tried it.

Kissare saluted her with his sword. "I'm being summoned away, fair Myone. But it was a good session. Until our next practice." He sheathed his sword, then vanished.

Myone twirled her golden sword around her body with incredible expertise. He could watch her do that all day.

Suddenly, she sighed and held her sword up so that she could see the hilt. "I know, I'm not supposed to practice with you. It was just this once. Promise." She paused to listen, then nodded. "You're tired. I'll take you home." She smirked at her weapon in a way that made her pert nose even more adorable. "I hear you, Kasumi. I'll let you rest, and soon we'll find you food. Please, don't yell at me. I'm doing my best to honor you and my position."

Sheathing her sword, she reached up to the gold pin that held her hair coiled around her head and released it.

Xev's breath caught in his throat as she shook her hair out and he saw the long, dark curls that begged him to sink his hands in them.

She was spectacular.

*Don't even go there, moron...*

But he couldn't help himself. He'd never known hunger like this. There was something about her that was just irresistible.

Suddenly, she turned to face him. With deep frown, she searched the shadows. "Is someone there? Hello?"

He froze as she looked right at him. Eye to eye. Terrified she might somehow see him, Xev stepped back further into the shadows. The last thing he wanted was for her to know he'd been spying on her.

Not the way to meet someone. People tended to react rather badly whenever they caught a perv watching them when they didn't know it. And he couldn't blame her for it if she did. Anyone would be justified in a screaming fit.

*I hate you, Shadow!*

This was creepy, and he seldom did it. No one wanted to be spied on. She would slap him if she knew, and he'd deserve it.

Even so, he wanted to think—

"What you doing, punkin'?"

Jumping in startled alarm, he cursed at Shadow's sudden question. Jerk! He knew better than to sneak up on him. "Why are you here?"

"Why are *you*?" Shadow wagged his eyebrows at him.

Disgusted with Shadow and himself for having spied on the poor woman, Xev shoved at his brother. "I was just curious."

A lecherous grin curved Shadow's lips. "I am, too. She's quite a beauty, isn't she?"

"Stop! You don't just ogle someone when they don't know you're around. It's creepy."

"Xev got a cr-uh-sh. Watching the enemy...getting some ideas he sh-ooo-uldn't."

He could have really done without Shadow singing those words to him—and in particular, the kissing noises that followed. "Stop with your infernal questions and idiocy. Have I told you what a complete and utter ass you are?"

"Many times." Shadow started braying like a donkey.

Rolling his eyes, Xev headed away from him.

Until Shadow caught his arm. "What's going on with you? You know something, don't you?"

"No, I don't."

"I'm not stupid, Xev. You have no reason to be here with the Sephirii." He glanced back toward Myone. "Not that she'd not reason to draw you over to the dark side that's actually light. But I know you. You didn't just happen to come here because you wanted to see how they live or scout out some woman. You're not me and you're not pervy. You had some other purpose to this. What was it?"

"I have no purpose to anything. Go back to your demons or whatever it is you do when you're not annoying me."

Shadow tsked at him. "The testier and nastier you get, the more I know I'm right."

Growling deep in his throat, Xev knew Shadow wouldn't give this up. He was more tenacious than a toddler after honey cake. What he wouldn't give to have one stupid brother who never noticed anything.

Which left him with two options answer the question or teleport out. Of course, if he teleported out, Shadow would only follow and continue to badger him until he answered the question...

Or gutted his brother.

Xev let out a deep, annoyed growl. "You have to swear yourself to absolute secrecy."

Shadow quirked an eyebrow at that. "Why? It's juicy, isn't it? Good and juicy."

"Swear it on your life."

Shadow took a moment to consider the matter.

"Seriously? You can't just say you'll keep your mouth shut?"

He scoffed. "Easy for you. You barely speak a word to anyone. Mal and I have to drag at least half the syllables out. Me, on the other hand—"

"Talk so much that you're lucky you still have a tongue?"

"See why it's hard for me to make that promise? Want to make sure I don't do anything to cause future harm to myself. Not that I particularly value life, but there are some deaths I'd really rather avoid. You know...dagger to the eye. Gut wound. Disembowelment...There really are a lot of very grisly ways to end a life. I'd rather not suffer any of those. So who's going to kill me and why?"

Xev sighed. "Fine. I'll keep my se—"

Shadow cut him off again. "Just kidding. I swear. You know I won't be able to sleep until you tell me. I can't stand a secret I don't know."

"Isn't that what makes it a secret?"

"From others, yeah. But why would you torture me, little brother? What did I do to you?"

Xev rolled his eyes. "Fine." Grabbing Shadow's tunic, he jerked him close so that no one would overhear them. "Braith's pregnant."

Shadow's eyes bulged probably as much as Xev's had when he'd been told.

"You're serious?"

"Why would I make that up?"

Shadow shrugged. "Cruelty. You are your mother's son."

"So are you."

Shadow grinned. "Makes us both dirtbags, doesn't it?"

"It doesn't make me a liar."

"True." Shadow sobered. "But that still doesn't explain why you're here. Unless..." He trailed off as he looked back to the courtyard where Myone had been.

Those weird gray eyes widened again. "Unless you were scoping out the baby daddy."

"What?"

Shadow gave him a knowing smirk. "Either you were scoping out the baby daddy or you were trolling. Since you don't troll the way I do, I have to believe it's the baby daddy that brought you here. Ooh, that's grisly. Braith got busy with a Sephiroth. That's a bet I wish I'd made. Dang, I'd be cleaning up, 'cause no one would ever believe it."

Xev really hated how astute Shadow was. He never missed any detail, no matter how small.

Shadow turned back toward him. "So who is it?"

"Shadow..."

"Don't Shadow me. I need his name so I can send a card or a gift. At least let me know who's going to be gelded when your father and our uncles find out about this."

Xev started heading back toward his room. "Want to know? Ask Malphas."

"Wait! No...What? You're kidding. Both of you knew this, and none of you told me? What did I do to make you both hate me so?"

"Stop your dramatics."

Shadow waved his hands in the air and acted as if he were having an attack of some kind.

"Aren't you a little old for this?" Xev asked.

"Oh, very. But it doesn't stop me. Now be a good boy and answer my question. No need in hunting down a demon when I have a perfectly good...Wait. Wait. Wait. I don't need you to tell me who. Oh my God, I'm an idiot. We're here in the Sephirii hall. There's only one person it could be...*her* Sephiroth. Kissare. None of the others ever go near her. Ever. She hates them." Gasping dramatically, Shadow doubled over. "Oh my God, the ice queen got frisky with her own guard!"

As he'd said, Shadow was far too intelligent for anyone's good.

Or sanity.

"Tell no one, Shadow. I mean it!"

"No fear there. I wouldn't betray Braith for anything. I like having my body parts attached to me. Like them so much, I've named all the important ones."

Grimacing at an image he didn't want in his head, Xev groaned. "So much more information than I needed."

Shadow grinned, then vanished. He was good at that.

And once he was gone, Xev realized that Myone had

vanished, too. *Crap*...He'd wanted to spend a few more minutes with her.

Not that he was *with* her.

It'd just been a welcome change. He wasn't sure why, but there was something about her that called out to him.

*I'm an idiot.*

No one would argue that. Certainly not his brothers or father. Nor his mother.

Still...

"Daraxerxes!"

He ground his teeth at the shrill scream that splintered his skull. How he hated that summons.

*Ignore it.*

But Azura would just send demons out to find him. And the last thing he wanted was for one of them to find him this close to the Sephirii stronghold. His luck, they'd concoct some lie, and his mother would think he was in league with them.

Yeah, that would be a disaster.

There was no need to delay the inevitable.

Irritated even more, he teleported to her throne room. As black as her soul, the walls reflected the torchlight around them. She had a blood-red rug underneath the two thrones on the dais where she and Noir held court.

Sterile and cold, just like both of them. Xev hated this room. It was bad enough when it was filled with demons and others wanting an audience with her. When they were alone...

It was chilling.

Like Malphas the night before, she paced the empty

area before her black, heavily carved throne while Noir sat on his, watching her.

As soon as she saw Xev, she turned and used her powers to pin him to the nearest black marble wall.

Closing his eyes, Xev wished he could figure out how he'd blasted her so badly all those years ago. But he'd only had that particular power surge on the night Chani and her mother died.

Never since.

And that really pissed him off.

Noir stood up slowly and approached him as he hung uselessly eight feet above the floor. "Have you really been shooting bolts at my daughter?"

This time, Xev didn't even bother to debate. "What are you talking about?"

"Don't play stupid." Noir used his powers to slam him on the ground as if he were nothing more than a bug.

His mother sighed heavily. "You done?" she asked Noir.

"For now. But if he goes near Anat one more time, I will chain him to her chariot and let her rip off whatever body part she chooses."

Depending on his mood, that might be worth it. Xev wiped the blood from his lip. "Is that all you wanted me for?"

"Just don't." Azura walked over to him. "Get up. I have a mission for you."

This he couldn't wait for. He pushed himself up with a sullen sneer. "A mission?"

"Your aunt is pregnant. We want to know who the father is."

Xev arched a brow at that. Who knew Mal's information would prove *this* valuable?

"My aunt?" he asked while he continued to play stupid with her. That was, at times, his most valuable play. "Which one?"

Azura glared at him. "Braith. Why would I care about the other two?"

He shrugged. "How should I know? I don't even know why you care about Braith." Xev scratched at his ear, only to learn he was bleeding from it, too. *Awesome.* "May I ask how I'm supposed to learn this from the aunt who doesn't speak to me?"

"You're always crawling around with my other worthless male offspring. Make yourselves useful. For once in your putrid life, go do something to please me."

Because that was what he wanted to do, please the beast who'd never shown him any affection. Yeah, he'd get right on that...after the Source froze over. "Will do, my bloodthirsty maternal unit."

With a sarcastic salute, he flashed himself out of her palace before she could blast him again, and back to the shadows he preferred.

At least here, he felt at home.

That was his thought until he felt something sharp and hot pierce his side.

*What the...?*

He looked down to see an arrow protruding from his flesh. It was followed by three more in quick succession.

Stunned, Xev staggered back. He tried to find his attacker, but all he saw was darkness everywhere. Using his powers, he sent out bolts blindly, hoping to hit whoever had attacked him.

Either way, he had to get out of here.

With no real destination other than someplace a demon wouldn't dare follow him, he stumbled through the shadows until he found the one opening he needed.

The only place he knew none of them would dare follow.

There was light ahead. He prayed those on the other side wouldn't attack him, too, but at least it was away from the ones currently using his body as a pincushion. He just had to get to it.

Unfurling his wings, he flew as he felt more arrows striking him. They caused him to dip and spin. Unable to stabilize his flight, he hit the shadow veil that separated the shadows from the world and flew through it sideways.

But he couldn't stay airborne. With a heavy thud, he hit the ground. He saw the four arrows in his chest. One in his thigh. More in his back that hurt so much...

*Focus. Find the anger.* He pushed himself up and tried to walk.

All he found was pain and agony as he staggered forward in case his assassin was still in pursuit.

His knees buckled and he rolled. He tried to tuck his wings in to protect them, but it was useless. They were as injured as the rest of him, and no part of his body wanted to cooperate.

When he came to a stop, he heard a sharp gasp. Before

he could see who had made the noise, everything went black.

MYONE STARED in disbelief of the demon at her feet. At least, she thought him a demon. With those sharp, beautiful features and black hair...

He had to be one of their ilk. Especially given the powerful aura he gave off. Even wounded and unconscious, there was something lethal and dangerous about him. Like a feral beast that had been taken down by hunters.

The fact he was wounded just made him deadlier, as such creatures usually struck out blindly in their pain.

Given the amount of injuries, he had to be a fierce, hunted demon who'd done something unspeakable. Why else would they have done this to him?

She should probably finish him off. It was obvious he'd infuriated someone to the brink of murder. Most likely, it was one of the gods she served.

"Myone!"

She jumped at the sharp call as she heard Kuru nearing her. "I'm here."

He pulled up short the moment he saw the huge demon at her feet. "What happened?"

"I don't know. I was resting when I heard an unexpected noise. I looked up, and he came rushing out of nothing. I think he's a demon."

Kuru shook his head. "Not a demon. He's a son of Jaden."

She stepped back from her intruder, startled by that knowledge. "What?"

"His mother's Azura. His father's Jaden. He's not a demon. He's a god."

*He's a god...* Those words echoed in her mind. "Are you sure? How do you know?"

He gave her a droll stare. "I serve Jaden. To my eternal regret, I know both of his sons."

She didn't understand what he was saying. "Regret?" Why would he be sorry that he knew Jaden's sons?

"One's demonkyn, and this one"—he toed at the unconscious god—"as I said, is born of Azura. He serves her instead of his father. He was so awful even at birth that Jaden spurned him."

Pure evil, then. Why else would Jaden have refused him?

Even so, she couldn't very well leave him here. Not in this condition. He was bleeding everywhere. If someone didn't do something...Well, she wasn't sure if he could die or not, but it didn't look good for him. It would be indecent to leave him here like this. Alone and bleeding. "Help me, Kuru. We need to have him tended."

"Have you lost your mind? Jaden has no use for him. You won't win any points if you help his vile offspring. He doesn't even acknowledge this one."

It made no sense that he'd claim a demonkyn demigod and not a son who was a full god.

But that, too, didn't matter.

"This isn't about Jaden. It's about doing what's right. He's been wounded and needs help." She knelt down to examine all the arrows protruding from his body. By their red color and tainted appearance, she knew they were demonic in origin and not from anyone on their side.

Someone had definitely wanted this god dead, and most likely, it'd come from his mother. Myone wanted to know why.

Brushing the blood-soaked black hair from his face, she saw just how much he resembled his father. No one would ever mistake his paternity.

But she saw nothing of his mother in him. Other than the demonic arrows. Had Azura ordered him killed? Myone wouldn't put anything past her. Killing her own child made much more sense than nurturing him.

There was something insidious about this, and she wanted to know what.

KURU LEFT MYONE'S ROOM, grinding his teeth. He still thought this was a bad idea. Women! He'd never understand them. No mercy should be given to an enemy, and Daraxerxes was definitely on the other side.

That was his thought until a shadow caught his attention. With his hand on his sword, he went after it.

At first, he thought he was imagining things.

Then he saw it move.

Faster than the being could react, he caught the demon and pinned it to the wall. Fire rippled over its skin as its wings spanned out. Red eyes glared at Kuru, who was unimpressed. He'd faced all manner of demons in service to his lord. This was just another bottom feeder he needed to dispatch.

"Wait!" it growled when he went to cut its throat. "I'm here for Daraxerxes."

Of course it was. "Are you the one who wounded him?"

The demon tilted its head. "You hate him, too." A statement, not a question.

"I don't know him well enough to hate him."

"You don't have to know someone to hate them. I find that particular kind of hatred to be even more powerful. Jealousy...It's far greater when the person is a stranger. There's nothing to buffer the hatred then. It's far more raw and potent."

"Shut up!" Kuru was a Sephiroth—they were supposed to be above such petty emotions. And he hated that he wasn't.

The demon clasped his hands around Kuru's wrist. "You covet leadership...Perhaps we can help each other."

"There's nothing you can do for me."

The demon laughed. "My name is Paimon, and there's *much* I can do for you."

## 7

Xev came awake to the scent of lavender and roses. Lifting his hand, he gasped at the wave of pain that racked him. Gah, his entire body ached.

Then he remembered the arrows. Most of all, he remembered the agony that had driven him unconscious.

*Am I dead?*

No. This wasn't any nether realm that he knew of. It was too pleasant. And if he was dead, he doubted he'd hurt this badly. Death was supposed to bring an end to his misery. Though with his luck, that wouldn't happen.

Somehow, his mother would find a way to torment him, dead or alive.

Looking around, he frowned. A wall of doors on his left were wide open, letting in a gentle breeze that kept the room cool. That wasn't the odd part.

He was in a strange bed, in a room he'd never seen

before—feminine and dainty, pink had exploded everywhere. And the sheets were made of the softest material he'd ever touched. Never in his life had he seen anything like this.

What had happened?

Where was he?

His last memory was flying out of the shadows...Well, it'd been more like half-controlled falling and tumbling. He hadn't flown that badly since he'd been a toddler first learning to use his wings.

"You're awake."

Rolling over, he turned to see...

*Ah crap.*

Not *her*.

Anyone but her.

Yet there was no mistaking the Sephiroth he'd seen practicing with Kissare. Only now, her hair was loose about her shoulders, flowing to the middle of her back. And those blue eyes seared him. More than that, she was so close to him that he could reach out and touch her.

It was tempting...

She was so incredibly beautiful. So dainty. He'd never seen any creature more enticing. Up close, he reminded her more of a tiny fairy sprite than a warrior, especially with that pert little nose.

With a worried frown, she brought a cup of water to him and sat on the edge of his bed. "Here. Drink slowly."

He took the cup from her hands, trying not to notice how perfectly delicate and manicured they were. "Where am I?"

"The hall of the Sephirii."

"This doesn't look like a hall."

A becoming blush stained her golden cheeks. "It's our barracks. You're in my room."

More to the point, he was in her bed, and that knowledge brought out all kinds of thoughts he didn't want to have while she was in the room with him. Mostly, because he was sure she'd slap him if she could read his mind.

"Any idea why I'm here?"

Myone blinked at his question in a way that said it confused her. "You're joking?"

"Sarcasm. It's my native tongue. Since I'm in your bed, I assume you know how I got in it." He glanced under the blanket and realized something quite embarrassing. "Naked. I just don't know why you'd bring me here and disrobe me."

That caused her to bolt from the bed and put more feet between them than he wanted. "Your clothes were ruined by all the arrows." She went to a small chest near the window and picked up a small bundle. "I have more for you. Perhaps you should put them on."

She was completely flummoxed, and that made him want to smile. She was even more exquisite up close.

And without thinking, he set the cup on the table beside the bed and drew back the covers to reach for the clothes in her arms.

With a horrified shriek, she instantly vanished. How weird was that?

Had he frightened her? He hadn't meant to.

"Uh...Clothes?" he asked. "I need something to wear."

They appeared in a pile at his feet, and then he understood what had caused her to bolt so unexpectedly.

Xev laughed at the sight, and at her reaction, which told him she was as innocent as she appeared. Just thinking of that also made him glad that she'd vanished when she had. He didn't need her to know how much he was attracted to her. That knowledge was dangerous to both of them.

MYONE STOOD in the hallway outside her room, trying to regain some semblance of decorum.

Her face was so hot, she was amazed her cheeks hadn't burst into flames. When they first brought Jaden's son in for treatment, she'd told herself it was because even the evil needed help. It was wrong to leave him for his enemies to find.

But when they'd removed those arrows and his clothes, and she'd seen the multitude of scars that marred his flesh...

When had someone *not* been trying to kill him? He was just a young man surely no older than she was, yet his body had been marred with scars. Not even their strongest or bravest warriors who'd been in battles for centuries carried the number of scars he did. His body was a road map of anguish.

That had made her hurt for him. No one should be subjected to so much pain.

To her dismay, Kuru had laughed about the scars. "He really must upset his mother a lot."

His comment had confused her. "What?"

He'd gestured at the young god's bloody body. "I've heard it said that Azura never spares a whip, and I've seen these scars on others who serve her. Judging by this amount, he must go out of his way to anger his mother. Probably a few others, too."

Without thinking, she'd placed her hand against a particularly long, nasty scar that ran from his stomach to his hip and up under his arm.

Poor thing. She couldn't imagine anyone hurting her like this. Not for any reason. While her mother had perished just hours after her birth, she knew her mother would have never beaten her, especially not like this. Nor could she imagine her father allowing it.

Why would Jaden not stop this or protect his son? She'd always thought of the light gods as being decent and caring.

This wasn't care. It was horrible, and it made her heart ache that his parents refused to protect him.

Even now, she saw those scars and wanted to know why his father hated him so. What he could possibly do to make a mother beat him until he bled. It just didn't make sense.

Clearing her throat, Myone knocked on her door. "Daraxerxes? Are you dressed?"

No answer.

She knocked again. "Daraxerxes?"

And again, nothing. Not even the rustle of cloth.

Myone scowled as she debated what to do. Should she go in?

*What if he's still naked?*

She covered her face with her hands, unable to believe how bold he'd been when he stood up. She would have died of embarrassment. But apparently, he had no modesty whatsoever.

Or maybe he'd wanted to shock her.

Maybe he was still trying to.

"This is ridiculous." She drew a trembling breath. "I'm coming back in. Please make sure you're dressed or covered."

Myone opened the door to find her room completely empty.

He was gone?

Why? She looked around the room and found no trace of him. Except he'd left something on her bed.

Even more confused, she went to see what it was.

A single red rose lay upon her pillow with a simple, handwritten note.

*Thank you.*

There was no other sign that he'd ever been here. He'd even changed her sheets so that they were no longer marred with his blood.

Her hand trembling, she reached out for the note that held his strong, masculine script. Two simple words, yet they touched her deeply. It made no sense.

Nor did the sensation of emptiness inside her.

*You're not sentimental. What's wrong with you?*

That was certainly true. Her father had raised her to be a warrior, as he was. Tough. Emotionless.

Just as her mother had been. They had no other purpose than to abide by the will of the gods they served. Her goal had always been to become the Sephirii second-in-command one day.

To stand strong at Kissare's side in battle and protect their gods.

She wasn't far from it. There was only one Sephiroth who ranked between her and Kissare. Sadly, that Sephiroth was also Kissare's brother, Tisahn. But she felt certain that if she worked hard enough, she could rise to Tisahn's position one day.

So why were her thoughts being wasted on someone she'd most likely never see again?

He was gone.

She had duties to attend.

Forcing herself to put him out of her thoughts, she put his note away and took the rose to her table.

It would be a shame to throw it out.

Wasteful.

That was the lie she told herself as she carefully put it in a vase with water and left it on the table beside her bed.

There was nothing sentimental about this.

She was being practical. Preserving a piece of beauty. Nothing more to it than that.

And she was too busy for such nonsense. He'd left her without so much as a goodbye. Obviously, they were strangers, and it was all they'd ever be.

"Peace to you, Lord Daraxerxes." And with that, she left the room.

Xev sighed as he watched her leave from the shadows he'd stepped into when he heard her returning.

*You're such a coward.*

He wouldn't argue that. But what was there to say? She was a tool of the Primals. He was their outcast.

They had no business together. No matter how much he might wish to know her better, he didn't dare.

Braith was one of the Primals. Her powers were absolute, and the others were already turning on her just for being pregnant. If they ever learned Kissare was the father of her child...

Kissare was dead. They would brutally kill him.

Given that, Myone was off-limits. Xev would never stand by and watch her pay the price for hormones he didn't even want.

Besides, he had something a lot more important to deal with.

Someone had come at his back. He didn't know who, but he was going to find out, and when he did, there would be an accounting. And the perpetrator would bleed a lot more than he had.

Turning around, he left and headed back to his own rooms. But as he flew, he wondered more and more about who'd come for him.

And why.

"Shadow?" he called as soon as he was in his bedroom.

"Don't you have a life?"

He snorted at Shadow's surly question. "Not really. And someone almost ended what little bit of one I manage."

Shadow appeared beside him instantly. He pulled his shirt on, then fastened his breeches. "What?"

"I was in Skatos when someone ambushed me."

Shadow blinked slowly as if digesting those words. "Is that why you've been silent over the last four days?"

Those words shocked him. "What?"

"Mal and I have tried to contact you several times. We were getting worried. Is that where you've been?"

Xev ignored the question. "Four days?" He was astounded that he'd been out for so long. His best guess had been a couple of hours.

Had Myone really been tending him for *days*? Why would she have done that?

"Four days," Shadow repeated. "One more day and we were going to send out hunters for you." He raked his hand through his unbound hair so that he could pull it back into a tight ponytail. "Ambushed you how?"

Xev opened his tunic to show his brother the healing wounds. "Used me as their arrow catcher."

The color faded from Shadow's face. "Shit...Who'd you piss off?"

"No idea. Other than my mother, but she wouldn't have done this in secret." She'd have wanted to see the look on his face while she ripped him apart. Her game was pain. She never went after someone in secret. "Who could go to your domain and dare this?"

Anger flickered in Shadow's eyes. "You don't think I—"

"If I thought you'd done this, we wouldn't be speaking. We'd be fighting. I know better. Who has access to the shadows?"

"Unfortunately, most demons. Some gods. It's not like it's a secret. It's basically open to anyone who as the powers to access it."

That was what Xev was afraid of. "So, it could be anyone."

"Yeah. But why come after you?"

"That's what I want to know. Azura had just put me on a mission for her when I was run down. So I doubt she was behind it." Then again, his mother was deranged. Capable of anything, anytime.

*She didn't do this.*

Yeah, as much as he'd like to think that, he did know better.

"How'd you survive it?"

Xev gave him a dry smirk. "Flew out of the realm to a place I didn't think a demon would dare follow me."

"Good call. But where wouldn't a demon go?" No sooner had Shadow spoken those words than he cursed. "Oh really? Sephirii? Are you out of your mind? What were you thinking?"

Xev had no idea why his brother was surprised. "Can you think of anyplace better?"

"Well, yeah, but the gods there would have taken your head for daring to fly into their palaces or temples."

"Exactly. The only chance I had was that the Sephirii would hesitate before they killed me." He closed his tunic. "Thankfully, my gamble worked."

Shadow nodded. "What did you tell the Sephirii?"

"Nothing. I don't really know anything other than I was shot. A lot."

Shadow sucked his breath in sharply between his teeth. "I don't envy you, little brother."

"I don't envy me either. Is there any way you can help me figure out who did this?"

"There's someone..." Shadow's voice drifted off as if he were thinking twice about it.

"Who is it?"

"Lombrey." No sooner had he spoken the name than the darkest shadow in the corner of Xev's room took on the form of a tall, muscular man. With hair darker than night, he had caramel skin and eyes as golden as Myone's wings.

That being said, he was as huge as Jaden. Maybe more so.

Given his own height, Xev didn't normally look up at anyone. But he had to this time. Lombrey towered over Shadow, who barely reached the middle of his chest.

More than that, there was a darkness in those eyes that rivaled Noir's. It was palpable, and it ignited every evil gene inside Xev's body.

When Lombrey started toward Xev, Shadow stopped him. "Xev's a friend."

Lombrey didn't speak. He merely froze then cast a sinister scowl toward Shadow.

"I know. Trust me. He's friendly. And he was attacked in the shadows four days ago. Did you see anything when it happened?"

Lombrey shook his head, then gestured at Shadow.

"Is he saying something?" Xev asked.

"No. He's telling me that I should be careful. He felt something the day you were attacked, but he doesn't know what it was. The one thing it wasn't was a demon. You have an unknown enemy. Watch your back."

Lombrey vanished.

"Who was that?" Xev asked Shadow once they were alone again.

"He's the darkness we all fear. His soul is made up of millions of screaming victims."

Well, that was terrifyingly ominous and it sent a shiver down Xev's spine. "What?"

Shadow inclined his head. "He's the eternal death that was created alongside the Primals."

Eternal death? That didn't make sense. "Isn't all death eternal?"

"No. Not all death. You can actually come back from a number of them. Except for his. Lombrey swallows the soul and devours everything he touches. He is the nightmare that haunts all creatures. That fear we have that if we die, there's nothing left of us."

"And he lives in Skatos?"

Shadow nodded.

"Why?"

"For an obvious reason, no one wants him. I stumbled

across him long ago and offered him a home in Skatos with me."

Xev was aghast. Shadow had more guts than anyone he knew. Still…"You have got to stop bringing home strays."

"Says one of the strays I took in?"

That was different. "I'm your brother."

"So is Lombrey. Not by blood, but by choice."

Xev wasn't sure what to say to that. While he'd known that Shadow kept odd company, this one beat all the others. "Eternal death, huh?"

"Better to make friends with him than become his enemy."

That was definitely true. He couldn't fault Shadow for that logic.

Xev nodded. "Just do me a favor and let me know if he ever comes for me."

Shadow let out a low, evil laugh. "That's the thing, little brother. He doesn't tell anyone. I won't know until he strikes, and you vanish from all realms. No one keeps a secret better than Lombrey."

*Lovely.* "Can he kill the Primals?"

"I don't think so."

"What do you mean?"

Shadow looked away from him. "He went after Lilit long ago. That's part of what's wrong with him now. Not only did he fail to kill her, she cursed him."

That stunned Xev as it was something he'd never known about. Not so much that Lombrey failed or that she'd cursed him, but that he attacked her to begin with. "Why did he go after her?"

"Noir told him to."

Of course he had. Leave it to Noir to try to kill his sister, and get an innocent party cursed in the process. Sounded exactly like something he'd do.

"As a result of that unpleasant nightmare, Lombrey will never trust anyone again."

Xev wasn't so sure about that, as he knew one person Lombrey trusted. "Except you."

"Yeah. That's a long, long story for another day."

"Fine. Keep your secrets." *And I'll keep mine.*

In the meantime, Xev had an assassin to find and a story to make up to tell his mother as to why he hadn't discovered a name he already knew.

Unlike Lombrey, he wasn't about to kill an innocent person just because a Primal wanted it that way.

He didn't care what they did to him. Pain he could take. They were old friends who'd shaken hands early in his childhood when he watched Azura kill Michi.

Honestly, Xev didn't know why he had any morals. The Source knew Azura had never tried to teach him any, and they made little to no sense to him. Maybe it was because of Michi. She at least had tried to teach him to be kind to others. To respect natural order.

Whatever the reason, he wasn't going to hurt Braith. She'd never harmed him.

But he had every reason to disappoint Azura.

Even if it cost him his life.

XEV WAS CHANGING clothes in his room when he felt a powerful presence appear behind him. An unmistakable one.

"Jaden." He spat his father's name. "To what do I owe this displeasure?"

His father let out a long, tired sigh. A tic started in his angular jaw. If Xev didn't know better, he'd swear he could hear the god counting to ten in his head for patience.

"Your brother told me you were ambushed."

"Shadow?"

"Malphas."

That made more sense. As a rule, Shadow avoided all of the Primals. But Malphas had been equally concerned when Xev told him about the attack.

*Why couldn't you keep your mouth shut, little brother?*

Because, for reasons unknown, Mal cared about him, and Xev wasn't going to curse his brother for that. Malphas and Shadow were the only ones in the universe who cared what happened to him, and he was grateful for them. "What else did he say?"

"You were injured."

"And?"

Jaden shook his head as if Xev's blasé tone irritated him. "And you haven't found out who or what was behind the attack."

What was his point, other than to restate everything Xev knew? "Okay."

The tic sped up. "Why do you make this so difficult for me?"

"Difficult for you? I'm the one who was used as an arrow cushion." And he still had no idea why his father was in his room.

Jaden's mismatched eyes glowed with irritation. "I'm here to ask if you'd like to move into my palace."

His father couldn't have shocked him more had he been the one who'd riddled him with arrows. Had he even heard those words correctly? "You want what?"

"I'm offering you protection."

Since when? His father had never cared about him before. Where was this protection when he was a kid and his mother had wanted him dead?

Or, more to the point, when Jaden had ordered him drowned?

The fact he'd show up now, pretending that he cared, infuriated Xev. How dare he! Where was this asshole when he'd been a boy and Michi was killed because Jaden refused protection to both of them?

He could have saved her. Instead, Jaden had wanted nothing to do with him.

"I don't want anything from you."

Xev started to leave, only to learn that he didn't have the ability to teleport. His father had locked him down the same way his mother did, and that only ignited more fury inside him. "Seriously? Release my powers. Now!"

Jaden refused. "I'm well aware of your feelings toward me, and I don't blame you for them. But you're now of an age where I know you don't allow your mother control over you. I admire that."

Oh, so that was why. Not that he loved him or was concerned about him. He admired the fact Xev wasn't stupid enough to do his mother's bidding or let her control him.

*Wow.*

This wasn't about Xev at all. Jaden was solidifying power. What better way than to put the son he'd denied under his roof? For what? So that Xev could help Mal wrangle demons? He'd really rather not.

His first impulse was to tell his father where he could stick that.

Until he realized his own selfish reason for wanting to stay with his father.

If he were with his sperm donor, then he'd have access to the Sephirii.

More to the point, access to one particular Sephiroth. Myone.

He wouldn't have to hide in the shadows to see her. His father had his own Sephiroth, Kuru, or whatever his name was. If Xev could befriend that Sephiroth...

Maybe, just maybe, he might be able to befriend Myone, too. Maybe they could practice together or share a meal?

*Don't even go there.*

It was an impossible dream. A stupid dream. And still it was there. Taunting him.

Pushing him over the edge of sanity.

Even now, he could see the kindness in her blue eyes. That gentle, unassuming touch.

*Don't!* his mind screamed again.

He didn't listen. Not when something so tempting was there to lure him. "Sure. I'll move in."

The look of shock on Jaden's face should have been memorialized. Xev was sure it was a look his father didn't get very often. It was comical, really, and was probably similar to the look he'd had when his father proposed this to him.

A few weeks ago, he'd have never agreed to it.

Things were different now. He had a new purpose. And someone he actually wanted to see. If living with his father was the price to pay for access to Myone, it was worth it.

She was worth it.

He only prayed that he didn't live to regret this.

## 8

Xev watched Mal as he finished practicing against Kuru in the garden of their father's temple. "Impressive."

Shaking his head, Mal angled his sword in Xev's direction. "Care to spar with me?"

"Don't want to damage your fragile ego. Be a shame to see it bruised after you went through all this to nurture it."

Kuru laughed, not realizing that he was the brunt of Xev's joke.

Until Malphas growled at him. Then Mal's expression turned speculative. "Why don't you two spar?"

"Kuru's too tired." Xev pushed himself away from the column where he stood.

That seemed to upset Kuru. "You think I can't hold my own?"

He definitely couldn't. As good as Mal was, he still wasn't in Xev's league, and they both knew it. Mal was young and lacked Xev's fury. Not to mention the fact that Mal wasn't even trying against the Sephiroth, and they both knew it.

Mal practiced for fun and to learn Sephiroth techniques. Same reason Xev watched them. Neither of them would ever teach a Sephiroth how they fought or give him pointers on how to defeat them or their kind.

However, Kuru's ego was weak, and Xev didn't want to get into a fight with him. Verbal or physical. "Didn't say that."

Fury flared in Kuru's eyes. He flung a sword at Xev, who caught it in one fist.

He shook his head. "You don't want to do this."

"Yes, I do. I'm not tired at all."

Mal laughed. "Go ahead, Xev. I'll get cleaned up while you teach him some manners."

Xev tested the heft of the sword, then gave Kuru a look of warning. "I'm not my brother, Sephiroth. Take heed and walk away while you can." Even in play, he was a lot deadlier than Malphas.

Kuru attacked.

Xev parried the blow. Then, without thinking, he zapped him with his powers.

Kuru went down, face-first.

*Oh crap!* Xev panicked as he realized what he'd done without thinking. He wasn't used to practicing. In his mother's realm, all fights were to the death.

Even a practice match.

"Don't be dead. Don't be dead!" Crap! He pulled the much smaller Sephiroth over. There was no telling what kind of tantrum or seizure his father might have over his little pet being hurt. Even if it was accidental.

"What happened?"

Xev looked up at the female voice, then cursed himself even more as he saw Myone there. "We were sparring and, I don't know...he fainted?" Maybe.

*Or I killed him.*

With a gasp, she knelt on the other side and felt for a pulse. "Did you stab him?"

"No." It was something much worse. Normally, a zap like that just pissed a demon off and made them do something stupid so that he could finish the fight easier.

He'd never zapped a Sephiroth before, so he had no idea what it would do to one of them.

Had he killed him?

"Kuru?" She slapped gently at his cheeks.

He came to with a curse.

Xev sat back in relief. *Thank the Source!*

Until Kuru cursed and went to stab him.

Myone caught his hand. "Don't you dare."

"He tried to kill me!"

Xev scoffed. "I don't *try* to kill anyone. Had I wanted you dead, you'd be gone."

Myone believed those words unequivocally. From everything she'd heard about Daraxerxes, he wasn't one to play at war. He had a furious temper and a sword arm no demon wanted to test.

Which was probably why he'd been ambushed by one of his mother's soldiers.

She helped Kuru to his feet. "You don't appear

harmed." Other than having been knocked out, which could have been accidental. "Perhaps you should return to the barracks."

His eyes still showing the depth of his fury, Kuru nodded, then vanished.

Alone with Daraxerxes, she glanced about nervously. He always seemed so massive and...masculine. Much more handsome than he should. "I should be going, too."

He bit his lip in an adorable way that showed her a strange hesitancy for someone she was sure never hesitated in anything. "Why are you here?"

"To see your father."

"Ah."

"Ah? Why the weird note in your voice?"

He smiled at her and shrugged in an adorable manner that strangely reminded her of a boy. "It was directed at me for being dense. Of course you're here for my father. Why else?"

She returned his smile. "Well, I'm glad you didn't kill Kuru."

"Me too," he mumbled.

That confession caught her off guard. "Pardon? You meant to do that?"

He actually blushed. "No, of course not. I didn't mean to hit him so hard. I'm not used to pulling punches. I forget that other creatures aren't as tough as demons."

That unexpected arrogance irritated her. "You really think a demon is stronger than a Sephiroth?"

Xev realized he'd just stepped into a treacherous pit. Her eyes were fired by her fury. And that offended tone warned him to walk his statement back. "Uh…" *Crap.* He didn't want to lie to her. Nor did he want to anger her more.

How could he get out of this?

*Help me!*

"You want the truth?" he asked her.

"Of course."

"If a war was to break out, it wouldn't go well for your species."

Myone glared at him and his audacity. Did he really think for one second that a demon could hold his own against her people?

He was deranged.

Or was he?

She forced herself to calm down as a bad feeling went through her. Kuru had been unconscious on her arrival. Daraxerxes hadn't even been breathing heavily.

Putting aside her own arrogance, what if he was right? The Sephirii always assumed they were stronger and better at fighting, but what if they weren't?

What if he knew something they didn't?

"You're not being mean, are you? You really think that."

"I don't think anything. It's the truth." That wasn't an obnoxious boast. He was speaking honestly.

Myone felt sick to her stomach. The last thing she wanted was to see her people harmed. If there was a war, they needed to know how to fight against their enemies. Both the demons and the dark gods.

"Can you teach me how to fight against them?"

Xev wouldn't have been more stunned had she slapped him. That, he would have at least expected. This...

"Seriously?"

She nodded. "I was born to protect the gods. I need to know how to fight demons. Was that not what Kuru was doing with Malphas?"

No. Mal had no interest in teaching Kuru any of their secrets. He only sparred with the Sephiroth to gain knowledge as to how they fought and to learn what sword skill they knew.

Mal had never once taught Kuru anything that would be beneficial to the Sephiroth in a real fight against any demon. Why would he? If they ever went to war, none of them would want a level playing field.

But if it would allow Xev some time with her...

He could share a few things to help her fight against them. It wasn't as if any of the demons meant anything to him. Other than Mal, he couldn't care less about a demon. All they'd ever done was make his life miserable. Abuse him at Azura's command.

Honestly, he hated them.

But he didn't hate her. She beguiled him.

"You really want to learn?" he asked.

She nodded.

*You know you shouldn't do this.* Training her would be all kinds of stupid.

*It'll keep her coming back to you every day.*

That was the one major advantage.

*Do it.*

Mal would kill him. Azura and Noir would want his throat for even considering it. Last thing they wanted was a Sephiroth who knew how to quell them or their army.

That just made it all the more appealing. Aggravating his mother was the only pleasure he had in life.

*Let the rain come down on me.*

Xev smiled at her. "Sure."

"Really?"

He nodded. "Come dressed and ready to learn skills you can't imagine."

"I will. Thank you." She rose up on her toes and placed a chaste kiss to his cheek, then she ran toward his father's area of the palace.

Xev stood there, completely stunned. She'd kissed him. Well, not really, but still his cheek burned from the softness of her lips.

Never had anyone given him something so chaste that had meant so much.

Touched him so deeply.

*This is madness.*

He couldn't argue that. Any more than he could argue how much he was looking forward to their first session.

PAIMON CLAPPED Kuru on the back as they watched Myone and Daraxerxes from the shadows. "What did I tell you?"

The demon had been right. There was something weird between Myone and Daraxerxes. "It doesn't matter.

No Sephiroth is supposed to mix with a Primal or their offspring. Myone would never break her vows."

Paimon snorted. "If you say so."

Kuru did, but it didn't mean that he might not be able to use this to his own advantage...

"Keep an eye on them, demon. Let me know if anything changes."

Paimon rolled his eyes as the Sephiroth flew off. Stupid insect had no idea the gift he was giving him. At least, not at the moment.

But Paimon knew. This was juicy. Unlike the others, he paid close attention to his enemies. While he commanded three legions for Azura, Daraxerxes commanded more these days.

Even though he was a traitor, Azura had yet to denounce him.

That galled him most of all. Xev might be her son, but Paimon knew he was a traitor. This attraction to a Sephiroth proved it, and one day, it would be his undoing.

*I'm a true son.* Yet Azura and Noir treated Paimon like an animal.

It infuriated him. What would it take for them to show the same loyalty to him that they showed to Anat and Daraxerxes? Why was he denied?

Because his mother was a demon?

It wasn't right.

Daraxerxes shouldn't have survived Paimon's attack. But maybe it was a good thing that he had.

Maybe letting the gods kill his enemy would be the best revenge of all. This way, he wouldn't risk dying for it.

**9**

———————

"Daraxerxes?"

Xev cringed at the name even while his heart quickened at the sound of Myone's voice. "Xev."

She pulled up short. "What?"

"I don't use the name Azura gave me. My name is Xevikan or Xev." The name Michi had given him when she took him in. That was the only name he'd ever wanted, and it was the one he'd bear to the date of his death.

"Sorry. I didn't know."

"It's all right. In case you haven't heard, I don't think much of the creature who gave birth to me."

"Understood. And there's no need to be polite. I've heard many rants from Cam about her."

"Bet you have." Xev scowled as he realized she held a practice sword. "Where's your real weapon?"

"She's resting. I almost never use her for practice. She doesn't like it."

That told him something very important about Myone. "So, you're one of the Mimoroux." There were ten of them who were allowed to carry a Seraph sword. Or, more to the point, the sword had chosen them to carry it. Those swords were inhabited by a war spirit who guided them and helped them in battle.

As such, they were the most cherished swords and warriors in their ranks. It was a high honor, indeed.

Myone looked away sheepishly. "My mother wielded her originally. After she died giving birth to me, Kasumi refused to allow anyone else to wield her."

That saddened him for her. He hated for anyone to lose their mother. "I'm sorry about your mother."

"Thank you."

Clearing his throat, he quickly sought to change the subject to a happier topic. "So how did you know you were her designated warrior?"

Myone's mind went back to that fateful day. "She called to me when I was a girl."

Barely nine, she'd been playing in the garden when she heard someone calling out to her. Thinking she was in trouble, she'd gone inside their home slowly. "Hello?" she'd called out, looking for her father, or someone else.

No one had answered.

Not until she turned around to return to the yard.

"Myone..." Definitely a female voice.

That had confused her, as there weren't any women in their home. Her father had refused to allow another woman near him after the death of her mother. His love for her had been so great that, to this day, he'd never even looked at another.

"Hello?" she'd called out again.

"In here, child." The voice had begun to hum.

Curious, she'd followed that hum into her father's bedroom. She stood in the doorway. "I'm not supposed to enter here when my father's not home."

"Come closer, child. I want to see you."

Those words had seemed eerie, and yet she'd been compelled against all reason to follow the ethereal voice that beckoned her to break her father's rules. So she'd walked into the bedroom, prepared to run if she heard any noise.

The humming led her into a small antechamber off to the side. Inside that antechamber where her father stored his clothing and weapons, there was a glass case on top of a pedestal table. Myone knew this was her mother's sword that her father kept in a place of honor.

The gold sword gleamed in the dim light. Intricately engraved, it was a thing of absolute beauty. Instead of leather, her mother had used a beautiful red silk scarf to secure the scabbard to her armor. The color of blood. It was a stark contrast to the gold.

"Hold me."

She'd blinked at the order. "What?"

"You will be my warrior, Myone. Don't be afraid. Come closer to me, child."

Biting her lip, she'd been terrified. Yet the gold had warmed her. As did the voice of the sword.

"Bond with me, and I will make sure that you never fall in battle."

Before she even realized what she was doing, she'd opened the glass and taken the sword in hand. The moment she did, pain tore through her so fiercely that she'd screamed out.

Her father had appeared in the room instantly, then cursed.

It was too late. Kasumi had claimed her. Even though no sword had ever chosen a child before, Kasumi had wanted her and taken her to be her initiate.

Myone had been training for war ever since.

Clearing her throat, she met Xev's curious gaze. "Kasumi can be bloodthirsty. She's not a good practice partner."

"Very well." He changed his sword to a wooden one with his powers. That was definitely impressive and reminded her that he was a full-blooded god. "You ready?"

She nodded.

"First lesson. Demons don't play by any rules. Nor do they follow them. There's only one law in battle."

"Don't die."

He saluted her with his practice sword. "Exactly. And if you do, make sure you take your killer with you."

She widened her eyes at that. "What?"

"Demon law. No sonofabitch kills me and lives. They will do whatever they can to take you with them. So expect that. And I do mean *any*thing."

"Good to know." She put her left foot behind her and fell into her practice pose.

He started to swing at her.

As she went to block that stroke, he reversed direction and went for her feet.

She jumped without thought.

Xev pulled back. "Good. You're better than most. Remember, they don't telegraph where they're going to strike, and they believe in misdirection."

She nodded. "May I ask you something personal?"

Xev didn't like the tone of her voice. But he was curious what she considered personal. "What?"

"Were you really suckled by a demon?"

That unexpected question brought a ferocious pain to his chest—one so bad that, for a moment, he couldn't breathe as he tried to determine the source of what he felt. Was it grief over Michi or rage that Myone would ask him anything about his mother?

He decided it stemmed from any mention of the fox he'd loved more than his own life. "An Inari, and she was goodness personified. Speak of her with only reverence in your voice." Michi's kind were often referred to by the name of the goddess she'd served. She might have been a demon, but there was no evil in her.

Myone scowled. "I didn't think any demon was capable of kindness."

Xev had to force his anger down. She wasn't trying to be insulting. Like most, she was ignorant and curious. He needed to respect that. "Forget what you think you know about demons. They're not all evil or bad."

"Like Malphas?"

That brought out a grin as he thought about his

brother. "Mal is his own kind of evil, but he's nothing like the ones who serve Azura. Think of demons as you would people and gods. Some of them are exceptionally kind and giving, and others will cut your throat without hesitation for something as simple as making the wrong comment."

She nodded. "Your Inari?"

"Absolute decency. Everyone should have a mother like her."

Tears welled in her eyes. "I never knew my mother. She died when I was born."

Feeling bad for her, Xev stepped forward and brushed away the single tear on her cheek. "I'm sure she would have been like my Michi. Just be grateful your mother wasn't Azura."

Myone didn't miss the bitterness in his tone when he spoke of the goddess who'd birthed him. "I'm sorry."

"Not your fault. That I lay fully on Jaden's groin and drunken stupor."

She let out a squeak. "You like to shock me, don't you?"

"I would say no, but you are awfully cute when I do." His eyes widened an instant after he spoke those words. "I mean, I—"

She cut his words off by placing her finger over his lips. "It's all right, Xev. I think you're cute, too."

Xev couldn't breathe as those words registered. She thought him cute?

Then, before he realized what she was doing, she kissed him quickly on the lips...and set him on his ass with one swift move.

Smiling, she planted her foot on his chest and held her wooden sword at his throat. "Is that demon-like enough for you?"

Stunned and aghast, he stared up at her in awe. "You did not just do that."

When he moved to flip her, she used her wings to hover over him.

*Wow.* She was a fast learner.

He growled, then flew after her.

Squeaking, she started altering her path in an effort to avoid him.

It worked until he used his powers to flash himself in front of her.

She collided with him.

Xev wrapped his arms around her and held her against his chest to keep her from falling. "If I were a demon, you'd have been stabbed, Myone. Remember to always expect the unexpected. They don't fight with honor."

"Do you?"

"Depends on who I'm fighting." He scowled, then shook his head. "No, it doesn't. I fight like a demon. Always."

"Then I will fight like one, too."

And he would spend the rest of eternity making sure no demon ever harmed her.

**10**

———

"The baby's here!"

Xev felt the color drain from his face as he heard the cry go up in the market where he was meeting with his brothers. Without being told, he knew the baby was Braith's. It was the only birth they'd all been waiting for.

And dreading.

Braith had yet to disclose anything about the father. Which meant he had yet to breathe a word to anyone. Even Xev's mother, who was furious over his excuses for not learning something he already knew.

Or, more to the point, disclosing what he knew.

The only thing that saved him was the fact that he was living with his father. No matter how much she wanted to, Azura didn't dare breach those walls to drag Xev to her hell. Or send her demons to Jaden's hall to fetch him.

All she could do now was shriek at him.

For the first time in his life, he had a modicum of peace, and for that he was eternally grateful to his father.

If only his father would free him completely from his mother's clutches.

Jaden had refused. *I don't want to get caught up in those politics.*

Bully for him that he had a choice. Xev was trapped, and he was tired of playing this game between them.

Not wanting to think about that, he held his goblet up to Shadow and Malphas. "To Braith and her son."

"To Braith and her son," they said in unison before clinking their goblets against his.

Shadow downed his in one gulp then laughed. "I have to say that I'm shocked Azura hasn't killed you for not telling her who the baby's father is. Respect."

Malphas snorted in what might have been agreement, but with Mal, one could never really tell. "Here's to grand stupidity on both our parts. I'm lucky Jaden hasn't gutted me for not telling him, either."

Xev reached to pour more ale from the wooden flagon on the table, only to realize it was empty. "Next round's on me."

He got up to get another flagon.

As he reached the bar, a much smaller person turned and ran straight into him. Normally, such a thing would have set his temper aflame.

However, the soft gasp caught his attention.

And when he looked down into a pair of celestial blue eyes, all thoughts of anger fled.

"Xev."

His name on Myone's lips always set fire to his soul. "Greetings, fair lady."

Her cheeks turned bright red. "What are you doing here?"

"Meeting with my brothers. You?"

"Here, my lady." The bartender handed her a bottle of wine.

"Thank you." She took it, then tucked it into a basket she carried. "I'm running errands for Cam."

Of course she was. Why else would she be in a place like this unless it was to serve her goddess?

The one thing Xev had learned over the last few months of training her had been the fact that she was rather boring.

As sick as it was, he liked that about her. Especially whenever she'd bring her lyre to practice. He loved to hear her play. Even though they were sweet, innocent songs, not the tawdry or bawdy songs he'd been exposed to in his mother's court, he found them oddly entertaining.

Yeah, there was something seriously wrong with him that he found everything about her perfect. Even when it irritated him, he liked it.

He indicated the basket with a jerk of his chin. "I take it the wine's for her?"

"To celebrate. At least, that's what she claims."

Xev forced himself not to react. Out of all his aunts, Cam was his least favorite. Even though she was a goddess of light, she was terribly judgmental. Maybe it came from the fact that she was the goddess of justice.

Or perhaps she just had an innate hatred for him, personally. Whatever it was, he wouldn't shed a single tear to find her gone, except for the fact that it would hurt Myone, who was attached to the goddess she served.

"I don't envy you your service to her."

Myone was stunned by his dry words and the sincerity she saw in his eyes. He really didn't like her mistress. "She's kind and fair."

"I guess she hides that side of her personality from me." He ordered more ale from the bartender then turned back to her. "Are you excited about Braith's child?"

Myone bit her lip at his unexpected question. "Honestly?"

He nodded.

"I'm petrified. Can you imagine someone so evil spawning a child? Just imagine what he's going to be like. No doubt he'll be even more repugnant than his mother." The instant those words were out of her mouth, she cursed herself for speaking them.

After these past months of training together, she'd forgotten who Xev's mother was. That he was a child born divided. Truly, he never showed her that side of himself. All he'd ever been was kind and gentle.

Instead of being offended, he laughed it off. "I don't have to imagine it. I live that nightmare every day. Hopefully, Braith will be kinder to her child than she is to others."

He took the flagon and started away.

Myone stopped him. "I'm so sorry, Xev. It was a thoughtless thing to say. Truly, I meant no offense to you."

Kindness softened his gaze. "Don't worry, Myone. In my world, that doesn't even come close to offending me. Have you met my brothers? Their kindest greetings are harsher."

She laughed at his charity. "I have, and I won't be unkind about them, as I know you're rather fond of their company."

"Then I shall be unkind enough to them for both of us." Xev smiled as she laughed again. The sound was so sweet and musical. He could listen to her laughter all day long.

But Shadow was already glaring at him and holding his hands up in irritation over his delay.

"And they are waiting for their drinks. It was nice running into you when you don't have a sword in hand to kick my butt."

"Again, sweet sir, you are far too kind about my inept abilities." Inclining her head, she left him.

Xev wanted to follow after her, but he knew better. Cam would never welcome him into her home. She wasn't known for tolerance. And, as noted, she really didn't care for him, and she never would.

Sighing, he returned to their table with the flagon and set it down.

*Don't do it.*

He knew better.

Sadly, he wasn't listening to his common sense.

"I need to run an errand."

"Want us to come?" Shadow asked him.

"I'm good." Xev left them before they could protest or

trail after him, or he could think better of this. This was one thing he needed to do alone.

He caught up to Myone in the marketplace, where she was buying cheese and wine for her goddess.

"Are you following me?" she asked in a teasing tone.

"If I was?"

She leaned in to whisper, "I'd tell you to be more discreet."

That enticed him. "You're not afraid?"

"You've had more than one chance to end my life, Lord Xev. Should I be afraid?"

"No," he answered honestly. "You're the only one I'd never hurt."

"Dary—"

"I know, Myone," he said, cutting her off. She was the only one who called him that, and he had no idea why it melted him when she used it, but it did. "Better than you do." He wanted to touch her but didn't dare.

If anyone saw them…

She looked around to make sure no one was too close. "I feel the same for you. We just have to be careful."

He nodded. "I also wanted to let you know not to worry if I'm not at practice later."

"What? Why?"

"I haven't done something Azura wanted me to."

She scowled at him. "Which is?"

"Give her the name of the father of Braith's child."

Eyes wide, she gasped. "Do you know it?"

"I've known it since before I met you."

"And you haven't told her?"

Xev shook his head. "I refuse to hurt Braith or her child. They don't deserve my mother's wrath."

Myone choked on her tears. He was even sweeter than she'd imagined. He was protecting a goddess known for her malicious cruelty. One who wouldn't have hesitated to attack him or give him up to his parents without a second thought.

And she was sure he wasn't doing it for Braith's sake. But to protect her innocent baby.

Myone knew the story of his birth, just as everyone did. The way his father had denounced him, and his mother had hunted him. It said a lot for him that he didn't return that favor to another child, but rather risked his own life to safeguard a baby he didn't know and that he had no vested interest in.

Just as his Inari mother had done with him.

And in that moment, Myone realized something.

She loved him.

He wasn't the monster he thought himself to be or that others accused him of being. If he was, he'd hand over the name of the baby's father and not think twice. He wouldn't care what happened to either of them. He'd be more concerned with his own welfare.

Instead, he was willing to bleed for a goddess who'd never cared to protect him. A goddess who'd ignored his pain.

Just as in all these months, he'd been so careful not to harm her during their practices. So charming and sweet with her. Nothing like his mother.

Nothing like anyone else she knew.

She saw Xev. The real him that others refused to see.

"What will she do to you?"

He shrugged with a nonchalance she knew he couldn't possibly feel. "I don't know. But it won't be pleasant. I'll be in touch when I can."

She took his hand and squeezed it. "Call me if you need me. I will come."

There was a dark shadow in his eyes that frightened her. "I won't risk you."

"Call if you need me," she repeated. She squeezed his hand one more time then left him.

Xev refused move for a full minute as he savored Myone's lingering touch.

Not even with his mother screaming a summons in his head did he move. He just wanted to stay here and feel the lingering warmth of Myone's hand on his skin.

But this couldn't be avoided. It was what he got for leaving his father's home. He should have known better. So long as he was under his father's roof, she couldn't summon him. Whenever he left, she had access to him.

*Why did the baby have to be born now?*

Sighing, he teleported to Azura's throne room. He'd barely manifested there before she hurled him against the far wall with such force that he slammed into it sideways.

*Ow.*

"Where have you been?"

Pushing himself to his feet, he sighed as he faced her. "My father's palace," he lied.

Azura glared at him. "You know what I mean! Do you have that name?"

He rippled his wings, then rolled his shoulders, trying to alleviate some of the pain that continued to plague his back from her attack. "No one knows it." Funny how he never minded lying to her. It didn't bother him in the least.

She blasted him. "You failed me."

The irony of that comment wasn't lost on him. It actually made him laugh as he caught himself with his wings and hovered in the room.

Which made Azura even angrier. "What's so funny?"

"Just thinking of how many times in my life my dear old mom has failed me."

That did exactly what he expected—set her off into one of her more stellar tantrums, where she blasted him so fast and furiously, he couldn't counter them all.

By the time it was over, Xev wished himself dead and never born.

It changed nothing.

He knew how much she hated him. It was entirely mutual. But at least this time, he had something to look forward to.

Myone.

All he had to do was survive this.

## 11

———

Myone knew this was all kinds of forbidden, and yet she had to know Xev was all right. She hadn't seen or heard from him in what seemed like forever.

Desperate, she knocked on the door of his room.

There was a muffled sound inside, but she couldn't quite make it out.

*Go home.*

That was the sanest thing. Too bad it wasn't in her to leave without an answer. So she pushed open the door.

The room was uncomfortably warm. The windows were shut, and it appeared as if no one had been here.

Until her gaze went to the bed.

Xev lay there, sweating.

She moved to stand over his inert body. "Are you all right?"

He remained as still as a corpse. "You shouldn't be here."

"I know." But she was so relieved he was in his bed, and alive. "I had to make sure you were all right."

Snorting, he rolled over to show her that he was anything but.

Her breath caught in her throat as she saw the bruises marring his face and bare torso. "What happened?"

"Motherly affection." He brushed his thumb over his swollen bottom lip.

Feeling terrible for him, she sat beside him on the mattress and brushed the hair back from his battered forehead. "I wish I could get you away from her."

"It's fine. I did what I set out to do."

She scowled at his odd words. "What was that?"

"Infuriate her."

Myone sat back and shook her head. "Maybe that shouldn't be your goal."

Sitting up, he snorted. "I can think of nothing better. Other than having you come check on me." He wrinkled his nose then cursed in pain. "Maybe have you kiss some boo-boos."

"You're silly."

Xev took her hand in his. Only for her was he ever silly. Anyone else...he was deadly.

Although, at the moment, he didn't think he could fasten his own sword belt, never mind hurt someone.

But Myone was here. To have her look at him like this, he'd endure a thousand maternal encounters.

"Daraxerxes?"

He cursed silently at the sound of Jaden's voice and the loud banging on his door. "It's my father," he whispered.

"I'll come back later." She vanished just as Jaden pushed the door open.

"Did I hear voices?"

Xev shrugged. "Why are you asking me? I don't know what sounds play in your head."

"You're not funny."

"I think I'm hysterical."

Jaden scowled as he finally focused his attention on Xev's damaged body. "What happened to you?"

"Ran afoul of the nightmare that birthed me. Thank you so much for that, by the way. You just had to get frisky with her, didn't you?"

He actually appeared sympathetic. "I'm sorry."

Hollow words. Especially since Xev knew his father didn't really care what happened to him. "We're all sorry for something. And I know that's not why you're here. Care to enlighten me?"

Jaden sighed. "I know who the father of Braith's child is."

Xev didn't move as he waited for his father to continue. When he didn't, Xev prompted him, "And...?"

"I don't know what to do about it."

"Why are you bothering me?" Was he seeking a conscience? "There's nothing to do. Leave her alone and let her raise her child in peace."

"You make it sound as if that's an easy thing to do."

Just like a Primal. They were forever meddling in things they should leave alone.

Like Xev's life.

He sighed. "It is. Just pretend you know nothing and go about your business."

"Is that what you do?"

Now his father had lost him. "How do you mean?"

Jaden's mismatched gaze intensified. "I know you keep things from me."

"Yeah, well. You're not special. I keep them from everyone." Except Myone. He loved her to distraction, and there was no need to keep anything from her. She never judged or held them against him.

Unlike his father. Xev didn't dare tell him anything, as he had no idea how his father would react to any given thing he said, thought, or did.

Jaden shook his head. "I know my siblings. They're not going to let this go. They will punish Braith for this."

"Why?"

"Because they know what she's capable of. The last thing they want is another person having power over her."

What could a Sephiroth do? They didn't plot mischief. He'd yet to meet one who schemed.

It was part of what made them so damn boring. And irritating.

And what made him treasure Myone most of all. She was never conniving or vicious. All they did was compliment each other.

Be nice. If only the rest of the world could be so decent, they'd all be better off.

"I don't see the harm in leaving her in peace."

Stepping further into his room, Jaden drew up a chair

so that he could sit beside Xev's bed. "Neither do I, but the others won't chance it."

Xev ground his teeth in irritation. After all this time, his father finally wanted a bedside chat. Seriously?

"So why does that bring you here?"

Jaden met his curious gaze. "I want to know from you how hard is it to be a child of light and dark."

Xev had to bite back a snide quip that he knew would cause his father to explode and probably beat him even worse than Azura had. "Don't you know?"

Jaden scowled at him. "Of course not. How would I?"

Xev looked away. *Say nothing.*

"What do you know?" Jaden asked.

*Don't say it,* Xev's mind repeated. That was the smartest thing to do. Unless he wanted to live with Azura again...and he most definitely did not.

But if he didn't answer, his father wouldn't let it go.

"Xev?"

He had to say something. So he decided to hedge a bit. "How often you slum with demons." Hence the birth of Malphas.

But Mal's mother wasn't the only demon Jaden had trifled with. "Why would a light god be so determined to hang out with demons?"

Jaden's gaze narrowed. "You have a theory?"

"I have an opinion."

"And that is?"

"That the demons we know and love were born from you."

Jaden paled. "What makes you think that?"

Think, nothing. Xev wasn't stupid. It was common sense. "I know for a fact that they're not from Azura. Someone had to create them." Who better than his father?

"There's always Noir."

Xev chuckled. "No. He's more monster than Azura. There's nothing in him that could create a benevolent race that can turn as vicious as a god. No reason why he'd bother."

The demons were as at odds as Jaden's eyes.

"I didn't birth them, I promise you."

Xev hadn't accused him of birthing them. He'd accused him of *creating* them.

Wordplay. His father was good at that. Cam wouldn't have bothered. Xev knew Braith hadn't done it, nor had Rezar, and Lilit had created her own special creatures.

That left his father. No one else would have bothered.

Jaden scratched at his ear. "I have another question for you."

"That is?"

"When this war breaks, whose side will you be on?"

That was an easy question to answer, and Xev was offended that Jaden would even ask it. "Whichever side opposes Azura."

Jaden nodded. "I don't blame you. And you still haven't answered my original question. How much of her blood is inside you?"

"What do you really want me to say? That I never feel the need to lash out and hurt something? That I only try to do good? Even if that were true, would you believe my answer?"

Jaden looked away.

"Exactly. If you're asking me how much of Braith's genetics this child will inherit, I have no idea. I imagine, like all creatures, he will be good and bad. The spirit that will sustain him will be whatever spirit's fed the most."

"Meaning?"

"If his mother hates him and teaches him hatred from birth, then he will know nothing of kindness or goodness. That hatred will be all he knows and all he practices."

"That was all your mother taught you, and yet you're not a monster. I've seen you do good. *Be* good. All the time you've spent here, you've never once struck out at anyone."

Nice of his father to finally admit that he'd been spying on him. Not that Xev hadn't known it.

No one, other than Myone, had ever trusted him without question. Not that he blamed his brothers for their mistrust.

Still...

His father shouldn't hold his birth against him, since he'd had no say in his own conception.

"My mother wasn't Azura. I was birthed by that bitch you chose, who cast me out to die while I was still wet from being born. But I was cared for and nurtured by another."

"You never speak of that."

Maybe not to him. "I refuse to sully her memory by talking about her lightly. She's sacred to me and will always remain that way. She died protecting me. I would give my life today if it would return her to the living. She didn't deserve what she got. And it infuriates me to this day that I wasn't able to save her."

Jaden actually winced. "I'm sorry. I never wanted your life to be so difficult."

"I never wanted a life at all." Because it had been nothing other than misery and misfortune from the moment he'd drawn his first breath and hadn't been smart enough to not expel it and refuse to draw another.

All he'd ever known was misery.

Except for the few moments whenever he was with Myone. Like his Inari mother, she brought him warmth and comfort.

Xev rubbed his thumb over the split on his lip and winced at the pain. Hoping to be rid of the paternal unit he'd rather not deal with, he answered Jaden's question. "There's no way of knowing how her child will be or what powers he'll hold. All I can tell you is the best way to keep him sane is to befriend him and show him something other than cruelty."

"If that doesn't work?"

"Guess between him and Braith, we'll have our asses handed to us."

Jaden raked his hands through his long, dark hair. "You really think he'll have more powers than we do?"

Xev shrugged nonchalantly. "I'm not as worried about him as I am Braith. Do you think you and your two snub buddies have the power to control her?"

Jaden frowned. "Snub buddies?"

"Cam and Rezar." The other two gods who walked around acting as if they were better than everyone else. Especially their other four siblings they detested.

"Rezar's powers equal hers."

Xev burst out laughing. "Glad you think that. But if I were laying odds, my money says she'd mop the floor with all three of you. Wring it out, then finish off Lilit, Noir, and Azura just for fun."

"Why do you say that?" Jaden asked.

"The one thing I learned in my childhood from Azura was the power of hatred. *Never* underestimate it."

Jaden scoffed. "The power of love is far greater."

His father was even dumber than Xev had thought. "Say fools and philosophers who've never really been screwed over. Believe me, I've known love, and it will inspire and has its place, but nothing, and I do mean absolutely *nothing*, tops hatred for spurring someone into action. Braith's love for that child and its father is what will keep her weak. She will be too afraid of losing them to do anything to anger her siblings where they're concerned. Take my word on this. Do whatever you can to make sure she lives in happy bliss with them."

"Why?"

"Because if anything interferes with her love and takes it away, then you'll face the unrelenting, absolute hatred I'm talking about. Don't make it so that she has nothing left to lose. Because if they're gone, then none of you will have any ability to control her. You will all die, screaming in agony."

"We can't die—we're immortal."

"Are you?"

Jaden stood up, and this time Xev saw the fear in his eyes. "What do you know?"

"That eternal death was born alongside the seven of you. He hides, but he's here. Are you absolutely sure that not even the great Primals are able to defeat him?" He left out the part about Lilit. Because he really wondered what had happened with Lombrey and her.

If Lombrey went after them, what would happen now? Would Lombrey lose, or would the Primals die?

Did anyone want to take that chance?

The color faded from Jaden's cheeks. "I thought that was a myth."

"I've met him. Pray you don't."

"Are you threatening me?"

"No, Father. I'd never threaten you."

Jaden returned his chair to the table then paused. "Your mother and Rezar are demanding the name of the father. Do you think I should tell them?"

"Depends."

"On?"

"How suicidal you're feeling. If you know nothing else, you know Braith's temper. As brave as I like to think I am, and as suicidal as I *know* I am, I haven't breathed a word of it. 'Cause the one thing I do know...You betray her and you will regret it."

## 12

---

TEN MONTHS LATER

Xev stood in the garden, waiting for Myone. It wasn't like her to be late.

He was just about to go seek her when she finally appeared in front of him. Tears streaking down her face, she grabbed him in a fierce hug.

Stunned, he held her while she trembled in his arms. "What's wrong?"

"Tisahn...he betrayed Kissare and Braith. He told the Primals who Monakribos's father was."

Xev's gut tightened at those words. How could anyone have been so incredibly stupid? "Do I want to know what happened?"

"They've taken Kissare." She was crying so hard now, her body was racked with the force of her sobs.

"I'm sorry."

She clutched him even tighter. "You were right about everything. Braith tore Tisahn apart. It was so awful,

Dary..." She broke off into more sobs. "Cam had to take his corpse away from Braith just so that she'd stop resurrecting him in order to torture and kill him, again and again."

That was what he'd feared.

Well, not exactly. It was even worse than his nightmares. Xev shuddered at the thought of her vengeance.

The goddess of destruction was good and tearing things apart.

Myone drew a ragged breath. "I wanted to be second-in-command. Not the leader, Dary. How can I lead the Sephirii? Especially like this? And after...after...after *that!*"

He cupped her face in his hands and gently tilted her head until she met his gaze. "Who better to lead them?"

"I don't know what to do. It was so brutal. So awful. She tore him into pieces."

"I know you, Myone. You will be their best leader yet." Xev kissed her brow and used his powers to knock her unconscious to save her from this. She needed a break from the horror, and there was nothing better than sleep to help someone heal.

It might upset her later that he'd done this, but he couldn't stand seeing her so distraught.

Swinging her up in his arms, he took her to his room and placed her on his bed. He covered her with his blankets then made sure she was comfortable. "Rest, my precious."

They all needed a break from the unnecessary drama of the Primals.

Not to mention, he wanted to see what was happening, and Myone didn't need any more nightmares.

Honestly, he didn't know what to feel right now. Unlike Myone, he'd been through so much that whenever things became unbearable, he went into a scary level of numb. As if all his emotions retreated because they knew their presence wasn't needed or wanted. That having emotions would only cause him more pain and trauma, and he'd had more than his fair share of both.

Right now, he felt nothing other than anaesthetized calm as he left her and went to where the Primals kept those they wanted to punish.

A small building in the center of their temples in Hurrian City. He knew this was where they'd have imprisoned Kissare. What better place for the creature they wanted to make an example of for all their subjects to see?

Unfurling his wings, he made sure to keep himself invisible as he flew by the first set of guards who lined the inner corridor. They didn't flinch as he swept past them.

When he neared the room where Kissare was imprisoned, he saw the primary guard, Atticus, slumped on the floor.

Xev went to the demon to make sure he was still alive. He appeared fine, which meant someone had drugged him or knocked him unconscious.

Only a god would have dared such.

Sliding into the shadows, he entered the inner room, then drew up short.

Even though the room was dark, he instantly saw the

Sephiroth who'd been chained inside a cell. That was what he'd expected to find.

What caught him off guard was the sight of Braith reaching through the bars in an effort to touch her son's father, who'd been beaten to the brink of death.

Even worse? They'd shorn the wings from his back.

Xev cringed as his own wings ached in sympathetic pain. With the exception of losing Myone, he couldn't imagine anything worse than enduring that punishment. Wings were limbs. Integral to them.

And in his mind, he saw the image of his mother slicing them off and handing them to Noir. Of course it would have been Azura who meted out such a horrific punishment for the Sephiroth. Her cruelty was legendary.

Swathed completely in black, Braith stood with her ebony hair flowing freely around her lithe body. She was a stark contrast to Kissare and his white hair that was marred by his own blood.

Even broken and bleeding, Kissare reached through the bars to embrace the goddess he'd fallen in love with. "Apollymi," he breathed, using an endearment that in the Sephirii language meant *the light of my heart*. "You shouldn't have come here."

"I had to." Choking on her grief, she cupped his face through the bars. "I drugged Atticus and have stolen the key." She released him so that she could pull it from the folds of her cloak and unlock the door to free him. "We can—"

"Nay," he said, cutting her off. He placed his bloodied and bruised hand over hers to stop her from opening the door to his cell. "I can't leave. It's the only way to protect you and Monakribos."

She sobbed at the mention of their young son, and Xev felt terrible for both of them. This was so unfair. They didn't deserve to have their lives destroyed because of love.

"I don't know how to live without you, Sare. I don't *want* to live without you."

"Shh," he whispered before he placed a tender kiss to her cheek. "You're a goddess. The most beautiful of all. You lived centuries before I was born, and you were fine without me."

"No. I survived and endured. The last thing I want is to be cast back to that lonely hell I used to call home."

"And now you have a baby who needs his mother."

She choked on a sob. "He needs his father, too. How can he ever learn kindness without you? I can teach him nothing save murder, torture, and hatred."

He buried his hand in her dark hair and locked gazes with her. "The other gods will never leave us in peace, Polli. You know that. We've broken their sacred law, and they are a hateful lot. My execution will make amends. Better they punish me, alone, than you and Kri. But I will come back for you. I swear it. No matter what it takes. Death cannot keep us apart. Nothing can. I love you too much to stay away."

"How will I know it's you?"

He took her hand in his and placed it over his heart. "You will know, and you won't doubt me. Ever. You'll see."

"Then I will wait for you. No other shall ever touch

me. You will forever be my only heart." She turned her black hair snow white to match his.

He gave her a sad smile. "You will always be my precious Apollymi." He kissed her lips. "Now go, before they find you and punish you, too. Raise our son and never let him doubt how much his father loves him. One day, I will return for you both. You can count on it."

She nodded and let go of his hand. "I will wait for you! Forever!" She turned and walked away, but even so, Xev saw her grief.

And her hatred. Just as he'd warned his father. She would never forget or forgive this transgression.

*Is this my future, too?*

Was this what would happen to him if they ever learned that he was in love with Myone?

In the shadows, he stared as Kissare sank to his knees and wept even harder than Myone had.

The mighty Sephiroth had been broken by their cruelty. Kissare was nothing more than a shadow of the warrior he'd been.

Xev wanted to help them. But there was nothing he could for him now.

So he went after Braith.

By the time he caught up to her, she was in her temple, holding her son in her arms.

The baby looked confused by her tears.

Braith straightened and turned toward him. Even though he was still invisible, she clearly saw him. "What do you want, son of my enemy?"

The fact she could see him was terrifying.

Xev started to flee, but he wasn't a coward. He forced himself to appear to her. "I heard what they did, and I came here to see if you needed anything."

She laughed bitterly. "I need my husband."

"I can free him."

More tears streaked down her face as she held a regal composure he didn't understand. "He won't let us." She placed a kiss to Monakribos's head. "And he's right. The others would never let us live in peace."

Then she turned to face Xev. "You are the son of Azura and Jaden."

"I am."

"You knew who the father was, yet you said nothing."

He stepped closer to her so that she could see his sincerity. "I didn't think it was any of their business."

She sneered at him. "You were afraid of me."

Damn, her powers were terrifying. "Only a fool wouldn't be. But that wasn't why I kept my silence. What they're doing isn't right. No one should pay for love with blood."

She pursed her lips. "There is something I want from you."

That sent a chill down his spine. "Dare I ask what?"

"*Your* blood."

He widened his eyes.

"Not your life, fool." She manifested a goblet in her hand and held it out to him. "Fill this with your blood."

"Why?"

"You're a god of chaos. A son of Jaden who was

fostered by an Inari demon. Give me your blood. I demand it."

He really wanted to tell her no, but this was Braith. The deadliest of them all. Given her powers, he didn't dare deny her. It never went well for anyone who did.

Besides, she could take it if she wanted. The fact she asked was a good thing.

So he took her goblet and set it on the floor, then sliced open his palm with his dagger so that he could give her what she wanted.

The cut burned like fire as he watched his blood pour from his fist into the goblet.

And once the cup was full, he handed it back to her.

Braith healed his hand then inclined her head to him. "Thank you."

Xev rubbed at the healed injury as he watched her staring down at the warm red liquid. "May I ask what you plan to do with that?"

A sinister smile curved her lips as she handed the cup over to a Charonte demon who'd come forward out of the darkness. "I intend to create an army to protect my son so that no one will ever be able to threaten him again. But don't worry. I will tell no one what you've done."

BRAITH'S WORDS haunted Xev as he returned to his room to find Myone still asleep.

A part of him wanted to let her rest and stay in blissful slumber as long as she could. The selfish part wanted her awake so that he could confess what he'd done. Have her soothe the terror inside him at the thought of Braith creating an army with his blood.

What would they do to him when they learned about his part in this?

Images of Kissare continued to haunt him.

Knowing there was nothing either of them could do, he decided to let her sleep longer, as he was terrified of how she'd react once she learned that Braith was using his blood to create a race to rival the Sephirii.

*No one is going to harm my child. I will burn down the world before I let that happen. Do you understand?*

He understood Braith's determination, and those words haunted him. Even now, he saw her mixing her blood with his and the Charonte's to create the Malachai race. If he'd had any doubts before as to his father's ability to create demons, that was put to rest when she began making her own.

As he'd told Jaden, he knew his mother didn't have the power to create. His father did.

And so did Braith.

*What have I done?*

Pulling Myone into his arms, he held her sleeping form as fear tore through him. He was the father of a new class of demon that was stronger than anything his father had made.

If anyone ever learned what he'd done, they'd kill him. He had no doubt.

Even Shadow.

He'd just unleashed utter destruction into their world,

given Braith even more power than she'd had before. Never mind the fact that her Charonte friend, Xiamara, was terrifying...

This was something else entirely.

Something with all three of their powers combined.

A Malachai race that she intended to infuse with the blood of her own son to make him even stronger, too.

Myone would hate him for this. He was sure of it.

Tears clouded his eyes as he stared down at her beautiful face. "Please don't hate me," he whispered.

He could bear anything else in this world.

But not that.

He'd rather have his own wings ripped out and be cast into eternal slavery to the gods than lose her. She was everything he wasn't. Good. Kind.

Decent.

He was a monster Braith had used.

"Dary?"

He opened his eyes to see Myone staring up at him. Unable to speak, he held her tighter.

"Honey, what happened?"

Rather than tell her what haunted him, he opted for the safer events. "I saw Kissare."

"What?" She sat up. "When?"

"After you fell asleep."

She gave him a pointed stare.

"After I made you fall asleep."

Shaking her head, she sighed. "Why did you do that?"

Xev cupped her cheek in his hand. "I can't stand your tears, Myone. They destroy me."

She covered his hand with hers. "I love you."

"I love you too. But we can't see each other anymore."

Shock filled her eyes. "What?"

"I can't risk them doing to you what they did to Kissare. I'm not worth it." He cringed at the hysteria he heard in his voice. But the thought of that being her...It was more than he could handle.

"They're going to execute him."

She winced. "I can't bear to let you go, Dary."

Xev kissed her. "We have no choice. For both our sakes, we can't be together."

Myone nodded. "I will go, but I'm never far away."

And that was the worst part about all of this.

## 13

Xev stood with his brothers on top of a hill as they watched the line of Malachai demons that seemed to go on into infinity in the valley below. They marched toward the lands Braith, who now went by Apollymi, had set up for them to make their homes.

While each of the Malachai had a pair of wings, the Primals had forbidden the demons from using them unless they were in battle, or were practicing for battle.

It made no sense, but then, neither did the gods.

"I can't believe she did this." Malphas crossed his arms over his chest. "Have you ever seen anything more terrifying?"

Xev snorted. "Azura on a rampage. A hungry Charonte. My father naked."

Malphas shoved playfully at him. "I'm serious. How many of them are there?"

"Thousands." Shadow let out a long sigh. "All fully grown. Ready to battle."

"Ready to protect Monakribos," Xev said, reminding him of the real reason they'd been created.

Mal shook his head. "Why do I have the feeling that we're watching the end of everything we know?"

Xev agreed with Malphas's observation. "They're every bit as powerful as the Sephirii." Or more so. That was his real fear.

"How did she do this?" Shadow asked.

Xev didn't speak. He still didn't dare. But he was grateful that Apollymi had kept her word and told no one of his part in the demons' creation.

He wasn't sure why, as the other gods were screaming for a scapegoat they could tear apart. It would be nothing for her to offer him up, especially after Kissare's brutal execution. Honestly, he was expecting it.

And yet both she and Xiamara remained silent. He had no idea why they protected him. But he was truly grateful for their silence.

*Daraxerxes!*

He winced at the strident summons in his head.

"Mom?" Malphas asked sarcastically as he saw his reaction.

"Who else?" Xev sighed heavily.

Shadow let out an evil laugh. "Give her my best."

"Yeah, I'll be sure and do that." Dreading her tantrum, Xev went to her throne room.

For once, she didn't attack him as soon as he appeared. Even stranger, they were alone.

That made every sphincter in his body clench so tightly that he was amazed he wasn't leaving a trail of diamonds behind him. "Something wrong, Mommy Dearest?"

Azura glared at him. "Oh, I think you know what's wrong."

There were so many answers he could give. But one in particular came to mind. "You birthed me?"

From across the room, she backhanded him. Xev cursed at the pain that exploded through his head. He hated whenever she did that.

"Don't be so impertinent." She closed the distance between them. "You helped out my sister, didn't you, brat?"

"No idea what you're talking about."

She cocked a brow. "You didn't give up blood for Braith to create her new army?"

Xev ground his teeth. A part of him prayed she was only fishing for information and had no idea what she was talking about. Maybe it really was just a lucky guess. "Are you inhaling herbs? Or are you just delusional by nature?"

She tsked at him. "You really think I can't smell your blood in their veins? That I don't know the powers of my own child?"

He forced himself to show no emotion, but inside, he was screaming. *I should have known better.*

"But more to the point, do you think your father won't know, too, as soon as he nears one?"

Xev's stomach hit the floor. There was a nice tidbit he'd never considered. No wonder Braith had said she wouldn't tell them. She didn't have to. They'd know instinctively.

Azura walked a small circle around him. "Just what do you think ole Jaden will do once he realizes what you've been up to?"

He'd slaughter him.

"Or Cam, or Rezar? While there's nothing specifically barring you from creating a new race, I'm not exactly sure they'll be thrilled by it. Especially a race that rivals their pets."

Xev felt sick as those words echoed around his head. Images of Kissare went through his mind.

What was he going to do?

Right now, he was going to continue to play stupid. Because really, this wasn't his fault. Braith had done this. He'd had no real choice in it.

Had he said no, she would have killed him.

"I have no idea what you're talking about."

Azura clicked her tongue. "I think you know exactly what I'm talking about." She stood up on her toes so that she could whisper in his ear. "Do you think Braith will protect you?"

No. He wasn't that stupid. She had as much love for him as his mother did. "I've done nothing wrong."

"You've done nothing right." She brushed her hand down his cheek.

Xev caught her wrist. "What do you want from me?"

An evil smirk twisted her lips. "A favor."

He laughed bitterly. "As if I'd ever do anything for you."

"Oh, I know you will. Because if you don't, I'll hand you over to the others, and if you think what was done to Kissare was bad...Well, you'll wish you had it that good." She manifested an amulet in her hand. "Take this and swap it for the one Jaden wears."

What in the name of the Source was she planning? "Why?"

"Because I want you to. Do it and I'll give you what you want most."

What he wanted most was Myone, but thankfully, his mother had never figured that out.

Or had she?

Forcing himself to betray nothing, he met her gaze. "And what is it that I want?"

Azura's icy gaze burned him with its coldness. "Your freedom."

Okay. That was a close second to Myone. He'd do most anything to be free of her and all their politics.

She pressed the amulet into his hand. "All you have to do is exchange this one for the one Jaden wears."

"That's it?"

"Yes."

It couldn't possibly be that easy. He knew his mother. There had to be a vital piece of information she was withholding. "Why?"

"I want the Eye of Verlyn that he wears. Bring it to me."

He studied the duplicate. It was a nice forgery, but his father wasn't stupid. "Won't he know the difference?"

"Do it while he's sleeping, and he'll never know. Bring me his medallion, and I'll set you free. That's all there is to it."

Why didn't he believe her?

Because she always lied.

She was setting him up. He felt it deep inside his gut. "Why don't you send one of your other demons or goons?"

"They won't be able to get near him. You live there. He'll know nothing if you flit around those shadows you love so much."

She was right about that. He could easily get into where his father slept and exchange the necklaces.

Still...it just didn't seem right.

*Don't do this.* Every part of him screamed out in warning.

Yet the thought of being free...of never being summoned again...

It was more than he could resist. He'd give anything not to have to answer to her.

But if his father ever learned of it, he would be furious. Justifiably so.

Not to mention his father treasured that stupid necklace. He always wore it. He probably valued it more than he did his sons.

"What does the amulet do?"

"It allows him to temporarily control others."

That didn't make any sense. "Can't he do that already?"

She let out a frustrated sigh. "Do you want your freedom or not?"

Of course he did.

"Or would you rather suffer and die as Kissare did? What do you think they'll do to you when I tell them that you helped Braith create a new race out of your blood so that she could fight their Sephirii?"

He winced at the very thought. The last thing he wanted was to do this.

But there was no one who would protect him. Definitely not his mother, who was threatening to throw him to the gods.

And he already knew where he stood with his father.

He had no one. If he didn't do this, she'd definitely see him dead or punished eternally.

If he did it, there was a chance he might go free and be able to run with Myone. Maybe. Surely some chance was better than none.

Taking the medallion, he inclined his head to her and prayed for the best.

XEV CREPT out from the shadows, into his father's huge bedroom. Oddly enough, he'd never ventured here before. Never really cared much about his father or how Jaden lived.

He'd kept to his side of his father's temple and never been curious about the rest.

Weird that his father had a massive carved bed that

held images of dragons on it. That seemed oddly whimsical for such a stern god. Xev would have never picked that out for his father. And he was grateful Jaden was sleeping alone in it. And clothed. Last thing he needed was more trauma.

As quietly as he could, Xev crept toward the overly large bed. Jaden was entwined in his furs, peacefully asleep and unaware that the son he hated most was about to betray him.

*Don't do this. You know she's lying to you.* She was keeping some secret hidden. She had to be.

*Why does she want it so much?* There had to be more than what she'd said.

Xev knew nothing about the amulet, other than the fact that his father never removed it. There was no telling why. It could be a treasured gift from someone. Or something he'd won in battle. Maybe a token from one of the other gods, or a demon...

Or it could have something to do with his powers.

Did Xev really care?

His gut told him not to do this. Yet if he didn't, Azura would see him dead. Or worse. There was no doubt about that at all. He'd never meant anything to her and even less to his father.

She wasn't leveling an idle threat. He knew that, too. Azura would see it through and hand him over to the others, gift-wrapped.

*I want to be free.*

That was the truth. If he could have that one desire... surely it was worth this risk.

Freedom.

He could be with Myone. That was the only thing that really mattered.

Holding that elusive dream close, he crept to the bed.

Jaden didn't move.

Terrified of his father waking and catching him, Xev used his powers to trade out the necklaces. Jaden growled and reached out.

Xev froze instantly.

Jaden rolled over, then quickly settled back down with a heavy sigh.

Grateful he hadn't soiled himself in panic, Xev sank back into the shadows and took the necklace to his mother, who was waiting for his return in her throne room.

Azura laughed as soon as she saw him. "Put it here." She held a chest out.

That was a little strange, but then, his blue-skinned mother had never been particularly normal.

Xev dropped the necklace into the box.

Before he could ask about his freedom, Noir came rushing into the room to grab Azura into a tight hug. "You did it!"

Azura laughed. "*We* did it. He's ours now."

Xev went cold as a bad feeling went through him. "What just happened?" What had *he* done?

Smiling, Azura approached him with a gleam in those white eyes he hated more than anything. "Thank you, my pathetic little waste. Without you, we'd have never been able to strip your father of his powers and imprison him. Never been able to control his demons. I owe you."

Xev felt sick to his stomach.

*What did I do?*

But then he knew. He'd shifted the balance of Primal power.

Deep inside where he didn't want to look, he'd known something like this would happen. Why else would she have made such a threat?

He wasn't that stupid. *How could I have fallen for her lies?* He'd just made her stronger at the expense of his father. Why hadn't he thought of that?

The other gods would kill him, anyway, once they found out about it. Even Malphas and Shadow.

And he deserved it.

His mother was now in control of everything. She had the greater power.

*It's all my fault.*

Terrified of what he'd done, Xev returned to the shadows with her laughter ringing in his ears.

But there was no reprieve there. Shadow met him with a scowl on his face that said he already knew what Xev had done.

"Tell me you didn't do it, Xev. Tell me that they're lying. You had to know better!"

He couldn't look Shadow in the eyes. "She promised me my freedom."

"Are you insane?"

"I was desperate. I had no idea what his necklace did. She lied to me." He didn't dare tell Shadow about the

Malachai and his part in their creation. That his mother had used them to blackmail him.

*What am I going to do?*

Everyone would be after him now.

"Do you understand what you just did? How much power you've given our mother?"

He did *now*. Xev wanted to scream from the nightmare he'd just created. "I can never go home."

"Forget that. You just handed over control of all demons to her and Noir. How did you not know what the Eye of Verlyn was?"

Maybe because no one had ever told him.

Besides, he'd been too worried about his own ass to think about his father's. "He doesn't control all demons."

"Except for the Malachai Braith created, and the Charonte, yes, he does. The rest sprang from his blood."

So Xev had been right about that after all. Maybe if his father hadn't lied to him, he would have known that, too.

Not that it would have mattered. He still would have agreed to it. His fear of Azura telling them what Braith had done with his blood had been too great.

"I had no idea what his necklace did, Shadow. No one ever told me."

"You had to know there was a reason our mother wanted it. A reason why Jaden never removed it."

Xev raked his hands through his hair. "What do you want me to say?"

"Nothing. Undo this. For all our sakes."

It wasn't that simple. Especially given the fact that

Azura knew he was the one who'd helped Braith create the Malachai. Her threat was still hanging over him.

*What am I going to do?*

But then he knew. He had to make this right. Even if it meant his life. He couldn't leave his mother with this kind of power.

Either way, Myone would never forgive him once she found out. She'd be worse than Shadow.

For that matter, he would never forgive himself. He shouldn't have betrayed his father. While they had their issues, his father hadn't deserved this, and he knew it. Had she been honest with him, Xev would never have imprisoned his father with Azura. Nor drained his powers. That had never been part of their bargain.

*Never make decisions out of fear.*

Michi had taught him that. She'd returned him to his mother out fear, and it had cost her, her life. The worst mistakes always came from that very thing. He'd known better, and he'd been a fool.

Fear clouded rational thought. Always.

*Make this right.*

Leaving Shadow, Xev returned to his mother's palace and went to the dark underbelly where she kept those she hated most. To where he'd lived at one time.

Before his father had given him a reprieve he'd repaid with betrayal.

*Don't think about it.*

But how could he not?

And sure enough, Azura had wasted no time in

capturing her enemy. He could hear his father's curses and demands that everyone else ignored.

"Let me out of here!" Jaden banged against the walls and cursed everyone.

This was probably the dumbest thing Xev had ever done in his life, but he had no choice. Shadow was right. He had to undo what he'd done.

He approached the reinforced iron door where Jaden was being held. "Father?"

"What are doing here? Come to gloat?"

Xev wanted to die in that moment. "It's not like that."

Jaden struck the door so hard that Xev was surprised that he didn't break through it on his own. "No? I welcomed you into my home! Why would you do this to me? You are vile! I should have killed you the moment your mother sent you to me!"

That set his temper off. There had never been any real welcoming into Jaden's home. He'd always felt like an outsider there.

Even all these years later.

Jaden had never been a father to him. Had he been such, Xev wouldn't have been afraid of his mother. But he knew his father would never stand beside him the way Apollymi stood by her son. Jaden would never summon an army to protect him.

Never once had his father held an ounce of love for either of his sons. He didn't stand by them. Hell, he barely acknowledged them.

How dare the bastard be so angry when all Xev had ever wanted was a father?

He glared at the door, grateful that it stood between them. How many times had he been caged here while his father slept in luxury?

All those memories tore through him now, awaking a hatred so feral, he couldn't see straight. "For all the years you didn't welcome me, Father. For every lash and insult I've been given in your name, and for all the years I was forced to serve them as an animal because you refused to acknowledge me as your son. She said that if I did this for her, that I'd go free. You owe me this!"

"I owe you nothing, save my hatred."

And that Jaden had given him in excess. "Then we are even after all."

Furious, Xev left him there as he'd done him and returned to his room. The only place where he felt safe.

*Let him rot!*

What did he care? Like his father, he was cold-hearted.

*That's not true.*

He loved Myone. More than anything else.

And this would kill her. If she ever learned what he'd done, she would never forgive him.

He could hear her in his head, chastising him. She'd be absolutely horrified by his actions. And honestly, so was he.

This wasn't the man he wanted to be. He wanted to be the man she thought he was. The man she made him feel like whenever she came around.

She didn't see an angry beast who wanted to lash out at the entire world. She saw the decency inside him that

Michi had created and nurtured. The part that only wanted to love and be loved.

To protect and be protected.

Why couldn't he just be *that* Xev?

*Go back...*

Torn by indecision, he didn't know what to do. He was damned by either option.

A knock sounded on his door.

"Enter."

It was Malphas. "Did you hear? Noir and Azura have imprisoned Jaden. They're going to unite the demons with Braith's Malachai and the Charonte and attack the Kalosum." The Kalosum consisted of the light gods—Cam, Rezar, Jaden—and their servants, the Naşāru and Sephirii.

It meant that Myone would be directly in the line of fire.

Because of him.

"Wait...what?" Xev asked.

"They're already uniting their armies to destroy the Sephirii, Naşāru, and light gods. The war's begun."

Xev wanted to vomit. "Why?"

"Braith because she's blaming them for killing Kissare, and she wants to protect her son. Noir and Azura because they want to put down Rezar and Cam so that no one will have any way to limit their powers. They won't rest until every member of the Naşāru and Sephirii are dead."

All he heard out of that was that they were going to kill Myone.

*I have to let Jaden out.* His own anger be damned.

Every part of Xev cringed at the thought of it. If he let his father out now, Jaden would never trust him again. And he couldn't blame him for that.

If he didn't...

Better he should suffer for all eternity than anything happen to Myone. There was no other way. He had to set this right and make sure she wasn't harmed because he'd been stupid and scared.

*I am so screwed.*

No matter what, he'd do this and then he'd beg her to leave with him. Maybe they could find someplace safe to live among the humans...or in another realm. Anywhere other than here.

*I don't care, as long as I'm with her.*

He held tight to that thought as he returned to where Jaden was being held.

This time, he opened the prison door before he spoke a single word to his father and risked getting angry again.

Xev wasn't prepared for the sight that awaited him. His father appeared frail. Brittle.

His long black hair hung around a gaunt face.

"What did they do to you?" Forget his powers—it appeared they'd sucked the very life force out of him.

Jaden jerked at the amulet he couldn't remove. "This weakens me. It feels like it's made me mortal."

Of course it did. Leave it to his mother to find something that would turn his father into a hollowed-out shell. He probably was mortal, and they would kill him soon.

Xev had been lucky that it hadn't affected him, too. No

doubt his mother would have considered that a bonus. Two gods in one strike.

"Why did you come back?" Jaden growled.

"To free you."

"After you did this?" Jaden backhanded him so hard that, for a moment, Xev saw stars. So much for being weakened. His father could still pack a punch.

Even so, he'd deserved that.

Pushing himself to his feet, Xev slowly approached his father again. "I'm going to make this right." He removed the scarf from his neck, then he used it to hold the medallion. With one quick yank, he pulled it free of his father's neck.

Jaden instantly recovered his strength. The color returned to his flesh and his hair returned to its thickness and dark hue. He went from appearing as a withered husk to a man in the height of his youth.

It was done.

Xev let out a relieved breath.

Until he realized what Jaden intended.

Faster than Xev could move, his father placed that amulet around Xev's throat.

He stared in horror at his father. "What are you doing?"

Jaden curled his lip. "Giving you what you intended for me."

He gasped in disbelief as he tried to remove the amulet that was taking away all of his powers as they'd done his father. "You can't leave me here...You can't conceive what she'll do to me for it!"

There was no pity or mercy in his father's mismatched eyes. "Like I care? Rot here with your mother and her demons. I never want to lay eyes on you again, you treacherous bastard! You are no son of mine!"

"Please, Father! Please! You can't do this to me. I freed you."

Jaden didn't even look back.

Xev sank to his knees as he realized what this would mean.

His only hope was that his mother killed him. But deep down inside, he knew he would never be that lucky.

**14**

---

"Did you hear?"

Myone arched a brow at Cam's question. At first, she wasn't sure if her tiny goddess was speaking to her or herself. "Hear what, my lady?"

"Jaden's son betrayed him."

Biting her lip, she carefully measured her words, as she didn't want to refute or upset her mistress. "I think we may be missing some of the story, my lady."

Cam arched a dark eyebrow. "How so?"

"You're a goddess of justice. I think it would be remiss of us to judge him before we heard his side of the story."

The petite goddess considered that as she picked through the fruit pieces on her platter. "Have you ever met Daraxerxes?"

"I have." Myone continued to stand off to the side of the table where her goddess sat, dining on her snack.

"You know his mother is Azura."

"I do."

Cam selected a piece of melon before she looked up and met Myone's gaze. "Yet you defend him?"

"Is that not what you've taught me, my lady? A presumption of innocence?"

She chewed her piece carefully as she considered the question. "What makes you presume innocence for the son of such evil?"

"I've never witnessed any malice from him. In truth, I've found him rather pleasant whenever we've interacted."

"People often hide their true natures. Even Azura can seem pleasant when you first meet her. Particularly, Braith can be loving at times. Yet both are quite deadly and obnoxious."

As was Cam when crossed. Xev had never hidden the fact that he had no love of her. "True."

She wiped at her chin. "You still think he didn't betray his father?"

No, she didn't. There was something they didn't know. Myone believed in Xev, and until she knew more, she wouldn't doubt him. "I only wonder why he'd do such a thing." Especially given his hatred of his mother. It didn't make sense that he would have betrayed Jaden. Myone couldn't imagine what would have driven Xev to do it. He had to have some reason for it. Something they didn't know.

In truth, she was worried about him. No one would tell her anything, and she hadn't been able to get any real word. If only they could communicate.

"I think you should order him released so that you can pass judgment."

Cam choked on her food. "What?"

Myone carefully kept her composure. "What if he is innocent and being punished for something he didn't do? Is it not possible Azura set him up?"

Clearing her throat, Cam shook her head. "I trust my brother. If Jaden said he betrayed him, he did so. Why else would he have abandoned his son to Azura?"

Because he'd always abandoned him. Xev had been an innocent babe when Jaden handed him over for his mother's original cruelty. Who knew his reasons now?

And Myone wanted to weep for Xev. No one would help him. She'd been trying her best, and there was nothing she could do.

That helplessness was incredibly frustrating.

Over and over, she'd seen the scars on his body from the day they met. She could only imagine what was being done to him now. But no one else cared.

Not even his brothers.

*Please be okay.*

But every day that passed with no word worried her more. Surely, he'd be in touch if he could.

The fact that there was only silence…

Was he even alive?

She had no way of knowing, and she cursed his father for his lack of regard.

*I will find you, Xev.*

She had no idea how. But she wasn't going to give up on him.

MYONE WAS sound asleep in her bed when she felt a sudden surge in her room. At first, she had no idea what it was.

Fully alert, she sat up, seeking the source of her unease. There was nothing there, except shadows.

Until she noticed the shadow at the foot of her bed.

Her scream caught in her throat. "Dary?"

The shadow didn't move. At least not at first.

Slowly, it turned to face her.

Pulling her feet up to her chest, she debated what to do. Should she run? Scream? Fight?

She decided to try speaking to him again. "Is that you, Dary?"

He nodded.

"Can you say anything?"

*Not really.* His voice was in her head.

"I don't understand. What's wrong?"

*I'm not really here. Just a part of me. I wanted to see you, and this was the only way I could.*

Tears gathered in her eyes as she let go of her legs and scooted closer to his shadow. "I'm glad you came. I've been terribly worried about you."

*Have you?*

She nodded. "I've asked everyone to get a message out, but no one's been willing or able to help."

There was no expression on his shadow's face, but she thought it might be smiling. *Don't worry about me. So long as I know you're all right, I'll be fine.*

"But I'm not all right. I wish you were here."

*This is for the better.*

It didn't feel that way. It hurt deep inside not to be able to reach out at touch him. "I miss you."

*Not nearly as much as I miss you.* His shadow began to fade.

"Wait!"

It darkened again.

"Will you come to me again?"

*I will do my best.*

"Then I will wait and count my heartbeats until I see you again."

Xev nodded and faded away.

WITH A RAGGED BREATH, he opened his eyes in his cell. Every part of him ached and was ravaged. So much pain.

But there, for a moment, he'd seen Myone. She was well. That little bit had given him peace. A tiny sliver to hold on to.

And she missed him. She hadn't forgotten him.

It was selfish that he held that close to his heart. But he needed it. Needed to know that he mattered to *someone*.

He stared at his filthy, broken hand and imagined her touch on his fingers. Her skin was like velvet. Gentle and soft.

He'd never feel it again. But if he conserved his strength, he might be able to find the energy to travel through the aether with his spirit and sit with her again.

If he could manage that much...

*Why?*

That one word lingered in his mind. Why was he alive? Why couldn't he die?

Was there any purpose to his life other than to suffer? Had there *ever* been a purpose for him?

Why hadn't his father just drowned him?

In that moment, he hated Michi for not letting the demons kill him when he was born. At least then, he would never have known this agony.

A tear fell from the corner of his eye, burning the cuts on his cheek.

*You're not alone.*

Myone was with him in thought and spirit.

But was that enough?

He wasn't safe. He had no real purpose or reason to be here. All he wanted was an end to this.

Closing his eyes, he forced that hopelessness away. *I will take one more breath.*

And one more.

Though the fight in him was gone, his life wasn't. Somehow, he would muddle through and live just for those snippets that Myone provided.

It was all he had to look forward to.

**15**

---

Something was wrong. Myone didn't know what, but she couldn't let it go.

Not now.

It'd been weeks since there had been any sign of Xev, and that wasn't like him. He might miss a week. Maybe two.

But he always came back.

He'd missed her birthday. He wouldn't do that. Not unless there was something really wrong.

Had they killed him?

Desperate, she made her way to his mother's temple. Thankfully, it was night here. She pulled her cloak down low over her face and did her best to blend in to the shadows. What she wouldn't give to have Xev's abilities.

But they didn't teach Sephirii how to sneak. They barely taught them stealth.

*Xev would be so good at this.*

Instead of swordplay, she should have had him teach her this. If she got him back, that would be their next lesson.

Skirting around the building, she tried to find a way in. Sadly, it was sealed up everywhere.

*Think like Xev...*

He'd go high. Removing the cloak, she flew up toward a balcony.

While many had lights, there was one in darkness. She headed there and landed carefully in the shadows, praying no one would see her. Someone shouted.

Myone froze.

Until she realized that they were just shouting, and not at her. Releasing a pent-up breath, she crept toward the door and tried the handle.

Luckily, it wasn't locked. She cracked the door open as little as possible and slipped inside a dark bedroom. It took several seconds before her eyes adjusted and she could see the ornate bed and dark red bedding and curtains.

As quietly as she could, she made her way across the room, to another door. A faint light illuminated the bottom, and as she approached it, she slipped on something wet.

Thinking it was water, she looked down and realized there was a puddle of blood.

Bile hung in her throat as she saw the body of a demon sprawled over a rack.

This had to be Azura's room.

Disgusted, she pressed her hand to her lips and lifted

herself so that she wouldn't track blood over the marble floor.

"Ugh!" No wonder Xev hated his mother so much. She was a monster.

Even more desperate now, she cracked open the door so that she could look down that hallway.

No one was there. Not in either direction.

That was good. But she had absolutely no idea where to go from here. Where would Xev be?

This was hopeless.

How could she even begin to help him?

The palace was enormous. Was he in a room? Or in another building?

How would she know?

Biting her lip, she tried to use her powers to locate him.

Nothing.

Not even a whisper. It was as if he'd never existed.

"Well, well. What have we here?"

Myone squeaked at the gruff voice in her ear.

A light flashed.

Using her powers, she teleported back to her room in Cam's temple, hopefully before who or what had caught her saw who she was. Her heart pounded so fiercely in her chest that she feared it'd explode. For several minutes, she didn't move as she waited for them to follow after her.

When they didn't, she began to relax. Maybe, just maybe, she'd escaped unscathed.

But it didn't ease her fear where Xev was concerned. If anything, it made it worse.

"Where are you, Dary?"

Would she ever see him again?

SEVERAL WEEKS LATER, Myone was still determined to find Xev. It'd been so long since his father had banished him, since she'd had any word of him, that she couldn't stand it.

She was done with these games.

Heartbroken and needing to find some tangible proof that he'd existed, she teleported into Xev's old room in Jaden's temple. No one had been here in a long, long time. Even though his bed was covered with dust and cobwebs, it was neatly made. His personal items were right where he'd left them, as if waiting for his return.

But no one had touched them in all this time. It was as if he'd ceased to exist the day his father banished him, and everyone else had forgotten him.

It didn't seem right that no one cared.

Even though she wasn't supposed to be here, she flew to Malphas's room a few doors down. *Don't do it.*

Ignoring her inner voice of reason, Myone knocked politely on his door. "Malphas?"

He opened the door wearing nothing more than a simple loincloth. "What are you doing here?"

Myone glanced away, embarrassed by his meager clothing. "Have you any word or news about your brother Xev?"

He let out a long, tired sigh. "No. Nothing. You just need to leave it alone."

Same answer from everyone.

Every time she'd tried to ask after him, she'd been told to leave it alone.

"Can I get a message to him?"

"No."

The coldness of his tone chilled her. "What do you mean, no?"

Malphas let out a long, sad sigh. "Look, I'm sorry. There's nothing to be done. I feel for you, but the best thing is to forget you ever met him." He shut the door in her face.

Myone stood there in horror as she digested the news. Tears filled her eyes as she tried to imagine the nightmare Xev had been damned to.

Something had happened to him. She knew it. Otherwise, he'd have still been coming into her room at night to visit.

She knew Xev.

He needed help, and she was the only hope he had.

*I have to find him.*

But how? Her last attempt to find him had been disastrous. She still had no idea what demon had discovered her. There had to be some way...

She gasped as she remembered one way to find him.

"Shadow?"

At first, only silence answered her.

Then Shadow appeared by her side. "You rang?"

"No. I called you."

He shook his head. "Yeah. What can I do for you, peaches?"

She frowned at his odd word. "Peaches?"

"Ignore me. I'm weird. Is there some reason you called for me?"

"I need to see Xev."

He sucked his breath in sharply between his teeth. "Sorry, love. That's beyond my pay grade."

She tried to understand his words. But he was so frustrating with all the odd things he said. Sometimes she felt as if they were speaking entirely different languages. "What?"

"Can't do it. Azura catches *you* there...Trust me, you don't want that. Pulling the wings off your kind is her favorite hobby. You don't want to give her a reason to hurt you. And she's not any more fond of me, either. I don't want to think about what she might pull off me if she finds me in her domain."

It didn't matter. "I have to see him."

"Why?"

*Because I love him, and I'm not about to abandon him the way the rest of you have.* But she wasn't about to answer that question with the truth. So she tried another tactic. "Please, Shadow? Can you not do this one favor for me?"

He growled deep in his throat. "Don't think I don't know what you're doing. Batting those baby blues. Giving me that helpless, yet I'll-kick-your-butt-if-you-don't-do-this stare. I'm trying to keep us both alive."

She batted her eyes at him again. Especially since he'd let her know that it was working. "I need to see him, Shadow...please."

He shook his head. "I need all my body parts attached."

"What if he's hurt?"

He snorted. "Oh, I assure you, he's hurt. There's no chance she hasn't hurt him."

"Then how can you deny me?"

Shadow really wanted to tell her where to shove her request. But one look at her desperation and he understood why his brother was a complete idiot for her. The concern in her eyes touched him. He would kill to have someone care that much.

Yeah. He'd be a fool for her too. Poor Xev.

Myone was going to get them all killed.

Worse, he knew she was right. There was no telling what Azura had done to poor Xev.

Those nightmares had haunted him, too. More times than he could count, he'd wanted to do something, but there was nothing to be done. No one could barter with Azura. She definitely didn't want anything to do with him. If he'd even tried, it would have only made things worse for Xev.

His mother hated him more than anyone. Just the sight of him sent her into an apoplectic rage. If she had any idea he cared about his brother, she'd worsen Xev's punishment just to strike back at both of them. She was that psychotic.

No, she was that vicious.

But if Myone thought she could do something...

Maybe she *could* help. It was at least worth a try.

Because Shadow couldn't stand the thought of Xev suffering either.

"Fine." He held his hand out to her.

She didn't hesitate in placing her hand into his, trusting to an extreme he couldn't fathom. *Damn.* He'd never been like that. *Because no one has ever betrayed her.*

She had no understanding of their nightmares.

No understanding of real brutality. What he wouldn't give to know her world. To dream her untainted dreams.

Because of that, Shadow dreaded doing this. He didn't want to open her eyes to the things they knew. To the horrors that haunted their existence. Like his brother, he wanted to preserve her innocence. To keep it sacred.

If only he could.

Trying not to think of all the grisly outcomes for them, he pulled her with him into his domain.

She gasped lightly but said nothing more as he took her through his dark domain, to the shadows where Xev was being kept in the lowest pit of Azura's hell.

The moment they stepped into his cell, she let go of his hand to rush to where Xev lay naked on the filthy, cold ground. No pillow. No blanket. No sign of any kind of comfort, other than the scurrying vermin.

"Xev?"

Shadow winced at the condition his brother was in. Scrawny from hunger, Xev was less than half the size he'd been before. Almost every bone in his body was visible. His hair had grown long and tangled into snarls that would have to be cut, as there was no way to brush them out. All of his features were obscured by a thick, unkempt beard. And his wings...

They were all but plucked clean.

Shadow hated this for him.

Yeah, Jaden could be an ass. Xev still shouldn't have handed him over to their mother.

That being said, Xev had been more than adequately punished. Shadow barely recognized his brother. This was not the warrior who'd stood by his side in battle.

And the moment Myone touched him, Xev let out a weak breath. "You can't be here."

"Neither can you." She looked up at Shadow. "Can you get him out of here?"

Was she out of her mind? Azura would kill them all if they tried to remove him. "No."

Her astonished look seared him all the way to his blackened soul. "No?"

"No," he said firmly. "If I did that, our mother would demand he return and that we be punished alongside him. Trust me, it would only be worse for us all." And for his own ass, which he really didn't want to put in the heated compost. "The best thing anyone can do is stay away from Azura's notice. Especially right now."

Myone was aghast. "You really won't help him?"

"I can't, and neither can you." Shadow went to Xev and met his agonized gaze. "I'm sorry, Xev. You know if I free you, it'll only make it worse."

"I know."

Myone wept at how weak those words were.

Xev placed a hand on hers as if she were unspeakably

precious. "You must leave...please. No one can find you here."

She started to argue, until they heard a sound approaching from outside the door.

Shadow grabbed her and pulled her back into the darkness with him.

From there, she saw the demons coming to torture Xev even more.

Unable to stand it, she faced Shadow. "Get me out of here."

He nodded then took her back to her own room in Cam's temple. Without another word, he left her alone with the nightmare of Xev's condition.

But Myone wasn't finished. This wasn't right. She had to get Xev out of there. No matter what it took. She wasn't about to leave him to suffer like that.

A sudden solution came to her mind.

*Apollymi.*

She was the only one with the powers to quell Azura. The dark goddess terrified everyone.

*Including me.*

True, but what other choice did she have?

This was probably the dumbest thing she'd ever done in her life, aside from falling in love with Xev. Yet it was the only solution she could think of.

Terrified, she teleported to the goddess of destruction's dark temple before her common sense could return and talk her out of this.

The huge marble complex was impressive.

And scary. It glistened in the dim light.

Apollymi's Malachai army kept growing in size, and mixing with the Charonte demons who served her as well. They were everywhere in and around the temple. Three of the Charonte were in the goddess's antechamber, where Apollymi sat on the floor, playing a game with her young son.

"No fair, Mama. You always win."

"Not always, Kri. Sometimes I let you win." Apollymi was returning the pieces to their engraved wooden box when she looked up at Myone.

The laughter in her gaze faded to hatred. "What are you doing here?"

"I've come on behalf of someone who once did you a favor...Xevikan."

Apollymi went still for a second, then she looked at her son. "Kri? Can you give me a few minutes with this creature?"

He nodded. "Sure, Mama."

She snapped her fingers for the three Charonte to accompany him as he left them alone. Rising to her feet, she used her powers to teleport the box to a shelf on her right.

Apollymi approached Myone slowly. "Why is he not here to ask for this favor himself?"

"He's being held by your brother and sister. They've done unspeakable things to him."

Fury ignited in her eyes. Her white hair turned black for a heartbeat before it returned to the color of snow. She hovered over the floor. "Thank you for letting me know."

Before Myone could ask what that meant, the goddess vanished.

Even though it was against their rules, Myone used her powers to follow after Apollymi. She wanted to make sure Xev was taken care of, and honestly, she was curious where the goddess was off to.

It didn't take long to find out.

Apollymi exploded into Azura's throne room. The force of it splintered both Azura and Noir's thrones and sent Azura careening. The smaller blue goddess landed in a heap against the far wall.

Noir instantly appeared in the room, where Myone was hidden in a corner by the shadows that Xev had once called home.

"What is the meaning of this?" he demanded.

Apollymi didn't flinch as she faced him. "You dared to harm someone under my protection?"

Noir actually paled. "Wait? What? Who?"

Apollymi held her hand out and, using her powers, yanked Azura up from the floor, into her grasp.

Azura did her best to pry her grip loose, but Apollymi wouldn't give.

"Release Daraxerxes. Now!"

Azura coughed. "He's my son." Her voice was weak and raspy.

"You never wanted him."

"So?"

Apollymi grimaced then slapped her so hard it broke Azura's nose. "You whore. You drop children like a bitch in heat and give them nothing. I despise you. Release him and never approach him again."

Then she turned toward Noir. "Same for you. You are never to bother that boy again."

"Why do you care?" Noir challenged. "He's nothing to you."

"He will be a tutor for my son, as he's the only chaos god I seem to be able to trust. Bring him to me. Now!" That last word clapped in the room like thunder before a fierce storm.

A chill went up Myone's spine at the command in Apollymi's tone. How she wished she could do that. But she lacked the confidence of the older goddess. Apollymi knew her powers and position and wasn't afraid of them.

No wonder her siblings were so terrified in her presence.

None of them possessed that level of confident fury.

Something proven when Noir immediately vanished to fetch Xev, proving he was every bit as terrified of Apollymi as Azura was.

Was that what made the elder goddess so feared? Could it simply be her fierce power, or was there something more? Had she done something to them early in their lives that caused them to fear her so?

Then again, they hadn't feared her enough to spare Kissare from their wrath. Or maybe their actions now were because they'd killed him, and they knew Apollymi had every reason to harm them over their cruelty.

Whatever it was, they seemed all too eager to appease her now.

Noir brought Xev into the room and laid him at Apollymi's feet.

To Myone's astonishment, Apollymi knelt down by Xev's side. There was actual sympathy in her eyes as she saw what they'd done to him.

Then she raked a hate-filled glower over her siblings. "He's your son, Azura. What is wrong with you?"

There was no pity or mercy in Azura's eyes. Only a sick, smug satisfaction. "Your son has yet to betray you, Braith. Talk to me after that happens."

Apollymi shook her head. "There is nothing my Kri could do to make me hate him. Blood of my blood. I carried him beneath my heart and cradled him in my arms long before I birthed him. I feel his pain deeper than my own. I weep for you that you're incapable of that kind of love."

She sneered at Noir. "Or you. Maybe if you could, you'd understand better what matters in this world. So I'm warning you both, this one time only, stay away from what I love. My wrath will be absolute, and I will spare no one from it."

She placed a hand on Xev, and they both vanished.

Azura glared at Noir. "You idiot! I warned you about her. Why didn't you listen?"

"I'm not the one who locked Daraxerxes in the basement." Noir kicked at his shattered throne. "I wish we could kill her."

"Don't even say those words out loud, lest she hear them. Did you see what she did to Tisahn?"

He laughed bitterly. "I never thought I'd meet anyone

who could make me cringe in their creative cruelty. But I surrender my crown to her. Her viciousness makes a mockery of mine."

Azura waved her hand and restored their thrones. "We cannot fight her, and she now has an army."

"She has two."

"You think I don't know that?"

Noir gave her a droll stare.

"Then what do we do?" Azura asked.

"Befriend her."

She was aghast at his suggestion. "How?"

Noir shook his head. "Damned if I know. But we'd best find some way before she finds a cause to hate us more."

Myone withdrew then, afraid they might find her there and take issue with her snooping. The last thing she wanted was to run afoul of them and risk their anger.

Apollymi might not care if they tortured a Sephiroth. Her luck, the goddess might gift-wrap her for them.

By the time Myone returned to Apollymi's temple, Xev had been restored to the god she'd fallen in love with. His wings were again full, his hair trimmed short about his angular features. He was still thin, but he didn't appear quite so skeletal.

Relief flooded her as she saw him hale and whole, and it took everything she had not to rush to him and hold him. But that was the last thing she should do in front of Apollymi.

So she stood there respectfully.

The light in Xev's eyes told her that he wanted to do

the same. That he was every bit as happy to see her and was struggling not to run to her.

Instead, he stayed by Apollymi's side. "I'm told that I have you to thank for my rescue."

"I did nothing." She bowed to Apollymi. "Thank you, goddess."

"Thank you for bringing it to my attention." Apollymi glanced between them, then shook her head. "Ugh. For the love of the Source...Embrace, you two. Do you think for one moment *I'd* betray you? You both reek of love, and it turns my stomach."

Xev hesitated before he ran to Myone.

"But," Apollymi said as he hugged her, "remember what happened to my Kissare. I am a jealous bitch. Make no mistake about that. But I'm not an unfair one. I won't see you suffer just because I did. Your mother is another matter, Daraxerxes. Jealousy flows thick in her veins and rots her heart. Or at least the organ that pumps blood through her."

"I know."

When Myone opened her mouth to speak, Apollymi held her hand up to silence her. "Don't, child. Keep what you have between you and no others. I don't want to know anything else. Ever. I will do no more favors for either of you. Ask nothing more of me. My pain is too great. Keep this"—she gestured at their entwined hands—"from my sight, too. My mercy has limits. Don't test it."

"Thank you," Xev said, inclining his head to her. Then he pulled Myone into the shadows with him so that Apollymi couldn't see or hear them.

Myone finally kissed him as she'd longed to.

Xev savored the taste of her. She was the only thing that had allowed him to survive the nightmare of his mother's punishment.

Had he not been able to send his spirit-shadow form to her, he'd have never made it through. She was his lifeblood.

Yet he knew they couldn't keep seeing each other. This had to stop.

It had to.

The gods were cruel, and they would never allow them to live and love in peace.

Pulling back, he stared down at her. "Myone—"

"I know, Dary. I know. But I couldn't leave you like that."

That was why he loved her so much. Why he couldn't lose her. "Thank you."

Nodding, she kissed him one more time.

Xev pressed her hand to his lips, then took her back to her temple where the Sephirii lived. This was her home. It was where she belonged.

With her kind. Those who were gentle and who respected others.

His was now with a goddess everyone feared. He was an enemy to his father.

Nothing would ever be the same.

**16**

———————

Xev watched as the Malachai army trained. There were so many of them now. And all because of him. Because of the bargain he'd made with Apollymi to save her son.

He didn't know which secret was the one most likely to end his life.

The fact that he was the donor for the Malachai race or his love for the Sephirii leader.

He was torn between the two. It didn't make sense, but he felt a paternal love for all the Malachai. Even Apollymi's son, who'd been born without any help from him. Kri was like a son to him. The more time he spent with him, the more he treasured the boy.

Maybe that was why Apollymi had chosen him to be Kri's tutor. She'd known that, by making him responsible for her son's learning, he'd become attached to Kri. And he was.

Kri fascinated him.

At times, it was like staring into a mirror. A child torn between light and dark. One who wanted to do good and one who wanted to please his mother and do whatever she asked of him.

Only in Kri's case, his mother actually cared for her son. Would kill to protect him.

Something Xev had learned his first day of tutoring the boy, when another demon accidentally caused Kri to stumble and skin his knee.

The boy had cried out, and an instant later, the demon had literally been reformed so that his innards were outtards. The demon had died screaming in agony.

It wasn't something someone easily forgotten. Xev was sure it would give him nightmares for a lifetime.

And since that day, he had made sure to protect Kri with everything he had, lest his own innards decided to take a hike outside his body.

It was why Kri, fully grown now, wore full battle armor at all times. No need to risk any injury, no matter how small, lest his mother retaliate against an innocent party.

Kri scowled at Xev. "Why can't I go out with you and your brothers?"

Xev laughed...until he realized it wasn't a joke. "Wait. You're serious?"

"Of course. I thought you liked me."

"I do, Kri. But your mother terrifies me. I don't even want to know what she'd do to me if I let you out of here."

Kri sighed heavily. "Not fair."

Xev clapped him on the back in an effort to cheer him.

"I know, little buddy. Be glad you have a mother who loves you. I'll trade any day you want to."

Kri screwed his face up at that. "No, thank you. Met your mom. Wasn't impressed."

"Exactly. But I can bring you back some snacks."

Kri laughed. "Human?"

"Sure."

"No. I mean can you bring me back a human to snack on?"

Xev laughed nervously. "Joke?"

"Only if you want it to be." Kri winked.

Shaking his head at his wayward pupil, Xev groaned. "I'm too old for your humor."

"I know, Gramps." Kri hesitated.

"Something wrong?"

Scratching at his ear, he shifted uneasily. "I wanted to ask you about something, but it's kind of personal."

Xev wasn't sure he liked the sound of that. Personal things with the offspring of Apollymi could easily get him gutted.

Or worse.

"Why do I dread those words?" he asked Kri.

"Not about you."

There was something very serious in Kri's tone, and that wasn't normal. He was usually a playful boy. So much so that it'd often been a struggle for Xev to get him to focus on his studies.

Now...

This matter weighed heavily on his shoulders. "What is it?"

With his mottled red and black skin, Kri was actually adorable in his sudden shyness. "I met someone."

"I imagine you meet a lot of someones."

Kri rolled his red eyes. "A female someone."

"Oooooh." Xev drew the word out as he suddenly understood.

"It's more than an *ooh*," Kri said testily. "She's..." His cheeks turned bright red.

"Special?"

Kri nodded. "I've never known anyone like her."

Xev knew that feeling a lot better than he wanted to. "Is she a demon?"

"A Malachai."

Now that was more surprising than it should be. It wasn't as if Kri didn't interact with other Malachai. Still...Xev hadn't given much thought to his being attracted to others of any species. The boy normally kept to himself.

But Xev should have known that, sooner or later, Kri would grow up and be attracted to someone.

"Really?" he asked.

Kri nodded. "She came to the city to join my mother's army." A smile brought out his dimples. "She's incredible, Xev. She actually flipped me onto my back the first day I met her."

Xev laughed. He'd been there, too. "I can tell you're taken by her."

"Not yet, but I want to be...I mean...Ugh!"

"It's fine, Kri. I get it. We all have that someone we hold in our heart."

"Yeah, but my mother will have a fit if she finds out. She doesn't want to share me with anyone."

"I wouldn't be so sure. Apollymi loves you. She knows you're not a child anymore. I'm sure she'd want you to be happy with your Malachai."

Kri snorted rudely. "She doesn't treat me that way. I swear, she still cuts my steaks for me."

That was true. Xev had actually seen Apollymi do that a time or two for her son. "Because you're her baby."

"I'm grown, Xev."

"I know." He leaned in and nudged Kri. "I still want to cut your steaks, too."

Kri shoved playfully at him. "Please don't. My ego's frail enough."

"Right."

"It is. Especially after the way Rubati threw me on my arse. It was completely humiliating."

And he'd obviously loved every minute of it. "I have a feeling you'll get over it."

Kri considered those words. "You really think my mother would be all right with this?"

"I do. Given how much she loves you, I'm sure she'd love grandkids even more."

That made the boy smile again. "Thank you...and don't forget my human snack."

Xev laughed as Kri bounded off, no doubt in search of his female Malachai. How he wished he had the same freedom to go after the woman who held his heart.

Even after all these years, he didn't dare. He and Myone still had to meet in secret for fear of what the gods would do to them if they ever learned of their relationship.

And he hated that most of all. But at least he finally had a place where he belonged. For better or worse, Apollymi accepted him. She didn't resent his blood. Didn't question his loyalty or insult him for a mother he detested.

She didn't look at him as if she despised him.

Grateful for that, he teleported to his room to change clothes before he met up with his brothers.

Xev had just entered his room when he heard Apollymi and his mother shouting at each other. While it was nothing unusual to hear his mother's strident tone, it was rare for Apollymi to resort to raising her voice. As powerful as she was, she didn't need to. She could make most crap their pants by doing nothing more than arching a single brow.

This fight was exceptional.

And *very* loud.

"You have to side with us!"

Apollymi laughed. "I don't have to do anything. You had your chance to side with me against the others when they demanded Kissare's life, and you didn't. Instead, you helped them kill what I loved. So why should I do anything for you now? Other than beat you where you stand?"

"They are going to bind us. Is that what you want? To be imprisoned for eternity?" Azura asked.

"They can't bind me."

"Of course they can."

Apollymi scoffed. "I have an army. Two of them, if you count the Charonte demons."

"Do you really think they'll fight for you?"

"Xiamara?" Apollymi asked the Charonte who was never far from her side.

"We will fight for Apollymi, if she asks."

Azura was still furious. "Well, bully for you. But what if they've found a way to bind the Charonte, too?"

"Impossible."

"Is it?" Azura asked.

Neither Apollymi nor her Charonte friend responded.

Xev wasn't sure what to think about the argument. Heading into the shadows, he went to spy on them.

Apollymi and Xiamara were on the opposite side of the room from Azura. He'd never seen Apollymi uncertain before.

Xiamara stood next to Apollymi. With her red and white mottled skin, the demon was strangely beautiful even with her horns, tail, and wings. There was something innately graceful and deadly about their species.

More than that, Xiamara was fiercely loyal to Apollymi. He knew she would die to protect her goddess friend.

Azura glanced to Apollymi then Xiamara. "Our demons are attacking the Sephirii at dawn. There will be war. You will have to pick a side, sister. I suggest you pick the only side that will back you, as you know what Cam, Jaden, and Rezar will do if you try to join forces with them."

Xev's heart stopped as he heard those words. Unable

to breathe, he stepped back and flew through the shadows with only one destination in mind.

Myone.

He had to warn her.

This time of night, she might be at dinner. But he hoped and prayed she was in her room at Cam's temple.

Alone.

He would teleport there, but if she wasn't by herself, he'd do more harm than good. There would be too many questions as to why he was there, given that everyone knew he served Apollymi. And Apollymi and Cam never spoke and never had anything to do with one another.

Thankfully, Myone was in her room, changing clothes.

She'd just pulled her dress on when he came out of the shadows behind her. "Dary!" she gasped. "You startled me."

"Sorry, love. I just learned that Azura plans to attack the Sephirii at dawn."

She stopped lacing her gown to gape at him. Her face went pale. "What?" she breathed.

"They're starting a whole new war, and it begins at dawn."

"You're sure?"

He nodded. "Heard it straight from Azura's lips. Prepare your troops. Whatever you do, don't get hurt."

She pulled him into her arms and held him. "You need to stay out of this."

Those words meant everything to him as he buried his face against her neck. "I will do my best. You stay to the rear of the fighting."

She sank her hand in his hair. "You know I can't. I'm their leader."

He pulled back to stare down at her. "Lead from behind."

Myone scoffed. "You know better."

"Then I will meet you at dawn and I will make sure no one hurts you in the fighting."

"Dary..."

He cupped her face in his hands. "I will protect you, Myone. I don't care what they do to me. You fight and I will guard you."

Myone wanted to argue, but she knew it was useless. And she couldn't blame him for that. She felt the same way about him. Theirs was an impossible relationship. Yet they couldn't stop what they felt. No amount of time had ever dulled their feelings.

No amount of distance.

If anything, their love grew stronger.

"I'll see you in the morning."

Nodding, he kissed her again. "Warn the others."

"I will. Wear your green armor so that I can find you in the crowd." That would make it easier for her to protect him as well. His green armor stood out from the normal gold and silver of the others.

"I'll see you at dawn."

~

THE SUN WAS JUST CLIMBING over the mountainous

horizon as Myone waited with her army at the edge of Hurrian City.

There was no sight of a demon anywhere. Nothing other than a calm morning dawning in a beautiful city.

With an irritated smirk, Kuru turned toward her. "Where are these demons you spoke of?"

Biting her lip, she scanned the horizon. "I was told they'd be here."

He and the others looked skeptical. "I don't see anything."

Neither did she.

In fact, it was so quiet, she heard her own heartbeat in her ears. Where were they?

Maybe Xev had been wrong.

Had they changed their mind and decided not to attack after all?

This was so embarrassing. She'd brought her entire army out and there was nothing for them to fight.

Where was a hole to swallow her when she needed it?

Kuru sheathed his sword. "Really, *kyra*? Where did you get your information?"

She ground her teeth at the way he used her title *kyra*, as if to insult her because he couldn't stand the fact that she was their commander. "It was reliable."

He gave her a smirk that she really wanted to knock off his arrogant face. "Then why are we here alone?"

Myone glared at him. "Don't you dare question me."

Sadly, she could see that they were *all* questioning her now.

The worst part?

They didn't trust her. It was painfully apparent. She wasn't sure if they'd ever really trusted her, and that hurt most of all. No matter how hard she tried, they never saw her as the same caliber of commander that Kissare had been.

And Kuru thought himself her superior. He wanted her position and made no effort to hide his ambition.

He looked at the others. "Let's go back to bed."

"You're not the commander," she reminded him.

"No, but I should be."

Those words stung as her army followed him away from where she hovered. A part of her wanted to throw her dagger into his fleeing back.

Xev wouldn't have hesitated to do it. Maybe she'd been with him too long, because right now, that temptation was so strong that she wasn't sure how she resisted.

*This is useless.*

Just as she started to turn away, she heard something. A faint whisper that caught her attention.

Then she saw the flash. No, not a single flash...a bunch of them.

"They're coming!" She'd barely uttered those words before a thousand demons manifested around them.

Because they'd turned around to go home, her army wasn't prepared for the onslaught.

Screams and shouts rang out, lost to the clanging of steel against steel.

With a battle cry, she went after a group of demons on her right. They scattered at her approach. But she gave them no quarter as she flew after them, intent on regaining her honor.

She banked to the left and lifted her sword to slice at another. Right as she would have decapitated the demon, she recognized the green articulated armor.

*Xevikan.*

Myone barely pulled back her stroke that would have wounded him. He feinted right, then took a position behind her.

"What kept you?" she asked.

"Demons...They're never on time. It's like herding a bunch of hungry cats in a mice factory. None of them listen or do what you want."

She would have laughed had she not been surrounded.

Xev grabbed her and wrapped his wings around her.

She was aghast at his actions. "You have to stop this. They'll get suspicious."

"Slap me."

She scowled at him. "I can't."

He took her hand and made it appear as if she did. "Ow!"

"You're awful."

"Then be my prisoner."

How she wished she could be. "Never!" She playfully pushed him away.

He tumbled through the air.

When a demon went for her, he grabbed him by the throat. "She's mine!"

Myone shook her head at his angry tone. They had no idea what he really meant. "I need to fight demons."

"I fight them all the time." He grabbed her from behind and turned her so that she could see the others. "Besides, they seem to be doing fine on their own."

"Who's your leader?" she asked him.

"Why? You thinking of cheating on me?"

She gave him a droll stare. "Who do I kill to end this?"

"They're demons. They don't really have a leader. They were told to come kill and create chaos. So that's why we're here."

"Great."

Xev started choking and making loud noises.

"What are you doing now?" she whispered.

"Evil, evil vixen!" he cried out. "No!" He grabbed her hand, then wrapped her arm around his neck. "Don't!" Next thing she knew, he'd blasted half of his own troops into oblivion with his powers.

"What did you do?" she whispered.

He continued to strangle himself with her arm. "Run!" he shouted to the demons. "They have a secret weapon!" He twisted out of her hold, kissed her cheek, and vanished before she even knew what he was doing.

To her shock and relief, the demons followed.

*What the...?*

Scowling, she turned around to see her confused army. While some had been wounded, the majority of them were fine.

But they all stared in awe of her.

Then they raised their swords in salute and shouted.

In that moment, she wanted to kill and kiss Xev for the honor. She was grateful, but inside she knew she hadn't really earned this.

At least, that was her thought until she saw the jealous sneer on Kuru's face as he glared at her.

She'd take the victory, if for no other reason than to see him seethe. Sure, it was petty, and she hated the fact that she enjoyed it. Maybe there was more evil in her than she wanted to admit.

Or Xev had more of an impact on her than she'd realized. Either way, she'd take it.

But what bothered her most was that she'd wanted to earn her command honestly, by hard work and merit, once Kissare was tired and wanted to retire. Kuru wanted to take her place by knocking her down and ruining her.

So there was no true evil in her for taking satisfaction in watching Kuru's malice ruined. What was in his heart... That was sour and needed to be watched, lest it grow and turn more malicious.

She owed Xev for solidifying her command. He'd risked his life by doing this.

And she wouldn't forget it. Had she not loved him before, she would now. Too few people put others before themselves, risked their lives for the ones they loved. He'd proven himself this morning.

Somehow, she'd pay him back. She had no idea how. But this sacrifice wouldn't go unanswered. Or unrewarded.

She just wished others could see the decent man he was and not judge him for the blood of his mother. For something he couldn't help. It wasn't his fault that his mother had chosen her path.

If only she could make Jaden see the truth of his son.

*I will open his eyes.*

She had no idea how, but she wouldn't rest until Jaden realized that Xev wasn't the villain he believed him to be. He was just an imperfect man who needed his father to be there for him.

And speaking of, her own father hugged her. "I'm proud of you, Myone. I wish your mother was here to see you. I know she'd be every bit as proud as I am."

She smiled at him. "Thank you."

He kissed her on her forehead. "You did well. But I am curious about one thing."

"That is?"

"How did you know they'd attack?"

Myone hesitated. She wasn't sure what to say. She didn't want to lie to her father, but the last thing she wanted to do was tell him about her relationship with Xev. He'd never understand. No one would.

He gave her a knowing smile. "You have a spy among their ranks, don't you?"

"I'd rather not say."

"I understand. Last thing we want to do is lose a valuable asset."

He had no idea. And she wasn't going to give him one, either.

Smiling, she inclined her head. "If you'll excuse me?"

"Of course."

Myone left the field. Making sure that no one followed

her, she made her way back to her room and the shadows there. "Dary?" she whispered.

He appeared instantly so that he could pull her into his brother's domain. "Are you all right?"

"Of course. Are you?"

His grin thrilled her. "Never better."

"What happened?"

Smiling, he disguised her as a demon, then pulled her through the shadows with him.

She had no idea where they were going until she saw the three dark gods in a large room. Apollymi stood while Noir and Azura sat on their thrones. All of them were agitated.

"How could it have failed?" Azura shot a bolt of fire at a hapless demon servant in the corner. The poor thing yelped then vanished.

Lilit appeared in the doorway. "Now, now, dear sister. Why so distraught?"

"We were defeated."

Lilit shrugged nonchalantly. "You still have demons aplenty to fight with. It's not like you value them."

Apollymi arched a brow. "Speak for yourself. I value mine."

"Do you?" Lilit asked.

Apollymi floated over to her. "Don't play your mental tricks with me. I have no time for them, and even less patience for you."

Lilit turned toward Azura. "Jaden and Cam are terrified of how close you came to winning. Had you possessed a few more demons, the outcome would have been different. And who says you have to go head-to-head with their Sephirii? Prey on their precious humans. Weaken them where it hurts most."

Noir stroked his beard. "She has a point. War is all about strategy. And they do love their little humans."

Azura smiled. "War is our daughter. They don't have that strength."

Myone placed her hand over her mouth to keep from making a sound to betray her presence. Anat was lethal and the divine spirit of war. She would be hard to defeat.

Apollymi folded her arms over her chest. "Why is this so important to all of you?"

Azura lifted her chin. "We need to put them in their places. Control them lest they control us. Look what they did do you. Aren't you afraid they'll take your son?"

"I have their word that they'll leave Kri in peace."

"And you trust them?" Noir asked.

"No."

"Exactly." Azura glanced to Noir. "The only way to guarantee peace is to hold all the power."

Apollymi scoffed. "*I* hold the power."

Noir cocked an eyebrow at her. "Do you?"

"You want to try me?"

"Then why is Kissare dead?" Azura asked.

That caused Apollymi to send a jolt of power through the room. It was so fierce that it knocked Myone and Xev off their feet and slammed Azura and Noir into the wall, while shattering their thrones. Lilit tumbled across the floor.

"Never challenge me!"

Azura came to her feet with a feral glare. "I was making a point, dear sister."

"You were pissing me off." Apollymi swept her gaze around her frazzled siblings. "War is never the answer."

Noir growled at her. "You're the goddess of destruction. How can you say that?"

"Destruction is different. War is needless and prolonged. I only torture those who deserve it." She pinned a menacing glare on Noir. "I don't torture for pleasure. Destruction serves a purpose. In order for good things to grow, you have to purge the bad. That's my job. I amputate the poison limb in order to save the body." She indicated Lilit and Azura. "You're the poison that infects the limb. Particularly you," she said to Lilit.

Azura rolled her eyes. "You're so sanctimonious. It's not fair that you were given so much power."

Apollymi raked her with a sneer. "And you can only control water and misery. Poor you."

"You shouldn't pick on her," Noir said.

"Or what? Your darkness will consume me? You control mortal death, not mine. I have no fear of you, brother."

Azura tsked. "But you fear Rezar."

"I fear none of you." Apollymi vanished.

Lilit laughed as she sat on the floor so she could rock back and forth.

Noir snapped his fingers and repaired their thrones. "I'm really tired of her tantrums."

"We all are." Azura sighed. "What's your problem?" she asked Lilit.

"Sorrow. Sorrow. All around. Tomorrow. Tomorrow. Nothing found."

Azura rolled her eyes. "She gone insane again."

"Not insane," Lilit said. "Just thinking. War is here and it's there. It shall be with us for a long time."

"Will we win?"

She laughed at Noir's question. "No one wins a war, silly!"

## 17

Myone was so sick of this war. The gods had dragged it on for so long that no one could remember when or how it'd started. She barely remembered a time of peace.

Just as she couldn't remember the last time she'd seen Shadow. He'd completely withdrawn himself from it. Not that she blamed him. She wished she could do that same.

Worse, Malphas had left his father's side to join ranks with the demons they fought. No one knew why. Only that he and his father had a falling-out, then he was gone.

He was their enemy now. And that made her heart ache. She lived in fear of facing him in battle.

The last thing she wanted was to kill him. Like it or not, he was Xev's brother.

"Are you all right?"

She let out a relieved sigh at the sound of Xev's voice

in the dim light of her darkened room. "I didn't think you'd come tonight."

"I almost didn't." He tucked his wings in so that he could lie down beside her in her bed and pull her back against his chest. "But I couldn't stay away from you another second. I had to come. I've missed you."

She'd missed him, too. And she needed him tonight. Needed to feel the strength of his arms around her. Until she saw the vicious wound on his bicep. "What happened?"

"It's a flesh wound."

"Dary!"

He sighed wearily. "My assassin is still around. Taking potshots at me. No idea why. Guess, even in war, he or she has nothing better to do."

They had tried so hard to find that assassin. Luckily, whoever it was, they were completely incompetent. Or Xev was just that hard to kill.

Either way, she wasn't happy about it.

"Have you seen Shadow?"

He shook his head. "No one has. He's determined to become his namesake. Not that I blame him. Wish I had that option."

"Some days, I do, too."

Xev nuzzled his face against her cheek. "Just let me hold you for a bit and forget that we're enemies."

"I'm not your enemy."

"I know. I should have new battle plans for you tomorrow. Laguerre has something she's planning, but they haven't told us what yet."

Even though she was sad, that mention of his sister brought a small smile to her lips. "Have you been taking more potshots at your sister?"

"Believe it or not, I've stopped."

Myone looked over her shoulder at him in total disbelief. "Seriously?"

He brushed strands of her hair away from her cheeks. "I guess I've finally grown up."

"Since when?"

"Since the demons do it for me." He grinned. "They hate her more than I do."

She laughed at his impishness. "I shouldn't find that funny."

"Don't worry. I don't think less of you for it."

Suddenly, Myone heard distant screams echoing outside her open windows. Cringing, she listened for a second, but they didn't dissipate. "Sounds like they're attacking the village."

"I didn't know." Xev released her.

She quickly left her bed and pulled her armor on as someone knocked frantically on her door. "I'm dressing. I'll be right out."

"We'll meet you in the courtyard, *kyra*."

Xev helped her dress. "Be careful," he whispered.

She kissed him as she took her sword from his hands. "Don't be seen."

Nodding, he stepped back into the shadows.

She took one last look at him there before she flew out her window and returned to war.

Xev wanted to follow and protect her, but he knew

better. They'd kill him on sight if they knew he was here, with her. He was a villain to the ones he fought for.

To the side he'd die for.

Only Myone knew where his real loyalty lay.

He and Malphas had a screwed-up truce they'd come up with to keep from killing one another. They did their best avoid being in the same battles. And he tried to keep Myone out of the battles he knew Malphas was fighting in. Source help them if they were ever forced to face off.

Neither of them wanted to kill the other. But they would do whatever they had to in order to survive, and they knew it.

Sooner or later, they were bound to fight against each other. Someplace. Sometime. It was something they weren't looking forward to.

All they could do was hope the war ended before it came down to that. Before Xev looked across the line of his enemies' faces and saw his brother's.

Which was why he was grateful Shadow was staying out of it. Neither wanted to fight him, either.

Each day was getting harder. He was so torn between his loyalty to Kri and Apollymi, what he owed them, and his love for Myone.

He didn't know how this would end.

*If* it would ever end.

The Primals seemed content to keep this war going for the rest of eternity, regardless of how many lives it ruined or ended. He had no idea why. All he wanted was to live in peace. He'd never understand the others, why they continued to seek misery when they could be happy.

What was inside them that made them so desperate to create their own hell? To wallow in it so needlessly. He'd never understand them.

He didn't need the world. He just needed one person.

Myone's touch was his paradise. She alone sustained him. "Please, stay safe." Because if he lost her, he had no idea how he would continue on.

## 18

Xev caught Myone's hand as she entered her room from the doorway.

She gasped.

"Sorry," he whispered, gently pulling her against him. "I didn't mean to startle you."

She leaned against his chest and held him close. "I've been so worried. Where have you been? It's been so long since I last saw you that I was afraid you'd been harmed."

He nuzzled his face against her hair, inhaling the warm floral scent that never failed to brighten his mood. "I've had to keep a low profile after our last battle." Which had only frustrated him even more. "Come with me?"

She nodded, trusting him completely.

He pulled her into the shadows, through the labyrinth of worlds until they were in his favorite one. His neon home that had become his second refuge after Myone.

"Where are we?" she asked.

"Trisa."

That only seemed to confuse her more. "What's that?"

He pulled her out of the shadows into the distant world in the Ichidian Universe. "Shadow and I used to spend a lot of time on this world. They're a peaceful race. Unlike any other I've come across. They don't lash out to hurt others. They strive to be better than that." He led her toward a small home at the edge of a walled city.

"Where are you taking me?"

"To a house I bought."

She paused with a furrowed brow. "What?"

Xev turned to face her. There were so many things inside him that he wanted to say and didn't know how. He loved her more than anything. She was his heartbeat. His soul.

The only light he'd ever known.

And every day he lived without her wore him down more. He didn't know how many more he could last. He needed her by his side.

Not just little stolen moments here and there. It was time to forget everything else.

Just be *them*.

"Marry me, Myone. I'm tired of war. Of the gods. Of chaos. I just want to live in peace...with you."

Myone froze at those words. She couldn't agree with him more—it was exactly what she wanted, too—but it wasn't that easy. They had enemies who would never leave them in peace. Obligations that they both owed.

"Dary..."

He silenced her with a kiss. "I know I'm springing this

on you. You don't have to answer me right now. Spend the night with me, and then think about it. We don't have to go back. Ever."

It sounded so wonderful. Like him, she was tired of the war that seemed to be without end. Tired of the gore and bloodshed. Of being ordered to kill for reasons only the gods knew.

But it just wasn't that simple.

Taking her hand, he led her to a small home that was absolutely perfect for starting a family. The front door opened into a living space with...Well, she didn't know what kind of furniture that was, but it appeared comfortable. Soft and pale blue, it looked like a cloud in the middle of the floor.

"What is that?"

He picked her up and placed her on something that was even softer than her bed. "It's a sofa." He jerked his chin toward the gleaming room behind her. "That's the kitchen. Down the hall are two bedrooms with private bathrooms attached to them."

She frowned at the words she barely understood. "Rooms for bathing?"

"And for other things. You'll like the plumbing here most of all. Shadow and I have tried to introduce it many times in our world. It hasn't caught on yet. Very frustrating."

For the sofa alone, she was even more tempted to stay here with him. Goodness, this was amazing. It was so comfortable here. There was a breeze even though the windows were closed. Truly magical. How could he keep the temperature so mild?

Best of all...no war. She could live here with him, and no one would pull them apart.

Closing her eyes, she smiled at the very thought. At the images of them happily living their lives free of the gods and others who would tear them apart. What could be better?

"Could they find us here?" she asked.

"In theory, but it wouldn't be easy for them. They'd have to search all worlds, and with the war, I don't think they'd bother."

That would be incredible. Not to have to see that look come over his face every time his mother summoned him. Or to hear Cam's call in her own head.

But she did have one concern. "What would happen to my army?"

"Kuru would take over, I imagine."

Myone winced. He was the worst commander she could imagine. His thoughts were only on his own glory and honor, not on what needed to be done to protect his soldiers. "He'd get them killed."

Xev ground his teeth, tempted to lie. But he wouldn't do that to her. They'd never be happy if they built their life on lies, and he knew that. Plus, she wasn't stupid. She knew exactly how incompetent Kuru was and what he'd do to her army without her. "Probably."

Tears filled her eyes. "I can't sacrifice those who depend on me for my happiness, Dary. They finally trust me, and listen to me when I speak...thanks to you."

"You earned their respect without me."

She tsked at him. "I've won battles without you, that much is true, but it's your information and support that lifted me to where I am. I wouldn't be here without you, and I know it."

Xev only knew one thing—she was his life. Without her, he had nothing at all.

Sinking to his knees, he placed his head in her lap, wishing for a future he knew they'd never have. A perfect home with just the two of them, and no one else.

She brushed her hands through his hair. "Do you hate me?"

"I could never hate you. You're my heart and soul."

Myone swallowed hard at the heartfelt words that tore through her. That made this all the harder. Damn the gods. Because all she wanted was to stay with him.

But even if they couldn't live together, she wanted to give him a part of her that she gave to no one else.

"I will marry you, Dary."

His jaw went slack, and he looked up at her. "What?"

She smiled at his shocked expression. "They can't take that from us. I won't let them. I *will* marry you."

And still, he didn't return her smile. His gaze burned her as he held his breath, as if afraid of what she was saying. The fear in his eyes was searing. "You understand what that means, Myone?"

That they'd kill them both if they ever found out, and that death wouldn't be kind or pleasant. That they could *never* tell anyone else, even though she'd want to shout it out from the rafters. It wasn't fair, but at least it was something she could hold on to. A promise for another day that would be between the two of them. "I do. And you're worth it. I have no life without you."

His fear melted under a shining wave of happiness that thrilled her. "Then stay here with me." He crawled up on the sofa so that he could lie beside her. "Let's never leave here. We'll forget all about our war and their stupidity and hatred."

"You know I can't. Would you really forsake your brothers?"

He laughed bitterly as he wrapped his body around hers. "I would forsake any and everyone for you. Besides, we don't even know whose side Shadow's on."

"I know you better than that, Dary. You don't believe for one moment he's betrayed you."

"No. He's the smartest one of us to let no one know where he is or what he's doing. But Malphas is as tired of this as I am. He's just waiting for his own army to turn on him and either kill him or imprison him. They have no real loyalty to him, and he knows it. It's just a matter of time before his traitor's exposed."

She felt that. Only the gods seemed to be indefatigable when it came to this misery, to the endless bloodshed and strife.

Myone tightened her arms around him, seeking to comfort him and be comforted at the same time. "Whatever comes for us, we will face it together."

Xev nodded before he buried his face in her hair. "I have no ally on my side. If anyone finds out I'm gathering information for you, I'm already dead."

Her heart pounded in fear of the thought. It was her worst nightmare. "Don't say that."

But they both knew it was true.

The dark Mavromino gods would take pleasure in killing him and making him an example for others. She couldn't even let herself *think* about what the gods would do if they ever found out Xev was on her side. While he did protect Kri, he also protected her. His loyalty was split evenly between them.

And she despised the fact that she did that to him, because it was hard to be torn in two. Maybe that was why this war wasn't progressing. She didn't *want* to win it.

Winning meant that he'd be punished.

If his side won, they'd demand her head.

This never-ending stalemate was the best they could hope for. It was the only way for them to remain together.

And it kept them eternally apart.

He kissed her hand. "My worst fear is having to choose between you and Monakribos. I love you more than my life, but he's like a son to me."

"I know."

And she did. They'd grown so close over the decades. More than friends, they *were* family.

This was so much harder than it needed to be. She didn't want to come between them. Nor did she want to kill Apollymi's son.

Honestly, she didn't want to kill any of them.

But if she didn't do as the gods commanded, they'd kill her and her soldiers.

She wasn't even sure what this war was over.

Cam and Jaden claimed the Malachai and demons were as evil as the Mavromino gods they serves and needed to be put down. She knew better. They were no more corrupt than those on her side.

Especially given the fact that the demons had come from Jaden.

None of this made sense.

And here they were. Caught in the middle. Unable to be together. Closing her eyes, she savored this moment of peace where it was just the two of them. Where there was no confusion or war. No one telling her what to do, or what to believe.

Just the strong heartbeat of the one person she knew for a fact would give his life to keep her safe. Myone breathed in his scent and let it soothe her. This was the only person in life that she could depend on.

Xev.

In all the madness that surrounded them, all the chaos that made no sense, she found her serenity with a god who was renowned for causing havoc. The irony of it wasn't lost on her.

"Don't ever leave me, Dary."

"You know I won't."

She brushed her hand over his wound as tears gathered in her eyes. But it might not be up to him. Life was so incredibly harsh and uncertain.

*Stay with him.* It was so tempting to be selfish. But how long would they leave them in peace?

Apollymi was so much stronger now than she was

decades ago, and they'd torn Kissare apart. What chance did they stand against her?

"Don't cry." Xev lifted himself up so that he could kiss away her tears.

"I can't help it. I hate that we can't be together."

"I'm always with you. Even when I'm not. You know that."

That made her cry harder.

"Myone, please. You're killing me." Xev tightened his arms around her.

All he wanted was to protect her. To give her whatever she wanted.

If only he could give her peace. Instead, he held her and promised to keep her safe. He would do whatever it took to make sure that those who ruled them would never cause her harm. While he might not be as powerful as the older gods, he wasn't completely at their mercy.

He had enough of his mother in him to do whatever it took to protect those he loved.

That list was small.

No one meant more to him than the woman in his arms. Not even Monakribos, when it came down to it.

*I will keep you safe.* He just hoped he survived.

## 19

Xev paused to take in the most beautiful creature in all the worlds. Tall and lithe, she was absolutely gorgeous. The epitome of feminine perfection.

Her long black hair fell in soft, thick waves to her waist. With the round face of an angel, she had large blue eyes and a pert nose and full lips. Her skin had a golden cast to it, as if it were made of gold or brushed with it. Even her wings appeared to be made of spun gold.

Though barefoot, she was dressed in a thin red gown that left one gold-kissed shoulder bare.

How he loved the sight of her. She was the peace he sought.

And it was a stark contrast to the battle armor Xev wore, his bronze chain mail that moved like articulated dragon scales, and gold greaves buckled over burgundy boots that matched his cloak. The center of his bronze breastplate had the head of a hideous, terrifying chimera that was meant to scare his enemies.

But never her. He never wanted to scare his Myone.

Xev's eyes twinkled with devilish joy as he snuck through the oracle chamber where she was finishing her prayers. The iron sconces threw their flickering shadows over the wall, giving him plenty of places to hide.

Without a word, he thought he was sneaking up on Myone without a sound.

Until she turned to face him with a chiding shake to her head. "You're not supposed to be here," she admonished him. "What if someone were to see you?"

Completely unrepentant, Xev gave her the kiss he'd been waiting days to deliver. He pulled back with a soft moan. "I had to come. I've information about my mother's battle plans you need to know."

Biting her lip, she cupped his face. "Dary, you must stop spying for us. They'll kill you if they find out."

He shrugged her concern away. "What are they going to do to me?"

"Cut out your heart and feed it to you."

He took her hand in his and pressed it to the center of her chest. "My heart is here, beyond their reach."

She opened her mouth to protest, but he silenced it with another tender kiss.

After a moment, he pulled back to smile down at her. "They're planning to attack at dawn on the north gate, where you're usually weakest. I'll slow them down as best I can to give you as much time as I can to fortify your positions."

Fear and concern lined her brow as she stared up at him. "Be careful."

"You, too." He lifted a lock of her hair to rub against his lips so that he could savor the softness of it. "One day, Myone, I hope to have more than just a kiss from your lips."

"You know better. We both do. Even this is more than either of us should allow. Why can't I resist you?"

"I live with demons?"

She kissed the tip of his nose. "You drive me to distraction and tempt me beyond sanity. Now go, before someone sees you. And don't come here again!"

Myone regretted those words as soon as she said them. His eyes showed the depth of his heartbreak. The depth of how much he loved her and how much those words cut him.

The last thing she ever wanted to do was hurt the one person she loved above all.

"Sorry I bothered you, *ägna*," he said, using the submissive demonspeak term for owner. The agony of her rejection was tangible as he dropped her hair and stepped back. "I will trouble you no more."

The moment his back was turned, silent tears fell from her eyes. She covered her mouth and sobbed where he couldn't see or hear. *Don't weaken.*

She couldn't keep risking him. She had to let him go so that he wouldn't be hurt.

Because of her.

And when he closed the door without looking back, she flinched as if she'd been struck.

*It's for his own good.*

"I love you, Daraxerxes. I do," she whispered. "I'm so sorry."

She turned to walk in the opposite direction when she heard a sudden commotion outside.

*Please don't be Dary.* Her heart lodged in her throat.

Then it choked her as she heard angry shouts. "Stop him! Don't let him escape!"

"Kill him!"

She gasped at the sound of that sharp command that was followed by the clashing of swords and the sound of fierce fighting in the main temple room. Wiping at her eyes, she flew to the door and threw it open to find Jaden there with Xev, surrounded by guards. They'd outnumbered him twenty to one.

On his knees with his hands and wings tied, Xev was cut and bleeding. Two of the guards held swords at his throat.

"What is this?" she demanded.

"We captured a Mavromino spy." Jaden gestured at his guards. "Take him and lock him up."

She paled at Jaden's cold words as they brutally hauled Xev away, making sure to cause him as much harm as they could while they did so.

Trembling, she approached Jaden slowly, knowing the older god could kill her or worse. But he was her only hope in saving his son. "What are you planning to do with him?"

"He'll be interrogated for information about their army and intentions."

She flinched at what that really meant. "You mean tortured?"

Jaden didn't respond. "We're at war, Myone. Don't underestimate our enemies."

Enemy? *Seriously?* "He's your son, my lord."

"Who came here of his own free will to gather information for his mother to use against us. You think that deserves my mercy?"

"And what if he didn't? What if he came to give us information to use against her, instead?"

Jaden laughed. "Do you know how he was conceived? Through lies and deceit. He was meant to be a tool to be used against us from the very beginning. And that's what he is. Don't ever be fooled by him. He was born of the lying, conniving Queen of All Shadows, and suckled on the breast milk of demons. Trust me. I made the mistake of trusting him once, and it almost cost me my life when he handed me over to her. It's a mistake I won't ever repeat. Keep your heart hardened where he's concerned, or else you'll pay dearly for your mercy."

She knew better, and it broke her heart that Xev's father was so blind where he was concerned.

Meeting Xev's gaze, she inclined her head. She'd get him out of this just as soon as she could. The one thing Shadow would still do was help his brother escape whenever he was captured.

Unlike his parents, she wouldn't abandon him.

But this was why she'd been so harsh. Why as much as she loved him, she had to find a way to let him go.

He shouldn't have to bleed for her love. And she was tired of watching him suffer.

IT TOOK three days before she was able to infiltrate Xev's cell with Shadow.

Three days.

He looked awful. They'd all but torn him apart.

And it broke her heart to see him repaid like this. His information had saved the lives of her soldiers. Just as it had before when he'd come to her.

And this was his reward.

Shadow let out a tired sigh before he used his powers to break the chains that held Xev against the wall. "You have got to find a better hobby, brother."

Xev gave a bitter laugh, until he saw her. "Thank you."

"Thank her? I'm the one got us here."

He tsked at Shadow. "And thank you. But I have to say, I like the fact she's not so demanding."

Shadow pulled a cloth from his pocket and handed it to Xev so that he could wipe his face. "Maybe, but I don't take a blood sacrifice."

"That's a low blow, Shadow," Myone said, hating the fact that he was right.

Shadow held his hands up. "Fine. You two can take it from here. Last thing I want to do is get caught and be chained to the wall beside him. Then we'd all be screwed."

He vanished.

Myone shook her head at Xev. "We can't keep doing this to you."

"Sure, we can."

"Why are you so determined to bleed?"

"Because all my happiness is here." He leaned down to kiss her cheek. "If I have to bleed for you, then I'll take it. The Source knows I've bled for a lot less."

"I think they addled your wits."

Xev laughed. "Shadow would say I never had any to begin with."

"He might be right, you know?"

"He thinks so." Xev leaned his forehead against hers and sighed. "I love you, Myone. Whatever price I have to pay, I will do so."

"I can't stand to see you harmed. A part of me dies every time they abuse you."

"Then I'll be more careful. Just don't let me go."

Those words hit her like a hammer. How could she deny him when he had no one else?

She pulled him against her and held on tightly. "I will never let you go, Dary."

"Then they can do whatever they want to me."

That was her nightmare. What they would do to him.

## 20

————

"Open your eyes."

Myone had no idea what to expect. When Xev had "kidnapped" her, she'd been washing blood from her hair and wings, trying to scrub the stigma of war from her skin. He'd dressed her in her best gown and blindfolded her, then taken her through his shadowed lands to...

She'd never seen anything like this. It was a darkened cavern where everything around them glowed brightly. "Where are we?"

"It has no name. It's a land in between nothing and everything." His teeth flashed white while he spoke.

The colors here were so vibrant. Her golden skin glowed, as did her white dress and wings. Laughing, she spun about. "Why are we here?"

"You wanted to get married." He handed her a bouquet of bright pink and white flowers.

Her heart pounded at the sight. No wonder he was dressed in something other than armor and had shaved his whiskers clean. He normally never did that—something she'd teased him over almost every time they were together.

"Seriously?"

He nodded. "Sadly, there's no one to perform a ceremony for us, but I don't think we need anyone." He stood in front of her and held his hand up. "Give me your hand, fair Myone, and I promise that I shall give you my eternity. So long as you walk by my side, I will need nothing else. No one else. I am your darkness, and I swear that I will keep you forever in the light. You are my air. My heart. My soul. There will never be another for me."

Tears choked her as she stared at those beautiful blue eyes that had captured her heart the first day she'd seen them. She took his hand and held it tight. "I promise to always be here to catch you should you stumble, and fall in love with you every single day for eternity. I take you as mine, Xevikan Daraxerxes, knowing all of your faults, and loving you because of them. Never fear that I'll leave you. Because you are everything in all universes to me. Without you, I have nothing. I am nothing." She kissed his hand.

"You are my wife."

"You are my husband."

He pulled her into his arms and kissed her.

Myone laughed as she held on to him for everything she was worth. How she wished she could scream this out to everyone. But they could never breathe a word of it.

It didn't matter. They knew they belonged to each other. No one could take this from them.

And one day, once this awful war was over, they would be able to have a life together. To have a family. Then they'd never be separated again.

Xev pulled a necklace from his pocket and placed it over her heart.

Lifting her hair while he fastened it around her neck, she frowned at the beautiful black wing. "What's this?"

"It's my wing." He pulled a similar gold one from his chest to show it to her. "I have one of yours that I'll wear."

Happiness warmed her. "I love it." She dropped the charm and kissed him again. "And I love you."

"Love you too."

*Daraxerxes!*

That screech was so loud that even Myone heard it in the aether.

Cringing, she sighed in sympathy for him. "What in the name of the Source does your mother want now?"

He let out a disgusted growl. "Who knows? But I better go see before she sends one of her pets after me." Sadness darkened his eyes as he cupped her cheek. "Meet me at our house?"

"I'll be waiting. Don't take too long."

"I won't." He kissed her one more time then vanished.

Myone took a moment to smell the bouquet he'd made for her as she let everything sink in. She now belonged to him...not that she hadn't before. But it was more real now.

He was officially her husband.

*Husband.* She'd never even thought about having one before. All that had mattered was her position.

Now...

She was absolutely giddy.

Clutching her necklace, she prayed for her husband and their uncertain future. There was so much against them. So many who'd want to kill them if they learned of this.

It didn't matter. They had each other. Somehow they'd find a way to defy the gods.

No one would ever divide them.

**21**

---

THREE MONTHS LATER

Xev paced the small apartment as he waited for Myone to meet him. Why was she late? They'd both been in battle earlier. His had been wretched.

Kri had been wounded and barely survived it. Apollymi was still enraged and throwing a tantrum that was manifesting in the human world as storms, earthquakes, and tidal waves.

Somehow, they'd managed to pull back in time to save the one true Malachai's life. For that, she was grateful, and so Xev was still alive.

Barely.

He wasn't sure he'd ever be able to hear properly again. Or see straight from the magnitude of her tantrum. But he wasn't dead.

From what he'd heard of the other side, Myone's battle

had been brutal, too. No one had told him if she'd been wounded in the fighting.

Now he was worried. No, he was terrified.

"Where are you?" he breathed.

"Behind you."

Relieved beyond belief, he turned to find her there, then froze.

There was more of her than he'd expected to find.

A *lot* more.

Stunned, he stared at her as he realized that it'd been several weeks since they last saw each other.

Either she'd been seeking a lot of comfort with food, or...

"Are you...?"

Smiling, she nodded. "I'm pregnant."

Tears welled in his eyes as he rushed to her so that he could splay his hand against her rounded stomach and pull her into his arms. "It *is* mine, right?"

Her smile faded instantly. She gave him a peeved glare. "Seriously?"

Laughing, he kissed her. "I'm teasing."

"You better be, you beast! I can't even believe you'd ask me that!"

But what held his attention was the blood on her armor. She was covered in it, and must have come here straight from the fighting. "Tell me you didn't go into battle while pregnant."

She visibly winced as she stepped away from him. He could tell she was upset by something more than his words.

Pressing her hand to her brow, she drew a ragged breath, as if what she had to tell him was more than she could bear.

After a few seconds, she turned to face him. "I think I might have killed Malphas today."

Those words hit him like a blow to his gut. For a full minute, he couldn't breathe as he stood there, reliving the past. Seeing his brother as a kid.

As a warrior.

Malphas dead? It just didn't seem possible.

While he wouldn't consider them particularly close, especially since the war had broken out, he'd never wanted Malphas harmed. Worse? She would have used the skills he'd taught her against his brother.

*It's all my fault. I did this. I killed my brother.*

But had he not given her that ability, he'd be grieving for Myone right now.

*Better Malphas than her.*

Granted it was true, he'd never hated himself more.

Damn.

Xev felt sick to his stomach. "Are you sure?"

Pain darkened her eyes as she nodded. "It was awful, Xev. I'm so sorry. It was the last thing I wanted to do. But the look in his eyes as he came for me...You wouldn't have recognized him. He was feral and terrifying. Relentless. For a few minutes, I really thought I was dead. He fully intended to kill me. I..."

Xev winced at what she described. "You had no choice."

Unshed tears glistened in her eyes. "I hope he survived.

I stabbed him and got away from him as fast as I could. It's possible that he didn't die. All I saw was him falling to the ground." She drew a ragged breath. "He didn't return to the fighting, and we didn't recover his body. So maybe?"

She was right. He was a fierce bastard. It was possible he'd lived. "Did you stab him with your sword?"

"No. My dagger."

"Then he has a chance." The dagger didn't have a living creature in it that would have infected Malphas. Even though Xev couldn't feel his brother in the aether, it didn't mean that Malphas wasn't there.

He could be wounded and hiding.

Until he knew otherwise, Xev was going to hope for the best and trust that Malphas was a fierce survivor.

She brushed her hand over the bruises on his face. "What happened to you?"

"Battle," he said simply. That was the least of his concern as he continued to stare at her belly where their child was growing.

*Our child.* It didn't seem real or possible. In all this time, he'd never once considered this. Never thought that he'd have a child of his own. Especially not one with Myone.

He was thrilled beyond belief, but beneath that was a terror so raw that it shredded his sanity.

"What are we going to do, Myone?"

"I don't know."

Neither did he. All he could do was see Kissare in that cell. Only now, it was Myone he saw in Kissare's place.

*I can't allow that to happen. Not to her.*

"Has anyone noticed?"

She screwed her face up. "Malphas did."

Of course he would. His brother had never missed any detail. Neither of them, actually. Shadow was probably worse about that.

But if Malphas realized she was with child, there were others who would, too.

"Anyone else notice?"

She shook her head. "Not yet. But I won't be able to hide it much longer."

True. While she was still small, it was obvious to him. With luck, someone else would mistake it for a bit of extra weight. But as she said, that wouldn't last.

Just like with Apollymi. Once the others realized she was with child, they'd demand the name of the father.

"What are you going to tell them?"

"Nothing."

He didn't like that answer, at all. "They'll feel his powers." Which meant they'd know the baby's father was tied to the Source. Only a Source god or one of their offspring could be the father.

That was a very short list. This wouldn't be the same as with Apollymi, where the father's powers had been overshadowed by hers. Kri's father could have been anyone.

Their baby wasn't that lucky.

Xev searched his mind for some way to protect them both. "Run away with me."

"We've already had this argument. Many times, Dary. They will find us."

She was right, and he hated that. "What are we going to do?"

"I don't know."

Neither did he. But whatever happened, they would face this together. "I'll find some way to protect you, Myone. I swear it." She would never suffer Kissare's fate. He wasn't his father and he damn sure wasn't Apollymi.

He would fight them with everything he had. There would be no bargain.

The only way they'd get to her was through him.

## 22

"What have you done?"

Myone froze at the thunderous sound of Jaden's voice echoing off the walls of her room. The ancient god didn't bother to announce himself. He merely appeared in her doorway without any preamble.

This was Cam's hall. Jaden had no business here. And he had no right to yell at her.

Rising from her desk, she set her quill down. "Can I help you, my lord?"

The expression on his face was terrifying and deeply unnerving. She wanted to run but refused to. "Don't play with me, woman. Have you any idea what they'll do to you? To Daraxerxes?"

She released the breath she'd been holding. So, it was exactly what she thought had brought him here.

The baby.

Jaden's eyes turned a deep, dark red as he glared at her belly. "Of all the creatures you could have chosen...My son? What were you thinking? Why would you do something so foolish? He's not even on our side!"

She had to bite her lip to keep from denouncing Xev as a traitor to his side. The last thing she wanted to do was betray him or cause him harm. But she couldn't stand here and let his father insult him. "He's not what you think."

Jaden entered her room and slammed the door shut with his powers. "You're such a fool to put any faith in him. Trust me. I made that mistake once and lived to regret it."

She stood her ground and refused to be intimidated by the much larger god. He might put her through a wall, but not before she said what she wanted to. "And you know nothing about Daraxerxes. You *never* gave him a chance."

"There you're wrong."

She shook her head. "I know what happened between you...and why. You never allowed him to trust you. Never gave him a reason to. At every turn, you've hurt him, starting with the moment he was born."

A tic beat furiously in Jaden's jaw. "And what do you think will happen now when the others learn about this? A baby shower? No. They're going to demand your life. Are you prepared for that?"

Myone lifted her chin defiantly. "Yes, I am, because I know Dary will protect his son. I know what he's suffered already to protect me from you and the others. Never once has he given me any reason to doubt him."

Jaden paled. "What? What are you talking about?"

She let out a tired breath. How many times had they been here? It felt as if they were on an endless loop. She defended Xev and Jaden dismissed her out of hand.

*Why do I bother?*

Because she loved her husband, and she would do anything to protect him. Even argue relentlessly with his arrogant father, who refused to listen to her.

She gestured at her window. "You know exactly what I'm talking about. The night you caught Dary here and had him dragged away for torture. I've told you time and again that he was on our side and bringing me information about Azura and her plans. Did you listen? No. Because he has to be evil, right? There's no chance that he could be decent."

She gestured to her belly. "Now you have proof of what I told you that night. He was always giving me information on how to defeat the Mavromino. That's why we've won so many battles against them. Dary's the only reason we've won so many battles against them," she repeated for effect, hoping to get through to him. "He's never been on his mother's side. Not once. As bad as he hates you, and he has every right to do so, his need to protect me, his love for me, has always overridden that hatred. For that matter, you hate him for trying to protect himself when his mother threatened his life if he didn't swap necklaces with you. He had no idea what your necklace or hers would do. But once he did, he went back for you and made it right, even when he knew you'd punish him for it. What he never dreamed was that you'd abandon him, again, to his mother for her torture."

She shook her head as she raked him with a scathing glare. "You left him there to rot, with no regard for his life or for the fact that he'd been lied to and threatened, and had tried to make amends with you. Had I not gone to Apollymi, he'd still be imprisoned by his mother...and you better thank the Source every day of eternity that you didn't suffer what he did when he went back and freed you. He didn't deserve any of that."

Tears blinded her as she remembered what Azura had done to Xev for that. "You are such a bastard. I hate you for what you've done to him. Just being around you sickens me. Do whatever you want where I'm concerned. I don't care. How a god as wonderful as Dary came from you and Azura, I will never understand, but I regret nothing because I know exactly what a wonderful man he is, in spite of everything you and Azura have done to him."

Jaden stared at her as if she spoke a foreign language.

And maybe she did. She was asking for kindness from someone who obviously didn't have any comprehension of it.

Poor Xev.

She'd taken the love of her own father for granted. He would do anything to protect her. She couldn't imagine having *this* as a parent.

Neither of Xev's parents cared if he lived or died. If he suffered. Neither of them should have ever had children. They didn't deserve them.

Heartbroken, she cradled her stomach, which was just beginning to show signs of her child that was forming there. She could never allow her son to know the pain of his father. To turn her back on him. Not for anything.

They would make sure their son had all the love and protection they could manage. No one would ever threaten him.

A tear fell down her cheek. "I will never understand you and your coldness."

Jaden sneered at her. "You have that luxury. No one has ever betrayed you."

That was a pitiful excuse, and she knew it. "My husband has known nothing except betrayal, and yet he loves in spite of it. More than that, he protects. No one is allowed to threaten me or his child."

Jaden tried to understand that. Was she right? Could he have misjudged his son so badly?

He hoped not. Because if he had...

Then he was the monster she called him.

Yet as he looked at her, he saw the sincerity. The love she held for his son. She believed in Daraxerxes with a faith no one had ever shown Jaden. No one.

Not even his sons.

*What do I do?*

His siblings would tear these two apart. Especially after what they'd done to Kissare. Apollymi would demand blood for blood. She would not take mercy on them, and there would be no way to talk her out of it. She'd be entitled to it.

Even if she had spared Daraxerxes before, she

wouldn't do it now. Her wrath would be absolute. And his son would pay the price for what they'd done to her.

Wouldn't matter that he'd argued against her punishment. She was all wrath now. All she wanted was to make the world burn, and tear all of them down.

Even Noir and Azura. They were just too stupid to realize it.

*And that is my grandchild.*

Jaden stared at Myone's stomach, awed by what she was willing to do for the idiot he'd fathered.

At the end for the day, he'd failed his sons, and he knew it. He'd never been there for any of them.

How could he fail another generation?

If what she said was true, Daraxerxes fought for their cause in spite of everything he'd done to him. In spite of the fact that he'd betrayed him.

Meanwhile, Malphas had turned on him completely. He didn't even know why. And that pain still burned deep inside him. He'd done everything he could for Malphas. He'd wanted his love. Had tried his best to keep him on the right side.

In the end, the demon in his blood had won out.

*Her child...*

There might still be a chance for him. He was part Sephiroth and held the blood of both sides. Would his mother's blood be enough to override theirs?

*I can learn from my mistakes. If Daraxerxes can be saved, maybe I can be saved, too.*

And maybe he could help them. Maybe he could do

what he should have done when the demon had brought his son to him as an infant.

"Perhaps there's a chance for the baby."

She stepped back from him. Suspicion hung heavy in her eyes as she wrapped her arms protectively around her stomach. "What kind of chance?"

It was a stupid one. But it was the only thing he could think of. "Marry me."

All the color drained from her face as if it was the most terrifying thing she'd ever heard. Her jaw went slack.

Jaden held his hands up. "I won't touch you." How disgusting did she think he was? He'd never hurt his son like that. "But it will shield you and your son from the others."

"How?" she asked, aghast.

"If you're my wife, they won't dare touch you. Apollymi snuck around with Kissare. That was her biggest mistake and what upset Cam and Rezar most. She hid her actions. Besides, we're at war with her. Her opinion won't matter right now. So long as we're open about our supposed relationship, Cam and Rezar won't be able to speak out against it. They have more important things to think about while we're at war. If I take you as my wife, I can bully them into accepting it."

Myone's head spun at what he was saying.

Marry her father-in-law? That was the craziest thing imaginable.

Wasn't it?

"Think about it, Myone," Jaden insisted. "I share the

same blood Daraxerxes does. The same basic powers, as does his mother. They won't be able to differentiate ours from his. When they sense the Source powers in your child, they'll assume it's from me. If we tell them it's my child, they will assume any deviation comes from the mingling of your powers with mine. No one will dare question the child's parentage. You both will be safe. As will Daraxerxes."

She wanted to deny it. But what he said made sense. Too much sense, unfortunately.

"And I will protect Daraxerxes as best I can. I swear it."

Did she dare trust this god? He'd betrayed her husband, time and again.

Moving back to her desk, she sat down as she grappled with this. "I need a minute. Because this doesn't make sense. Why would you help us after everything you've done to Dary? You're an unforgiving asshole."

He winced at the words that they both knew were true. "You're right. I am. From beginning to end. I won't deny it. But you have no idea what I've had to navigate through with my siblings. The eggshells I walk on every day because of them. I'm not perfect, and I've made a lot of mistakes. There's a lot of bad blood between me and my siblings. A lot of things I regret, that you can't imagine. I can't fix what I've done. But I don't want you or your child to pay for my mistakes. Or to be punished by their cruelty."

He let out a bitter laugh. "And you're right about Xev. I should have protected my son. But I knew if I let him into my heart, his mother would have used it against me. I would have been at her mercy and everyone would have suffered."

That didn't placate her at all. If anything, it made her hate him more. "So you let him suffer in your stead?"

At least he had the decency to look ashamed. "I can't change the past, Myone. But I can give your son a future. If you'll let me."

How easy he made it sound. But this would kill Xev. She could hear the screaming fit already. And who could blame him?

For once, she wanted to join his tirade.

Even if it made sense.

Sighing, she nodded at Jaden. "I need to talk to my husband about this."

He went to her door, then paused. "Don't take too long. The one thing we learned with Apollymi, that"—he indicated her belly—"won't stay hidden long."

No kidding. She still had nightmares over all of it. "I know."

Inclining his head, he excused himself and left her to think about what he'd offered.

Myone sat in silence, considering her options. She could run away like Xev wanted. Those hours they'd spent on Trisa were wonderful. It was where she'd conceived their son.

She would love to raise him away from war and politics. Just the three of them. Closing her eyes, she could picture it so plainly. Their little house with Xev and their son.

But how long until they were hunted down out of

spite? Azura wouldn't let him go. He was one of her top generals.

Apollymi relied on him to guard Monakribos. Kri relied on him as his best friend, confidant, and advisor.

While he would give her the information she needed to fight their army, he still protected Kri, and she respected that. They had an unspoken pact that she would never lead her army directly against Kri and his forces.

Just as she'd tried her best to avoid Malphas.

*Yeah, look how that had ended.* Over and over, she kept replaying that last fight where she'd stabbed Malphas.

The look in his eyes as he'd fallen away from her, toward the human realm—it was hard to live with the guilt. What would she do if she were responsible for Xev's death?

Or that of her child?

*What am I to do?*

"Is something wrong?"

She gasped at the sound of Xev's voice coming out of the shadows behind her. "I was just thinking of you."

"With *that* frown? Whatever I did, I am so sorry. I won't do it again. You just have to tell me how I screwed up and I swear I'll fix it...and bring you your favorite food from Trisa."

Laughing, she held her hand out to him. "You did nothing wrong."

"It didn't look like nothing. It looked like I left the toilet seat up or ate your last friggle. Again, whatever I did, I am forever sorry." He took her hand and kissed her cheek. "Better yet, can I blame my brother or father for it?"

She laughed again. "You did nothing wrong, but in this case, you *can* blame your father for my mood."

Relief spread across his handsome features as he moved to sit down beside her at her table. "Whew. I'd much rather he have your ire. So what did he do, and do you want me to kill him for it?"

She loved whenever he teased her like this. If only she was in the mood for it.

"No," she said sadly. "But you might kill him when I tell you what he said."

That caused one of his dark eyebrows to shoot up. "What?" While he might not be demonkyn by blood, his voice had a very demonic sound to it.

"Don't take that tone, Dary. It's not necessarily a bad thing."

"And that just made it worse." He stood back up. "What in the name of the Source would he have to say to you?"

Given his mood, she wasn't sure if she should tell him, but if she waited any longer, it would just make it worse. So she took a deep breath and blurted it out. "Well...he *propositioned* me."

His jaw dropped, then his cheeks darkened with color as his eyes glowed with rage. Both wings shot out. "I'll kill him!"

"Not like that! Ew!" She screwed her face up at the very thought, then cringed. "Well, kind of like that, but not the way you think. Calm yourself, Dary!"

That didn't work quite the way she'd hoped. He hovered to her right as if he was about to fly out the window. "Wait. What?"

She pulled him to sit down beside her. "He knows I'm pregnant."

He looked as if he'd bitten into something rotten. "Is that his thing?"

"Would you stop?" She shoved playfully at him. "He knows you're the father."

Xev sobered instantly as he realized what that meant. "What did he say?"

"You can imagine."

Yes, he could, and none of it was good. "Does he plan to tell the others?"

She shook her head. "He offered to marry me."

Xev choked as he felt his anger surge forward again. At this rate, he was going to kill his father before the night was over. "He offered to do *what*?"

"No. Now. Wait. Stop!" She grabbed him to keep him at her side as he started to get up and leave again. "Breathe, Dary. Just breathe and think about it before you go after him."

He was thinking, even though his wings were twitching...and so was his eye. Thinking of how much he wanted to beat his father until he bled. Thinking of how much of his mother he had in him right now, and how he should have left his father chained in that room.

And then he began to calm down a bit and really consider what she was saying.

To his utter disgust, it actually made sense. As much

as it galled him, it made sense. It made sense...He kept repeating that to his lizard brain that was having a hard time grasping all this without sending bolts of power toward his father.

Myone played with his hair, which went a long way toward calming him. "He said he wasn't going to touch me. It would be in name only, to protect us."

That was the most surprising part of it all. "And you're sure it was my father who said this? *My* father. Big, tall... asshole?"

She snorted. "Positive. Big. Tall. Asshole."

"My *father*?" he repeated. He just kept doing that, as he was having a hard time fathoming everything she was telling him.

"Your father."

He still couldn't quite wrap his mind around it. "Did you hit him in the head with something? Did he have a battle wound? Aneurysm? Hangnail?"

She laughed and rolled her eyes. "I think it was a change of heart."

"He has no heart to change."

Myone tsked at him. "I know, but people can change."

"He's not a person."

"Gods can change. Even Apollymi learned to love." She leaned against him. "Stop being so contrary, Dary. Don't let your anger get in the way."

Maybe, but he had a hard time believing it. This was his father they were talking about. Jaden was barely one step up from an amoeba. All he could see was the look in his father's eyes when Jaden had left him to his mother's tender care after Xev freed him.

He couldn't bring himself to ever forgive his father for that nightmare.

But as much as he hated to admit it, Myone was right. He needed to put his anger away and think clearly. What she said made sense.

If she was the wife of his father—he shuddered at the very thought—it would mask the baby's powers. He couldn't deny that. Because they were so closely related, no one would know.

This could very well be the best chance she had. The only chance, really.

Damn them all for it.

Xev placed his hand on her belly. He still couldn't believe that there was a part of him in there. That she loved him enough to risk so much. To risk her life.

This wasn't really his decision to make. And he wasn't about to make it for the one it would impact the most.

"What do *you* want to do?"

She didn't hesitate. "I want to be with you, Dary. But I want you both safe. You and our baby."

He loved her for that. "Do you trust my father?"

"I think I do. At least on this matter. You didn't see him when he came to me. He was being honest. He regrets what happened with you."

*Sure he did.* She might believe Jaden, but Xev wasn't so easily won over.

He clenched his teeth as he debated the best course of action. "I still don't trust him. At all. But I trust you.

Whatever you decide, I will back you with everything I have. I know that when it comes to him, I can't make a logical decision. My emotions are too invested in my hatred, and they always will be." He sighed. "I just wish this was all done with and we didn't have to live in fear."

"Me, too."

Taking her hand, he pressed her fingers to his lips and kissed them. "Just promise me one thing."

"Anything."

"Whatever happens, don't let my son grow to hate me."

Myone cupped his whiskered chin in her palm and forced him to look at her. "I will *never* let our son hate his father. How could he?"

"I'm a monster, Myone, and I lead others of my kind. I hate everything I'm forced to do."

Those words broke her heart. "What do you mean?"

"You are the only thing I don't regret. But everything else...I don't know how much longer I can hold on. I'm so tired."

She pulled him into her arms and held him. "It'll be all right."

Xev drew a ragged breath as he let the warmth of her arms wash away the horrors of his memories. The nightmare of his day. Too many battles. Too many bodies. He was done with war.

Done with killing.

But there was no end in sight.

He'd never understand the joy his mother had in

taking lives. Why Noir wanted to destroy everyone around him. Or Apollymi.

Or Kri, for that matter.

They'd laid waste to an entire human village today. He couldn't get the sound of innocent screams out of his head. People begging for mercy.

Or death.

The carnage...

The smell of burning flesh.

He well understood the need for revenge. Wanting to make someone pay for having wronged him.

Killing for killing's sake?

What the hell? It was twisted and sick. The only thing he'd learned in all this was that everyone bled. It didn't matter if they were gods, demons, humans, or other. Pain and suffering was universal.

Creatures who declared themselves superior or completely different from others were more alike than they were different. It didn't matter their species or country. They all were veterans of this war, brothers and sisters of misery, who cried out for mercy when they were dying.

And he was tired of serving it up to all those he met. Old and young. Innocent and guilty.

He needed a reprieve.

Sighing, he lifted his head to meet her gaze levelly. "Marry him and protect Jared."

She scowled at him. "Jared?"

"Our son. Our descendant. Let us hope that he's a much better man than his father is. That he has his mother's heart."

Brushing his hair back from his eyes, she winced. "You sell yourself short, Dary. I hope he's just like you. I can think of nothing better."

"And I hope he has much better judgment than his mother. Poor thing, she chose such a loser to marry. Both times."

She laughed so hard, she actually snorted, then playfully slapped at his arm.

Sobering, she sighed. "To Jared. And I will make sure that he never hates his father. He will love and respect you every bit as much as I do."

Someone knocked on her door. Myone gasped at the sudden sound that intruded on their moment.

With a sad smile, Xev gave her a quick kiss, then vanished.

Heartbroken that he had to leave so quickly, Myone took one quick look around to make sure there was no trace of him. Which saddened her even more. She would love to be able to keep something more than her necklace. And even that, she had to hide.

It wasn't fair.

One day, though, they wouldn't have to keep this secret. They'd be able to let everyone know they belonged to each other.

But that wasn't today. Today she was living for that future moment when they would be a family and there would be no more lies or secrets.

# 23

Xev hid in the shadows of his father's temple as he watched his wife marry his father. It was a bitter pill to swallow. Never had he hated his life or father more than he did right then.

Truly, the sight sickened him. There were flowers and sheer material draped everywhere. It was disgustingly sappy.

The kind of wedding he'd wanted to have with Myone.

Instead, they'd been forced to marry in secret.

His aunt and uncle stood to the side as witnesses to the event. Cam wore gold in honor of Myone, while Rezar was dressed in the same dark gray Jaden wore.

A gray that was definitely fitting for Xev's ill mood.

While it galled Xev to see them there, at least their approval meant that they would make sure no harm came to Myone or Jared.

*It's for the best.*

Didn't feel that way, but he kept lying to his emotions, hoping they'd give in and stop making it hurt so deep inside his soul that it felt as if he were on fire. As if a part of him was being flayed with acid. It burned on a level unimaginable.

He wanted to charge in and separate them, to scream out that *they* should have had a wedding like this, surrounded by family instead of doing it in secret for fear of being killed because they dared to love each other.

It wasn't fair or right.

Who should have to stand by and see this?

"How are you standing here and not screaming?"

Xev didn't respond to Shadow's sudden question in his ear. Although it had startled him so badly, he was amazed he wasn't hanging from the ceiling by his fingernails. He turned his head to give his brother a droll, irritated smirk. "Where have *you* been?"

"Staying out of everyone's hair while y'all do your best to end each other."

"Then why are you here now?"

"Heard about this and didn't believe it. Had to come see for myself. Lend you some support. Either to comfort or kill someone. Your choice."

Xev glanced over his shoulder to see his brother eyeing them all with the same level of disgust he was sure was etched on his own face. "Yeah, well, here we are. Still haven't decided if I should go into a killing frenzy or not."

"Grisly." Shadow handed him a flask. "I'm sorry."

"I'm sure I'll live." Mostly because the gods didn't love

Xev enough to kill him. They only wanted to torture and punish him for the stupidity of being born.

"I'm sure you won't want to," Shadow said.

He had no idea. The temptation for Xev to fall on his own sword had never been greater. He handed the flask back to his brother.

Shadow took a deep drink, then sighed. "I assume the kid she carries is yours?"

Xev didn't reply.

"You know I'd never betray you."

But why chance it? Especially with his luck. Last thing Xev wanted to do was strangle Shadow with his intestines.

Better to say nothing and just...

He didn't know. Words, like all rational thought, had fled him.

Shadow patted him lightly on the shoulder. Weird. Comforting someone wasn't really Shadow's style, but Xev appreciated the gesture.

"I understand. I doubt I'd say anything either. She is beautiful, though. Even with that little bump. I vote we tie Jaden up and beat the shit out of him later."

That succeeded in making Xev smile. "Hide his body in the desert?"

"Now you're talking. Maybe make a gift of him to your mother?"

"Nah. I did that. It didn't work out well for me, if you remember."

Shadow sucked his breath in through his teeth. "Yeah, sorry. I forgot. Bad choice of words." He shuffled his feet, then changed the subject. "Did you hear about Malphas?"

That did the trick and took Xev's mind far away from the moment. He still couldn't believe what had become of his half-demon brother.

A farmer.

When Myone had said people changed, Xev had never expected *that*.

He smiled at Shadow. "Caleb now." After Myone stabbed him in battle, Malphas had fallen to the human realm, where a woman had found him and taken him in. Not only had she given him a soul, she'd renamed him, too.

Now, Caleb wanted nothing to do with them, and he was lucky enough that he was able to get away with his wife.

Instead of returning to their ranks, Caleb had sealed away his sword and was now living with Lilliana on her farm, happy as he could be, with no plans to ever return to their war.

Xev was happy for him and wished them all the happiness in the world.

"Yeah. I can't believe you two. Women..." Shadow shuddered. "Source save me from love and feminine wiles."

Xev turned away from the wedding to shake his head at his brother. "There was a time I would have agreed with you. But it's not what you think. Although this"—he gestured toward his father and Myone—"is all kinds of screwed up. It's not normally like this. Usually, we're very happy."

Sighing, he folded his arms over his chest, wishing

he'd been as lucky as Caleb had been. How he wished he could lay his sword down forever and live in peace. "You can't imagine how Myone makes me feel."

"Stupid?"

He shoved at Shadow. Leave it to him to be an ass in any given situation. "No. She heals me."

Shadow snorted. "You don't look healed. You look like you're about to puke. You're standing here while she makes a vow to your dad. Buddy, this is all kinds of messed up."

*It's not a real wedding. It's just to protect her.* But Xev knew they could never say that out loud. To anyone. Everyone needed to think this was real.

That she was Jaden's wife.

Even Shadow. They just didn't dare risk anyone saying something by accident. No one could *ever* know.

Whatever happened, Xev had to make sure his wife and child were always protected.

He met Shadow's sympathetic gaze. "Can I ask a favor?"

"Knock you unconscious until it's over?"

Actually, he hadn't thought of that.

Not a bad idea, really. It had a lot of merit.

But sadly, it wasn't the favor he'd had in mind. "No. Can you be serious for a minute?"

Shadow scoffed. "Have you met me?" He shook his head. "Serious doesn't look good on me. Besides, I don't need you to insult me. I have creatures lining up all over to tear me down."

"Would you stop? I need my big brother right now."

"I knew better than to come."

Xev smirked. "And yet you did."

Shadow looked away and cursed. "I did, didn't I?" He shoved at Xev. "I know what you want. You want me to promise that I'll help keep them safe, too."

"Exactly."

He glared at Xev. "You know how I feel about all this, right?"

"I do. I also know if you promise me, you'll do it."

All the humor died on Shadow's face as he sobered. "What if I can't?"

Xev's stomach shrank. Did Shadow know something he didn't? "How do you mean?"

Shadow let out a tired breath. "This is a brutal war, Xev. We don't know who's going to win, if *anyone* wins, or when. It could go on for centuries more. I can promise I'll do everything I can for all of you. That's the best I can do."

"That's all I can ask. Thank you."

Nodding, Shadow clapped him on the back.

They fell silent for a few minutes, until Xev noticed the weird clothes Shadow was wearing. Solid black breeches and a tunic that appeared to be one piece, with a color that fastened tightly around his neck. "Where have you been?" It was a rhetorical question, given that he already knew from the type of clothing.

"Mostly hiding on Trisa." Shadow gave a wicked grin. "They think I'm a god there. It's kind of nice. I find being worshiped suits me."

Of course it would. Personally, Xev couldn't stand it.

Fawning of any kind had never been something he could stomach. He'd rather fight than be worshiped.

Unless it involved Myone. Then neither of those options appealed to him.

He just wanted to sit quietly with her and enjoy her company.

But the more he thought about Shadow spending time on Trisa unsupervised, a bad feeling went through him. "Please tell me you're not messing with the natives."

"Define *messing with*."

"Their history. Their culture. Their *genetics*." Particularly that last bit, as Xev cringed at the thought of a world populated by a bunch of Shadowlings.

Talk about grisly...

Shadow rolled his eyes. "I'm being careful, especially when it comes to the frolicking. Besides, I like being evasive."

That was true, and it did have its advantages.

Right now, Xev would like nothing better than to vanish into nothing and tell no one other than his wife.

If only he could.

But at least the wedding had finally ended.

Myone stepped away from his father, off to the side with Cam who was congratulating her.

Xev winced as bile rose up in his throat.

Then his gaze went to Shadow. Once again, his brother had been here for him. Even though he hadn't called for him, Shadow had heard what was happening and came, knowing Xev was in need.

While he felt alone most of the time, he knew he could count on his brother when he really needed him.

And always Myone.

She had never once let him down.

He prayed with everything he had that he would always be here for her. That no matter what, she would be able to rely on him for the rest of eternity.

*Don't ever let me fail her or the baby.*

MYONE JERKED at the pins in her hair as she desperately sought to remove the remnants of the wedding she'd despised and had really wanted nothing to do with.

It'd been so incredibly hard to stand there, uttering vows that stuck in her craw. She'd wanted so desperately to scream out that it was a farce, that no, she had no intention of swearing her love and affection to someone she could barely tolerate.

While she was grateful Jaden wanted to protect them, she had wanted to scream at the injustice of it.

He wasn't the one she wanted to be loyal to. Silently, she'd been saying her vows to Xev the entire time. Telling herself to just get through it. Do nothing. Say nothing.

Protect her baby and real husband.

She felt a presence at her back.

Turning, she moved to attack her intruder.

Until she saw Xev there. Relieved beyond belief, she pulled him into her arms and held him.

"You're choking me!" he gasped.

"I should. I should beat you, too."

She felt him smile against her cheek. "If it would make you happy."

That made her laugh. "You know I could never hurt you. Not intentionally. Even when I want to kill you." She kissed his cheek. "You were there today, weren't you?"

"Of course I was."

Never had she loved him more. "I could feel you there, watching us." She cupped his cheek. "Are you all right?"

"Not really. You?"

"No." She laid her head on his chest and held him as tightly as she could. "Tell me again that this was the right thing to do."

He let out a tired sigh. "I hope so."

Either way, it was done and over with. She just hoped they hadn't doomed themselves or their baby with what they'd done today.

**24**

———

"That was an amazing battle!" Kri clapped Xev on the back so hard, he actually staggered from the blow. Tall and handsome, the Malachai was almost a head taller than Xev these days. He was a massive beast and a fierce warrior.

But Xev didn't share his glee.

*Yeah, it was awesome,* he thought sarcastically. He was covered in blood, entrails, piss, and vomit. None of it was his, which he was grateful for. But still...

*Amazing* wasn't the word in his mind. *Disgusting. Awful. Nightmarish. Gross.*

Lots of other adjectives.

None of them made him feel like celebrating. He wasn't even glad he was alive at the moment. Rather, he felt awful for all the lives they'd taken. Not just today, but every time they fought.

And for what?

He still didn't know why they were fighting. 'Cause his mother wanted to control his father? Noir wanted more respect?

Apollymi wanted revenge for Kissare by taking the lives of everyone else's husbands and fathers?

None of this made sense to him.

He just wanted a bath.

Most of all, he wanted Myone.

"Come celebrate!" Kri offered him a goblet of wine.

Xev took it and drank deeply while Kri and his wife hugged and cheered. How he wished he shared that joy in their victory. He just couldn't muster it.

*Xev?*

He froze at the sound of Myone's voice in his head.

*Would you like to meet your son?*

His breath caught as he finally found something to smile about. *That* was worth celebrating. Tears gathered in his eyes as a real smile spread across his face. He couldn't remember the last time anything had made him this happy.

Not true. He felt like this every time he saw Myone's face.

Throwing his head back, he shouted in joy. He handed the goblet back to Kri and pounded him on his massive shoulder. "I'll be back to celebrate. I need to bathe."

Kri grinned and inclined his head. "That's the spirit, my friend."

Without another word, Xev flew to his rooms. He wanted to go immediately to his wife, but there was no way he'd meet his son while smothered in death. It clung to every part of him and clogged his nostrils.

He took the quickest bath of his life and had barely dried himself off before he teleported through the shadows to make his way to Myone's bedroom. In fact, he was still dripping, and his hair hung in wet curls around his face.

He didn't care. All that mattered was seeing his wife and son.

When he started to step out of the shadows, he saw his father with her.

Jaden turned toward him. "It's all right. Come meet your *brother*."

Xev didn't need the reminder of their pretense. His father had never once referred to Jared as anything other than his own son, and Xev wasn't about to correct him now.

His legs and wings trembled as he approached her in full reverence of what she'd done without his being here. And he hated that, too.

While he'd been taking life, she'd been giving it. He sank to his knees beside her bed. Laughing through her tears, she pulled back the soft white blanket to show him the tiniest creature he'd ever seen, sleeping soundly in the cradle of her arms.

Humbled to the core of his soul, he had no words. All he could feel was an overwhelming sense of love unlike anything he'd ever known. The need to protect that innocent child was so overwhelming that he couldn't breathe for it. This was his son.

*Blood of my blood.*

That surge of love and emotion was followed by a wave of profound hatred that was indescribable. He no longer saw his child in Myone's arms. He saw himself there.

While he'd known his father had turned his back on him, it wasn't until this moment that it hit home just how cold and uncaring his father had actually been.

The viciousness it'd taken for both of his parents to lash out against him when he'd been the most helpless of creatures.

*What was wrong with them?*

His breathing ragged, he looked up at his father and shook his head. "How could you abandon me to Azura?" Having never been around a babe before, he'd never really understood his parents that day.

What it'd taken for his father to be so cold as to order his death. And for his mother to send him into Azmodea to die as a helpless infant.

Now, he did.

They were broken.

At least Jaden had the decency to look away. "Be grateful every day of your life that you will never know the regrets that haunt me." And with that, he vanished.

Haunted *him*? Was he serious?

Myone reached out and took his hand. "I believe him, Dary. I saw the look on his face when he first held Jared. He regrets everything." She brushed her thumb against his whiskered cheek. "Please don't let your past destroy this moment."

She placed his hand on Jared's chest so that he could feel the rise and fall of the baby's sweet breaths. "This is our future. And he's beautiful."

Yes, he was. Unspoiled and untainted. And much better than Xev deserved.

Jared would never know the fear and pain of Xev's childhood. Never doubt that he was loved.

Or protected.

Whatever it took, Xev would keep his son safe.

Myone sat up and put their son in his arms. Xev tried his best not to cry as he held him, but he couldn't stop the tears that began to flow over this tiny miracle she'd given him. She kissed his cheek. "I love you both."

"Love you more."

"I know." She brushed her hand through his wet hair, then nuzzled his neck.

Xev couldn't believe how beautiful their son was. Such tiny little wings, hands, feet, and ears. Bald as he could be. Yet perfect in every way.

*Just don't ever hate me, little one.* That was all he asked.

He never wanted this baby to feel toward him the way he felt toward his parents. Never wanted Jared to think that he'd abandoned him.

"I will always be here for you. Always."

"He'll know that, Dary."

Would he?

Because Jared was going to grow up thinking Jaden was his father. And that was the most sickening part of all.

**25**

———————

Xev stood in the shadows, watching Jared play with a wooden sword. At six, he was incredible. Every bit the warrior his mother was. Maybe even more so.

He'd been Kri's tutor when he'd been that age. Had taught the Malachai everything he knew.

It pained him that he couldn't give the same lessons to his own child. That he had to stand in the shadows and watch him grow up without his real father by his side.

Why did the universe hate him so much that this was his fate? He'd never understand it. All he wanted was to be a part of his child's life.

Instead, he was banned from it.

Relegated to the shadows he'd learned to hate as much as he hated his father and mother. They had made the choice to ignore him. To cast him out of their lives.

He'd had no choice with his son. This decision had been forced on him. It wasn't right.

"Jared?"

Xev smiled at the loving tone Myone always used with their child, and that flooded him with warmth. It reminded him so much of Michi and her kindness toward him. How he missed her even after all these years. He could still feel the warmth of her fur underneath his cheek when he would lie on her to sleep. The tenderness in her hugs when she'd hold him and promise him that everything would be all right.

How he wished that she'd been able to keep those promises to him. And he prayed that he could keep the same ones he'd made to Jared.

His son ran out of the room and then back again.

Waiting until he was sure no one else was coming into the room with them, Xev stepped out of the shadows.

Jared looked up and smiled. "Uncle!" He ran to him.

Kneeling, he caught him in his arms and held him close to his heart. How he wanted to correct him and tell him that he wasn't his uncle. But he didn't dare.

For now, this was enough.

"Keep your voice down, little bit. We don't want to draw attention."

"Sorry," Jared whispered. "I was just excited to see you."

Those words made Xev's heart soar. "Me too. I think you've grown at least a foot. Maybe more." He ruffled the head full of bright red curls, amazed by them. Neither he nor Myone had any idea where the boy had inherited those. But it didn't matter. He was otherwise an exact copy of his mother, and for that, Xev was grateful.

It wouldn't have done them any good had his son favored him, even if Xev did look like his father. Better not to have anyone question the child's paternity.

"Do you know where your mother is?"

Jared nodded eagerly. "She's talking to a group of her soldiers in the other room. Do you want me to go get her?"

"No. Stay with me until she's finished."

"Okay." Jared took his hand and showed him the mock battlefield he'd created on the floor with his hand-carved wooden soldiers.

Xev wanted to be happy for his son, but the sight broke his heart. At this young age, his boy was already preparing for war. "Battle isn't so glorious, Jared."

His son ignored him as he continued to fight his mock battle. "Do you fight in the war, Uncle?"

"I do."

"Do you win?"

Xev sighed heavily. "No one wins in a fight, kiddo. The best option is to avoid it whenever you can. Even if it means looking like a coward. Better they think you're craven than you take a life needlessly."

That was what he envied Caleb for the most. The fact that his brother had been able to actually refrain from any violence. That his sword was now encased in stone, where Caleb vowed it would remain.

It said a lot about Caleb's love for Lilliana.

Jared screwed his little face up. "That's not what my father says."

*That's because your grandfather's a moron.* "He doesn't participate directly in them. He sends soldiers like your mother out to fight and die in them instead."

Jared frowned as he considered that. Xev didn't want to disillusion his son, but he wanted to make Jared aware of the reality they faced every day.

More than that, he wanted to keep his son out of war entirely.

A sharp gasp caused him to look up and see Myone in the doorway. She quickly closed the door and moved to join them.

"Is everything all right?" she whispered.

He nodded. "I wanted to bring Jared a gift."

Jared stopped to look at him. "What?" he asked, flashing a set of dimples.

Xev pulled out a small bag of fried treats. "They're called friggles. They're quite delicious, and your mother loves them. So you might have to fight her for them." He handed the bag over to his son and watched as Jared took one and sampled it.

His eyes flared. "Yum!"

Laughing, he grabbed the whole bag from Xev's hand.

Xev smiled as he watched his son eagerly shove an entire handful into his mouth.

Myone laughed. "You spoil him."

"It's my job."

She tsked at Xev. "Jared? Would you mind going outside to play for a few minutes so that I can speak to your uncle in private?"

"Sure, Mama." Jared pushed himself up. "Thank you

for the friggles, Uncle." He kissed Xev on the cheek then started for the door.

"And Jared?"

He turned toward his mother with a heavy sigh. "I know, Mama. Don't tell anyone he's here."

"Thank you, baby."

Nodding, he ran from the room and quickly shut the door.

She saw the sadness in Xev's eyes as he watched him leave. "You want me to call him back?"

"Yes and no." He let out a tired sigh before he pulled her into his arms and kissed her cheek. "It would scar him for life if he ever saw me holding his mother like this."

Myone closed her eyes and savored the sensation of Xev holding her. It'd been too long. The kiss he gave her set fire to every part of her.

If only it could always be like this.

Laughing, she pulled back. "It would definitely make him wonder why his uncle was molesting his mother so."

"Indeed." He nuzzled her neck. "I miss our time alone."

"I do too." Now that they had Jared, it was almost impossible to be together. She didn't dare leave this realm or even venture into the shadows for fear that Jared might need her. He was a wonderful boy, but he was too inquisitive, and too quick to get into things he shouldn't.

If she so much as blinked, he found things best left alone. She loved her boy, but he kept her on her toes.

"Why is this so complicated?" she asked.

"Because my family sucks."

She laughed at Xev's standard answer. "I need to give you a heads-up. We're marching tomorrow."

"I actually knew that. We were given that information two days ago."

She arched a brow. "Really? How?"

Xev rubbed at his eyes. "That's why I'm here. I have bad news for you. Apparently, you have a traitor in your ranks."

Her heart sank. Although it made sense. She still couldn't stand the thought of one of her soldiers turning against them. "What?"

He shrugged. "I don't know who yet. But one of your team is definitely leaking information to my side. We know every move the Sephirii and Naşāru plan to make, in great detail."

"Who are they telling it to?"

"Azura."

She cursed as she realized just how dangerous that was. "And you've no idea who it's coming from?"

"If I knew, I'd tell you."

That he would. He wouldn't risk her getting hurt. "What should I do?"

"Keep your eyes open. Given what Azura knows, it has to be someone high-ranking. Maybe Naşāru or one of your Mimoroux, but I don't know yet. As soon as I find out, I will tell you."

A knock on her door startled them.

She saw the sadness in his eyes and felt it all the way to her soul. Why did someone have to disturb them right now?

Tapping his heart twice as their silent signal to let her know he loved her, he vanished.

Myone cursed that she couldn't have had more time with him. It wasn't fair.

After making sure there was no trace of him, she went to the door to find Cam standing in the hallway, a stern glower on her face. So tiny that she barely reached Myone's shoulder, the goddess had dark skin and beautiful golden eyes. Her black hair was wrapped in a white scarf, trimmed with gold that matched her elegant gown.

"Is something wrong, my lady?" Myone asked.

The goddess of justice stared at her in awe. "Are you aware of the powers your son holds?"

Of course she was. *Unless...*"Are there new ones he's learned?"

Cam crooked her finger for Myone to follow her.

Confused, she left her room to trail after the tiny goddess, down the sterile hallway to the temple courtyard, where Jared was surrounded by four members of the Sephirii Mimoroux. She had no idea why she'd been summoned until she realized her child was talking to the swords.

*All of them.*

Her jaw went slack. No one had ever been able to talk to more than one sword, and then only rarely. Even her own didn't speak to her much. Mostly Kasumi telegraphed her emotions to make Myone know what she was feeling. Actual words...

Those were few and far between.

Yet as she moved closer, she saw the ethereal fey

spirits gathered around her child as if they were play-mates. Even though they belonged to her elite Sephirii commanders, they were out of their swords and actually frolicking. This was unheard of. Like shimmering ghosts, they surrounded him, humming and playing.

They were soldiers...playing? It didn't make sense, yet there was no denying what she saw.

How she wished Xev was here to see this. She'd love to know what he thought.

"Is this possible?" she asked Cam.

Cam shrugged. "I've never seen anything like this. Maybe it's from Jaden's powers?"

Or Xev's. Could there be something in his blood that made the Seraphs reach out to their son?

"Takara summoned me."

Myone turned to her right to find her father standing over them with the last of the Seraph swords in his hand. "What?"

"Takara called out to me," he repeated. He held the legendary sword out to her.

For the last two thousand years, the Mimoroux had only consisted of nine members instead of ten because Takara had refused to allow anyone to wield her. She'd just been completely stubborn in her refusal to accept any warrior.

All these centuries, she'd lain so silent that they assumed her spirit had died. As such, the Sephirii had created a place of honor for her in their gathering hall where everyone could see her.

But again, they'd assumed she was dead.

Now...

Myone scowled as she took the vibrating sword from her father's hand.

Takara refused to allow her to even touch her. She scalded Myone, who quickly let go. The sword clattered against the marble floor, then it stood upright and began to spin by itself. Faster and faster.

A bright light emanated from the hilt, blinding them.

That light began to bend until it formed a tiny, beautiful woman who stood no more than three feet tall. Her skin and eyes shimmered gold, while black hair cascaded over her shoulders to her hips.

Dressed in a flowing black gown, she had long, pointed ears and eyes like a cat. A small gold crown held her hair off her face in an intricate twining of hair and gold. Diamonds and rubies dangled from the crown around the delicate shape of her face.

She was absolutely beautiful as she headed toward Jared, who watched her curiously.

Inclining her head to him, she curtsied. In return, he gave her a formal bow.

Takara laughed at him. "My shiori. It will be my honor to help you in war."

Myone started to deny it, but her father stopped her. "She's chosen him, and there's nothing you can do."

Every maternal instinct inside her rebelled at those words. Even though she'd been a girl when Kasumi chose her, she'd already begun her training. Jared was barely more than a toddler. "He's too young."

"To battle, yes. But she's made her choice, and we have to honor it. We will train him for command."

This was unheard of. No sword had ever chosen a child so young, especially not Takara. She was the oldest and strongest of the swords.

Whoever wielded her was their leader.

*Their undisputed leader.*

Myone gasped as she realized that she wouldn't mind relinquishing command to her child in the future. But not until he was ready. And not for many, many years to come. Like Xev, she didn't want to see him in battle. Didn't want to watch him kill or be wounded. "His father will demand the strongest, most enchanted armor ever created."

"I know Jaden will."

She had to stop herself from correcting Cam. It wasn't Jaden who would be screaming out in protest over this. Xev would have much to say about their son being a Sephiroth. Especially if this war didn't end.

Because if it didn't end, there was a very real possibility that Jared could face his father in battle.

That was the last thing she wanted.

No. They had to find an end to this. She refused to lose either of them.

## 26

Jared stopped playing, then turned to the darkest part of the room so that he could frown. "Why do you watch me so much from the shadows?"

Xev arched a brow at Jared's pert question. And at the fact that his son could see him when he shouldn't have a clue that he was here. "Pardon?"

"You're there a lot. Sometimes you come out, but a lot of times you don't. It's really disconcerting when you're there, watching me for no reason. Why do you hide so much?"

Xev let out a long sigh at just how powerful Jared had become. At eight, his powers were staggering. He could only imagine how much more powerful he'd be as a man. "There are times when you're busy and I don't want to disturb you."

"Like when I'm sleeping?"

"If you're asleep, how do you know I'm watching you?"

Jared gestured to the table where his sword was kept. "Takara tells me. She can sense you too."

"Sense me how?"

"Your powers. They're close enough to mine that it awakens her whenever you're near. Especially if I'm asleep. She finds it very disturbing, and unsettling."

Far be it from Xev to unsettle his son's creepy sword that raised the hair on the back of his neck. He'd never liked Seraphs. Especially when he fought them in battle. "Then I'll try not to disturb your sword in the future when I come to visit."

Jared nodded then frowned again.

Leaving the shadows that kept him safe, Xev duplicated his scowl. "Is something else wrong?"

"I was just curious."

"About?"

"Why I'm not supposed to tell people that you're my father. Why do you and Mama believe it'll upset them?"

Those words struck him like a blow. Had Myone told him?

"No. She's never spoken a word about it to me. No one does. But I hear what you think, and I don't hate you. Why would I hate someone who's always been so kind to me? And that was before I knew you were my father. But I don't understand..." Jared paused as if he were listening to Xev's rapid-fire thoughts. "Oh, *that's* why. Would they really kill you and Mama?"

Kneeling in front of his son, Xev cupped his cheek. "I'd rather not find out."

Jared nodded. "Neither would I. Others can be...difficult. But you're wrong about my fa—grandfather," he quickly corrected himself. "He loves me absolutely. He thinks of me as his son. There's nothing inside him other than love whenever he's around me. If not for you and Mama, I'd have never known he wasn't my real father."

While that relieved some of the fears he'd had where his father was concerned, it made Xev feel a bit guilty that he'd doubted Jaden.

Jared cocked his little head as if he were hearing something else. "Don't worry, Papa. I won't betray you or Mama. I know how to remain silent." With the sagacity of an ancient, he took Xev's hand. "You can teach me anything you want. I'm happy to be your son. I don't see evil in you. I know you love me, and I love you too."

Xev had no words. All he could do was scoop the boy up and hold him.

It was such a strange sensation. He'd never felt so naked in front of anyone. And here he'd thought that only Myone could see the real him.

His son saw him even more clearly.

Why were his powers so strong?

"Mama thinks it's because I was conceived in love. She wonders if Monakribos is just as strong because he was conceived the same way."

That actually explained a lot. And why Xev's powers were often unstable. He could only imagine what his parents must have thought when he'd been conceived. His father had been drunk, and his mother...

She would have been filled with hatred. Not love.

And if Shadow had been conceived in love, it

explained why his powers were so strong, especially given the fact that he was only a demigod.

Xev didn't even want to think about it. But it made a lot of sense. They did share a lot of the same powers. Though, to be honest, Jared might be a bit stronger, because his powers were drawn from both sides, whereas Kri's only came from Apollymi.

A chill went down Xev's spine as another thought occurred to him.

*Balance in all things.* Was that what his father had been thinking when he claimed Jared as his son? That the Primals couldn't complain about his son, since they'd allowed Kri to live?

Jared was the balance for Apollymi's son.

Both of them were sons of Sephirii and gods.

Xev didn't like where this was going in his mind. Being one of those creatures that the Source had used for balance, he knew it didn't usually end up well for them. Lilit came to mind, too.

They always seemed to end up shafted in the end.

Jared smiled up at him. "It'll be all right, Papa. You'll see."

But Xev didn't have his son's optimism. Life had taught him an entirely different lesson.

*Duck and cover. Pray the shit flies overhead and not all over him.*

Why didn't he have the power of clairvoyance? Instead, he was left with hope, and he hated it. Hope carried him forward even when he didn't want it to. Even when he was bereft. When he wanted to lie down and give up.

It hovered there like an eternal pall that forever haunted him.

How he hated that bitch. Hope was the worst.

Because it wouldn't let him rest in peace. So long as hope was there, he kept going forward in spite of all common sense. In spite of every obstacle.

Especially when he had this tiny little boy to consider. He couldn't stop now. Jared's fate was tied to his. He couldn't let his son down.

He couldn't fail Myone.

They were both in this because of him.

"I believe in you, Daddy."

Xev held his son close. "I believe in you too, Jared."

Somehow, he'd figure this out. He had to. Because this wasn't just his life. Everything he loved was now at stake.

## 27

## EIGHT YEARS LATER

Xev cursed as a pain ripped through his chest. In an instant, he knew exactly what it was.

Caleb had just unsealed his sword and was getting ready to use it. Xev felt it move through the aether like an electric charge. Which meant every demon under his mother's command had felt it, too, and knew that Caleb was back in play.

Crap! They'd all be after his brother now.

What could have possibly happened to make Caleb leave his farm and wife, and rejoin their war? The last time Xev had seen his brother, Caleb had been adamant that he would *never* touch that sword again.

Even worse?

Both Myone and Jared were headed for battle. There was no way to let them know about this, and Xev had no idea which side Caleb would fight for.

*Please, let it be ours.*

He wanted to go after Myone and Jared and let them know. But if he did that, he'd have to fight, and while he'd done some shaky things in the past to protect his wife and son, he didn't dare do them right now. Kri wasn't a child anymore. He was sharp, battle-honed, and suspicious by nature. If Xev did anything out of the ordinary, Kri would know.

And he was being watched by too many to risk it. Because he was second-in-command, and close to Kri, there were many who wanted to watch him burn. Those who'd do anything to see his demise or defeat.

He still didn't know who was after him or who the traitor on Myone's side was. If either one saw him protecting her or Jared, it was over.

It was too big a risk.

All he could do was pray that his brother, wife, and son kept away from each other, and wait for news.

*Screw me...*

Azura glared at the demon in front of her. "Repeat what you just told me."

"I saw Malphas fighting with the Kalosum."

Those words brought a level of fury to her she wouldn't have thought possible. Which, given the state of fury she normally lived in, said a lot.

That anger vibrated through her body, making her limbs shake. Unable to stand it, she blasted the demon in front of her and watched as it died screaming in agony.

Noir picked just that moment to enter the room. Whether he did it on purpose or just to piss her off, she had no idea.

Until he spoke. "Killing messengers again, are we?"

"Shut up, Noir. I've no time for you. And even less patience."

He toed at the dust on the floor that used to be an almost-competent demon. "I see. May I ask what has set you on fire this time?"

"We've lost Malphas."

"How careless of someone. Any idea where they last put him?"

She glared at her brother. "You're not funny."

"I'm hilarious. You've just never fully appreciated me."

She scoffed. "Either find something useful to say or go find a demon to flay."

He considered that. "I do like flaying demons. They're quite entertaining when they beg for their lives."

She let out a long-suffering sigh. "Fine, then, since you're looking for something to torture, bring me the heart or head of Malphas!"

He arched a brow. "You do remember that he's a son of Jaden, right?"

How dare he pick at that festering wound. *Ugh.* What she wouldn't give for the ability to slap him without his hitting her back. "Since when does Jaden care about his children?"

"Probably as much as we care about our daughter. However, if one of our siblings attacked her, I do believe we'd be demanding a proper gutting from them."

He was right about that. Anat was mostly an annoyance that she avoided. But if anyone attacked her, there would be hell to pay.

But that wasn't what irritated Azura. "Why are you being so reasonable? Isn't that against your nature?"

He shrugged. "Self-preservation is always my priority. But while you're contemplating Malphas's death and dismemberment, have you considered something?"

"What?"

"Why the defection to the other side?"

Azura paused at the obvious question that had yet to occur to her. Why *would* a demon of Malphas's caliber switch sides? He hated his father.

He hated humans.

His brothers were on their side. So why would he suddenly reappear after all this time on the wrong side of the war?

Unless...

"You may have a point," she said speculatively.

"Of course I do. And unlike you, I'm not overreacting."

Those words irritated her. As if he wasn't known for throwing his own tantrums—most of them far bloodier than anything she'd ever conceived.

Noir approached her purposefully. "Think about it. One of our most vicious soldiers suddenly stops fighting. For no reason whatsoever. Poof, he's just gone one day. No rhyme. No reason. No trace. Then, just as mysteriously as he vanished, he shows up years later on the side of our enemies. What does that sound like to you?"

"Stupidity?"

He rolled his eyes. "Love, dearest sister. Love. Someone tamed our favorite animal. We just need to find out who."

"Then we destroy them."

"Exactly."

XEV DRIFTED BACK into the shadows, grateful that he'd chosen not to interrupt his mother at that particular moment with the message Kri wanted him to give her.

That message could wait.

Right now, he had to find Caleb. Luckily, the solstice was coming. At least he knew where his brother should be this time of year.

*Why didn't you stay hidden, Caleb?*

Taking that sword out had been the worst mistake he could have made. What had happened to change his mind about fighting?

Didn't matter. Xev had to make sure Caleb knew what was coming. Most of all, he had to help him keep Lilliana safe.

## 28

Xev hated being in the village that was near the farm where his brother lived. Ever since Chani had died, he'd done his best to avoid the human world.

Trisa notwithstanding.

Mostly because there he didn't have visions of a sweet little girl and her mother being burned alive. Everything here reminded him of that awful night.

But he had to warn his brother. Caleb needed to know Azura was looking for him, hellbent on destroying his life.

Besides, he owed Caleb for the last battle his family had been in. His brother had fought with Myone and Jared against Caleb's former army. Had he not been in that battle, his mother wouldn't know Caleb was back in play.

The least he could do now was help protect Lilliana and her people.

If he couldn't have his happily-ever-after with Myone,

then he would do whatever he could to help Caleb have his.

Not that he blamed Caleb for losing his heart to the tiny blonde woman. She was adorable and sweet. He well understood how Caleb had lost his heart to one such as she.

Xev watched as said tiny woman ran off into the crowd of people in her town to celebrate the solstice. Their loud shouts and cheers rang out in the night as they partied, unaware of how close death trod next to them.

Or the fact that they had a god in their mix who fought with demons against them.

When Caleb started after his wife, Xev blocked his way.

The minute Caleb saw him, he cursed under his breath, then smirked. "Do you mind?"

Xev grinned. "Never. It's one of my more irritating qualities."

"Yes, it is. Out of my way, idiot."

Why did that amuse him? Really, there was something wrong with him. "She's fine. Myone's in the temple, keeping an eye on Lil."

Caleb sighed. "We have to stop these talks. Every time I see you, my sphincter clenches. Can't you ever just say *nice weather* or *how are the crops growing?*"

"How do you know I wasn't planning on asking that?"

"Were you?"

Xev gave him a grin he knew would irritate Caleb. "No. But you shouldn't jump to conclusions."

"I hate you so much."

"I know. But you need to put that aside. We have bigger issues." He sobered. "My mother knows that you have a weakness."

All the humor fled from Caleb's face instantly. "What do you mean?"

Xev hated to be the one to tell him this. Caleb was so happy. Why couldn't he stay that way?

Because life sucked.

The gods were capricious, and they were never meant to be happy.

"It didn't take much for Azura and the King of All Darkness to figure out why you vanished, and then showed up fighting on the wrong side. Evil as they are, they still know nothing changes someone like love."

Caleb cursed. "How could I have been so stupid? Do they know who she is?"

Xev shook his head, grateful for that small mercy. "Not as far as I know. But let's face it, I'm not my mother's confidant. She thinks you and I are still fighting and not talking. That gives you an advantage." Because she would have no idea that he'd warn his brother.

He saw the relief in Caleb's eyes. "You have any other good news to tell me?"

"My boy's now commanding his own legion. He's third-in-command."

"I have no response to that. Though I feel like you're looking for a congratulations."

"Little bit." After all, he was proud of Jared. Terrified of the fact his son was fighting in this useless war, but it didn't change the fact that he was the youngest Sephiroth in history to attain a command of that magnitude. As his father, Xev couldn't be prouder. "Could you sound more insincere?"

"Not sure I should be happy he's helping to kill my kind."

Xev looked around the crowd that surrounded them, a crowd his brother had been happily blending in with and calling family these last few years. "You sure the demons are still your kind? It looks to me like you've upgraded."

Caleb glanced around and something Xev couldn't name darkened his eyes. "Xev...may I ask you a favor?"

His jaw went slack. That wasn't like his brother. Caleb never believed in owing anyone anything. "You're asking me a favor? There must be sun shining in Azmodea right now."

"Not funny."

"Not trying to be. Just amazed by words I never thought to hear from your lips." Which told him just how important they had to be for Caleb to say them. His brother never asked for help.

Even so, Caleb hesitated before he spoke them. "I need you to help me protect Lil."

That was what Xev had expected. It was all their fears —losing what they loved. "You know I will, especially after everything you've done for me and Myone...and Jared. I owe you."

"Don't forget it." And with that, Caleb left to go after his wife.

Xev followed after him.

Inside the great hall, Lilliana was in a group of

humans, drinking mead and laughing. Caleb paused as if to savor the moment.

Then he moved to the left.

Scowling, Xev followed.

But there was nothing there.

*What is he doing?*

"Here, kitty, kitty, kitty," Caleb said.

What was going on? Why would his brother chase a cat?

Caleb turned around, searching the crowd around them. "Where are you?"

Xev was about to ask what was wrong when Caleb ran back to Lil.

"Lil?" he called out. "Lil!"

"She's right here," Myone said as he joined them.

Caleb pulled his wife against his chest and held her the way Xev held Myone every time he went to see her in her room.

It was really odd.

"Caleb?" Lilliana asked.

"There's something here. Something from the Mavromino. I saw it."

Myone began looking around. "Dary!"

That explained the cat. It must have been a demon stalking his brother.

Xev was by her side instantly. "I'm here."

"We have an enemy in our midst. Help me find them."

Xev inclined his head to her before he stepped back and vanished so that he could search for the culprit.

Myone sighed as she looked at Caleb and Lil. "I assume Xev told you the news?"

"That our enemies know how to break me? Yes."

Myone winced at the way he stated that. She hadn't quite thought of that yet. "Then we need to secure you both."

Caleb started laughing. "You want to take me to Katoteros? Are you out of your mind?"

"You have a better idea?" she asked.

"Start pulling off my body parts and feeding them to me. That at least would be entertaining."

Lil scowled at them. "What are you talking about? What's Katoteros?"

"The realm where my kind lives. We'll be able to protect you there."

Lil blinked twice. "Leave my home?" The pain in her voice made Myone's heart ache.

"You have no choice, sweetie." Myone jerked her chin toward Caleb. "Neither of you can stay here after this. They'll come for you now that they know you exist and where to find you."

Lilliana let out a tired sigh as she faced Caleb. "I'm so sorry."

"For what?" he asked.

"Telling you to take out your sword. This is all my fault. I should never have asked you to protect my people or my village."

He pulled her against him. "No, precious. It's not your fault. They would have found me eventually. You didn't do anything wrong."

Myone patted her on the back. "Caleb's right. They would have come here sooner or later. They're relentless."

With a ragged breath, Lilliana nodded. "I shall miss our cottage. But as long as I'm with you, everything's fine."

Caleb tightened his arms around her. "We'll be back here again to pick those vegetables I hate. I promise."

She smiled. "I plan to hold you to that."

Myone hoped for their sakes that happened, but the one thing she'd learned was to plan for the unexpected. Nothing ever worked out the way anyone planned.

Finally, Xev made his way back to them.

"Did you find anything?" she asked.

"No. Whatever it was, it's gone. Demons have a bad habit of doing that."

"Then let's take them to Jaden's temple."

Xev hesitated. "You sure he'll welcome Caleb back?" After all, his brother had turned on them and led legions against the Kalosum. Given his father's record, Xev had a hard time believing Jaden would just let that go.

"He has a human wife. I'm sure Jaden will allow them to stay for her protection."

That rather stung. *His* wife led their army, and his son was their third-in-command. Yet they'd stone him if he dared show up there. His father would most likely cast the first one.

But this wasn't the time to worry about that. Caleb and Lil were under fire.

They were all that mattered right now. Not Xev's petty feelings where his father was concerned.

He inclined his head to his wife. "Get them to safety. Let me know if you need anything."

Myone kissed him, then took Caleb and Lilliana with her and vanished into the darkness.

Xev stood in the village, surrounded by humans. Something wasn't right. Whatever Caleb had felt, he felt it too. It slithered over his skin like a living, breathing creature.

Something was coming for all of them.

The end was near. He could feel it.

He just prayed that they all survived.

## 29

A YEAR LATER

"Where's Caleb?" Xev asked his son, breathless from the strain of trying to get to his brother in time. He'd flown and raced through the shadows, doing his best to get here before they left.

Jared frowned at him. "He just left with his army. Why? Is something wrong?"

Xev winced as fear tore through his body. "Your mother's with him?"

"Of course."

*Damn it.* He was too late. Why couldn't he have made it in time? "It's a trap, Jared. They lured Caleb and your mother out of here so that they could attack the civilians here."

Jared paled. "What?"

"I just found out about their plan. The Mavromino lured your mother's army out on purpose so that they could attack.

They're coming right behind me. We have to secure the children and women. They'll hit us where we're weakest. You stay here in case they break through. I have to get to Lil and warn her. She'll be their primary target. If they reach her first, they can neutralize Caleb's forces and crash the gates."

Jared shook his head. "Stay here? I can't do that."

Xev wanted to correct him. But this wasn't the time or place. He had to get to Lil before they found her.

He took his son by the arms and did his best to reason with him. "Send a messenger to Caleb and Myone. Let them know. I'll take some men and hold them off as best I can. But you have to stay here. No one else can hold them if they break through. We need you here."

Jared inclined his head. "Then I'll stay. Good luck."

They'd need more than that. They were going to need a miracle.

"Dary?"

He didn't respond to Myone's call. Numb, he couldn't move or speak. His knees were pulled tight against his chest with his arms wrapped around them. Silent and cold, he sat on the edge of a cliff, high above the smoldering remains of their defeat.

Technically not *his* defeat, but still.

Caleb's screams continued to echo in his ears, even though his brother had long fallen silent.

He'd broken his promise and failed his brother.

All he could see was Lil's body...Caleb's grief.

*I failed.*

"Dary?"

"What if it'd been you?" The words were barely audible. Because that was his nightmare. Over and over, he saw Myone instead of Lilliana. Heard his screams merging with his brother's.

She pulled him into her arms. "I'm right here, baby."

But for how long? What would happen if she fell in the next battle?

Myone forced him to look at her. "I'm not human, Dary. I'm a trained warrior. They won't kill me like that."

She said that, but he knew better. He'd seen so many fall. Sephiroth and others.

Even demigods.

"Caleb's destroyed," he whispered.

"I know, and I'm so sorry."

No, she didn't know. There was no way to describe what it'd done to him. His brother had been shattered to the core of his being. He would never be the same.

And Xev understood it. If he lost Myone or Jared, he wouldn't survive.

Worse? Caleb blamed him for not being there. Even though he'd done his best. Had tried to stop them. None of it mattered. It hadn't been enough. They'd broken through and killed everyone they found.

*I should have gotten here sooner.*

*Caleb's right. It's all my fault. I did this.*

Pain radiated through him, alongside the guilt that

would never give him peace. His family was whole. Caleb was alone again.

The injustice burned deep inside them both. How could he make this right?

But he knew that he couldn't. Nothing could. Caleb would never get over this.

Damn the universe. Damn their parents. Damn everything.

Myone tightened her grip on Xev as she felt him trembling in her arms. She'd never seen him like this. Like Caleb, something inside him had appeared to break. "I'm so sorry, Dary." She didn't know what else to say. Her heart was broken for Caleb.

Lil had been such a kind and gentle soul. She hadn't deserved her death.

But then, who did?

"Is there anything I can do?"

He shook his head.

So she held him, hoping to soothe some of the agony she saw in his haunted gaze.

"What are we going to do, Myone?" he whispered.

She didn't understand the question. "What do you mean?"

"How does this end?"

How she wished she had an answer. But she didn't have those powers. "I don't know."

Xev closed his eyes and pulled her against him, terrified of tomorrow. Terrified of finding her the way Caleb had found Lil. Over and over, he saw Kissare. Saw the images of war in his mind.

His panic attack was absolute. The gods were never going to let them live. There was no happy ending possible.

They wouldn't let them go. He knew that now.

They were going to lose because the gods wouldn't be happy until they made all of them bleed.

He just didn't know how bad this was going to get before it broke him, too.

## 30

---

"What are you doing?"

Xev cringed as he heard Paimon's voice in his ear. Furious, he turned on the demon and shoved him back into Skatos. "What are *you* doing here?"

Paimon spat at his feet to let him know what he thought of him. "I was sent to find you."

"By?"

"Your mother wants you."

Xev scoffed at the demon he hated more than anything, especially after everything that had been done to Caleb. He didn't believe the liar for one second. "She didn't call me."

Paimon looked past him to where Jared and Myone trained with her guards. "Why are you watching *them*?"

Xev forced himself not to show the terror that one

question evoked inside him. Last thing he needed was for this weasel to know anyone about him or his family. "None of your business."

Paimon wouldn't let it go. He looked from Xev back to his family. "What are you hiding?"

Xev kicked him back into the darkness, away from where Paimon could see Myone or Jared. "I don't owe you an explanation."

Without another word, he flew to his mother's throne room, hoping Paimon followed.

*You better be right behind me.*

He didn't stop until he was in front of Azura, inside her throne room. "Why would you send a maggot after me?"

She rolled her eyes before she took a seat on her throne. "You didn't come when I called."

He let out a bitter laugh over her lie. "You didn't call."

She blasted him. "I called."

Xev hit the wall so hard that it felt as if he'd broken every bone in his body. That ended any desire he had to argue with her. But he knew that she hadn't called him. What sick game was she playing now?

And why?

Tasting blood in his mouth, he pushed himself up from the floor. "May I ask what you needed, Mother Dearest?" Other than to knock him around for fun?

When she spoke, her voice was hysterical. "You've been seen at your father's."

That sucked all the air from his lungs in a rush, as it

was the last thing he'd expected her to say. Someone had seen him?

How would she know?

Not that it mattered—her fury was absolute.

Xev felt the pressure on his throat increasing until it cut off his windpipe. He struggled to breathe.

Azura walked slowly toward him. "I knew I had a traitor in my midst." She kicked him over. "I should have known it was you! You worthless dog! Why didn't I drown you, like your father said?" She planted her foot on his throat.

Suddenly, Noir was beside her, pulling her off him. "Before you kill the boy, give him a moment to explain."

"Why?" she demanded furiously.

"Because the news came from an enemy who wants him dead. Why would you believe them? After all, enemies never lie...do they?"

"Oh, shut up." She backed away.

Wheezing, Xev sat up and rubbed at his throat as he continued to struggle to breathe. He would ask what was wrong with her, but he knew that list was far too long to be tallied.

Noir actually had pity in his dark eyes as he held his hand out to Xev.

Was he serious?

Xev hesitated before he took it and allowed the older god to pull him to his feet. A part of him really did expect Noir to use it to sucker-punch him. He was stunned that the god refrained.

"Have you been with your father, boy?"

"I've been spying on them, yes. Have I been around Jaden? No. I hate that bastard." It was all true. He did spy on his family. Just not for the reasons they thought.

Noir gave Azura a hard stare. "Given everything the boy's been through, why would he ever be on his father's side? Think, Azura. What would he have to gain?"

"To get back at me. He hates me!"

"That's not a reason to side with his father." Noir shook his head then shoved Xev. "Get out of here, and watch your back. Your friendship with Monakribos has put a target on your forehead. Others have noticed how much Apollymi and her son favor you, and they're not happy about it."

That was scary, indeed, but nowhere as scary as Noir being nice. That was the stuff of legends and horror stories. "Why are you being nice to me?"

"I'm not stupid. As I said, you have Apollymi's favor, and more importantly, her son's. I do not want to cross my sister." He glanced over to Azura. "And neither does your mother. You should go see if they need something from you."

Xev saluted him then left, but he didn't go far. Only to the shadows so that he could watch them.

Azura was livid. "I can't believe you! How do you know he wasn't lying?"

"He has no reason to side with his father, especially after what happened with Malphas."

"Why would Paimon and Kuru lie?"

Kuru? Xev went cold at the mention of Myone's second-in-command.

Seriously? Kuru? Were they aware that Xev was here, and they wanted to screw with him?

Noir stared at her. "You're not really asking me that, are you? Paimon has hated him since the moment he was born. He's always been jealous of the fact that Daraxerxes is your son. Kuru wants to lead the Sephirii. He'd say or do anything to take that position, including working with you in order to sell out his own people so that he can kill his commander and replace her. He's giving you something he thinks you want to hear so that he can gain your trust. Daraxerxes is an easy target that Kuru knows because Daraxerxes used to live with his father, and he leads the largest contingency of Apollymi's forces outside of her son. Hell, the boy probably pissed on Kuru's leg when he was a kid, for all we know. Whatever Kuru's reasoning, I'd trust your son long before I'd trust a Sephiroth."

"I trust neither."

"Yet you were willing to kill your son over the word of the other. Maybe the boy's right to hate you."

That made her eyes flare as she glared up at Noir. "I can't believe you're defending him."

"Neither can I. And given that I am defending someone I can't stand the sight of, you might want to take a moment and think about what that says about you." With those words spoken, Noir left her.

Xev stepped back further into the shadows as he

digested what he'd overheard. He'd never known Noir to show that kind of empathy before.

Honestly, it shocked him.

Weird, especially given how much Noir hated him.

But that wasn't what was important.

He had to warn Myone about Kuru. No wonder they hadn't been able to find him. He was right there, beside her.

A traitor.

Always the one least expected. But that made sense. Kuru was privy to everything the Kalosum planned or did. Who better to have as a spy?

His heart pounding, he quickly returned to Cam's temple where Myone made her home. This time, he made sure that no one knew he was there and that no demon followed him. He'd deal with Paimon later.

Right now, he had to make sure his wife and son were taken care of.

Xev wasted no time rushing to Myone's private wing. Thankfully, she and Jared were alone in her war room, going over notes about their battle plans, when he arrived.

He took a moment to make sure no other demon, including Paimon, was anywhere around him before he stepped out of the shadows, into her room with them.

Myone looked up with a gasp. Rushing forward, she smiled at him. "What are you doing here? You said we wouldn't see you for a while."

"I learned something you need to know." He glanced to Jared. "Can we speak in private?"

While they trusted their son, Xev wasn't sure if Jared

needed to know this quite yet, which was why he was guarding his thoughts carefully on the matter. Kuru had been a lifelong friend and mentor to the boy. Last thing Xev wanted to do was hurt him.

Granted, Jared had gotten better about intruding into people's thoughts as he'd aged, but he still had a nasty habit of overhearing said thoughts, usually at the worst times.

Myone kissed Jared's head. "Why don't you go find Kuru—"

"No!" Xev snapped louder than he meant to. Then he quickly dropped his voice. "Is there anyone else for him to go to?"

"Lyla?"

He nodded.

With an arched brow, Myone turned back toward their son. "Can you confer with Lyla about our plans?"

"Sure." Jared picked up his notes and quill before he left them to their conversation.

After Myone let him out and made sure the door was locked, she returned to Xev's side. "What's going on?"

He tried to think of some easy way to tell her, but before he could stop himself, he simply blurted out, "Kuru's your traitor."

The color faded from her cheeks as she gaped at him. "Is this a joke?"

"I would never joke about something like this."

She sat down slowly as if she couldn't quite believe him. "Are you sure?"

"I heard it directly from Azura's lips. He's working with Paimon to take command from you."

A light curse left her lips. "I knew it. I mean, I didn't, but...something hasn't been right. I've suspected him at times. I just didn't trust myself. I thought I was imagining things. Being foolish. I should have listened." She stopped babbling to stare up at him. Her face paled even more. "There's only one way for him to take command, Dary."

"Kill you." Though those words came out emotionless, he wasn't calm inside. He was seething on a level that was terrifying.

What Kuru didn't understand was that Myone was the only reason their side still stood. If anything happened to her, Xev would rip down their army so fast, Kuru wouldn't even be able to say *stop* before Xev tore his head off and pinned it to a wall.

Myone was the single greatest fighter they had. But as great as she was, she was no match for Xev, Malphas, or Monakribos—or even Rubati, Kri's wife. Any more than Cam or Jaden could stand before Apollymi. Rezar might be strong enough against Cam, but not with Noir and Azura combined.

They had no one on their side who was really capable of keeping the Mavromino from victory.

All these years, Xev had been the only thing that had kept them from winning.

At times, he had guilt over it. But the one thing he knew for a fact was that if the Kalosum lost, Myone's head would be the first one the Mavromino would claim as a war prize. She was their commander.

And there would be nothing he could do to save her. As much as Kri and Apollymi valued his service, it wouldn't matter. Myone was the greatest prize, and he'd be powerless to stop them. She'd be the example they'd make to the others to show how merciless they were.

That, he could never allow.

He would do whatever he had to, to keep her safe. Even if it meant losing his life and defying all the others.

"Do they know about you?" she asked.

He started to lie to her, but he couldn't bring himself to do that. "Not exactly."

"What do you mean?"

"Paimon told them I was a traitor."

She sucked her breath in sharply. "And you live?"

Well, obviously, as he wasn't dead. But he held back the sarcasm he would pour all over his brothers. "Only because Noir didn't believe him. He knows how much Paimon hates me, so he told Azura they couldn't trust him to tell the truth where I'm concerned."

"Thank the Source." She pulled him into her arms and held him close. "You need to stay here. You can't go back."

"You know I can't do that." They'd never accept him here. His command position was too high. They'd never believe the fact that he'd been helping them the whole time.

And if they thought he had swapped sides, that would make it worse. Traitors could never be trusted.

Just as they'd never trust Jared if they had any idea who his real father was. As Jaden's son, they respected him and followed him without question. Xev would never take that away from his child. Not for anything.

No, this was for the best.

For everyone.

Myone shook her head. "We have never found out who tried to kill you."

He snorted. "Does it matter? I have many enemies, and I'm always careful. It's you who needs to be on guard. I have no evidence that you can use against Kuru. Only the conversation I overheard." Which gave her nothing she could use to remove Kuru from his position. She was stuck with a traitor by her side.

Nodding, she rubbed his arm. "I'll be careful."

Those words rang hollow to him. He didn't want to see her hurt for anything. "Don't let him at your back, Myone. I mean it."

"I won't. Don't worry."

He cupped her chin and forced her to meet his gaze. "If I lose you, I will tear down your entire army. My wrath will be immeasurable and unquenchable. I will leave nothing of the Kalosum standing...other than Jared."

Myone wanted to chastise him for that threat, but how could she? The love in those blue eyes seared her soul.

Lifting herself up on her tiptoes, she pressed her cheek to his whiskered jaw and savored the sensation of his arms. "I won't break your heart, Xev. Don't you dare break mine. I expect to spend eternity punishing you for leading your army against me."

"I'm going to hold you to that." He took her hand and kissed her palm.

Aching, Myone watched him leave her yet again. It was so unfair.

And now she had an enemy to contend with. One that left her furious. What angered her most was the fact that Jaden expected treachery from his son and trusted Kuru without question. Yet it was Kuru who was betraying him, while Xev was the only thing standing between Jaden and the defeat he feared most.

Unlike the others, Myone wasn't stupid. Even with the assistance of the Chthonians and others, she knew that they were no match for the Malachai that Apollymi had created or the Charonte who fought with her. As strong as the Sephirii were, there was something in the Malachai that was infinitely stronger.

It took everything they had in battle to hold them off. They were terrifying in their bloodlust and skill. Terrifying in their beauty.

The Sephirii were going to lose this war. And she had no idea how to stop it.

"You're troubled."

Myone jumped at the sound of her son's quiet voice behind her. For a man so large, Jared, like his father, moved with incredible stealth. She would never understand their ability to do that. Although Xev made more sense, given that he'd spent most of his life trying to avoid his mother and her minions.

Jared...

No one had ever made Jared feel threatened or unwanted. It was just a peculiar trait he'd inherited.

She smiled at her son. "I'm all right."

He gave her the same look Xev did whenever she lied about her feelings. They both knew whenever something bothered her. No matter how hard she tried to hide her feelings from them, she couldn't.

Sighing, she laughed. "Yes, my dearest love, I'm troubled by something."

He moved to sit beside her. "You know you can talk to me about it. I already know Kuru's a traitor. You can tell Xev not to worry or panic next time his name is mentioned. I've known for a while now that we couldn't trust him."

She gaped at his nonchalant disclosure, though why she was surprised, she had no idea. Jared's powers seemed to grow stronger every day. "How did you know?"

"Suri told me the first time he betrayed us."

That was even more shocking as she'd never heard of anyone's sword betraying them before. "His *sword* told you?"

Jared nodded.

"Do all our swords speak to you?" He hadn't talked about that since he was a boy. For some reason, she hadn't considered the fact that their Seraphs would still be speaking to him now.

"You told me not to talk about it to anyone, as it made everyone, even you, uncomfortable."

"Yes, it does." As did the mind reading. It was very disconcerting to have someone traipsing inside your head without your permission. She loved her boy, but she didn't want to be on guard all the time. Plus, she knew how harshly others would treat him over those powers.

Rubbing his arms uncomfortably, he refused to meet her gaze. "I try hard not to read minds or speak to the swords. But sometimes it's impossible. No matter what I do, it's just there."

She held her arms out to him. "I'm so sorry. I never meant to make you feel uncomfortable about something you can't help, baby." Baby...he was twice her size. Even so, she still saw him as that tiny little boy who used to crawl into her lap for comfort and kisses.

If only she could still scoop him up in her arms and hold him that way. All she could do now was wrap her arms around him and hug him close.

Which she did. Brushing her hand through his hair, she wished she could keep him safe from all threats.

He gave her a squeeze before he pulled back. "Suri will testify against him, if you wish her to. She doesn't want to serve a traitor any longer."

"How long have you known this?"

"Since he first aligned himself with the demon, Paimon, while he was carrying Suri. But don't worry, I've been watching him for you. Suri's been keeping me informed every time he's met with the other side. He's not done anything more than plot or give them information about us so far, which is why I hadn't mentioned it. But since Xev told you, I didn't want you to worry unnecessarily about what he'd been doing and how much harm he's caused us. I've mitigated most of it by making sure Xev had counter information."

She chuckled, grateful for how lucky they were to have Jared on their side. "You are such a good son. You should have told me about Kuru as soon as you knew."

"You have enough concerns with command. Besides, he isn't a direct threat. At least, not yet. My job is to watch after you and protect you. I'm not about to let Kuru or anyone else do you harm."

Sometimes she forgot just how young he was. He had ways about him that made him seem ancient. And then other times, she looked at him and saw nothing other than her tiny baby she'd once held in her arms. It was so hard to reconcile those two images in her mind. "I'd give anything if you didn't battle beside me."

"I know, Mom. But Takara isn't going to let me get hurt...and neither are my parents. I'm well aware of how much the two of you go out of your way to keep me safe."

She smiled at his impudence. But he was right. She'd seen Xev protect him in ways that left her husband vulnerable and exposed. She was often amazed that he hadn't outed himself in battle as Jared's protector.

Or her own. It was one of the main reasons she did her best to keep them both out of any fight where they faced Xev directly. As much as she hated for her son to fight, she had twice the risk with Xev. One, that he'd be wounded or die. Two, that he'd do something profoundly stupid to keep them safe.

As for Jared, she always kept him close in battle. As

had Caleb before his wife died. They had made sure that no one cornered him.

Now...

This was getting worse and worse.

Biting her lip, she tried to think what she needed to do. "We can't leave a traitor in our midst."

"Don't worry, Mom. The thing about traitors—they always expose themselves."

True, but not always before they did irreparable harm.

Or got someone killed.

## 31

"Xev?"

He looked up at Shadow's hesitant tone. "Yes?"

Shadow crossed Xev's bedroom to where he sat on the floor, sharpening his sword. He sank down beside him to watch him work.

Weird.

When Shadow didn't speak, Xev stopped sharpening his blade to frown at his enigmatic brother. Wow. This wasn't like Shadow. Moody sullenness was Caleb's territory. "What's going on?"

Still, Shadow sat in silence.

"Is Caleb all right?"

Shadow let out a tired breath. "He's not dead. Not that I'm sure that's a good thing where he's concerned. Pretty sure he wishes himself dead, every second of the day."

Xev hated the fact that he concurred. Caleb was in bad

shape, and there was nothing any of them could do to make it better. "Then what's wrong?"

Shadow looked up, grudgingly, before he raked his hand through his brown hair. "I think I screwed up."

That was nothing new. "Who hasn't?"

Shadow gave him a pained expression that said he didn't appreciate Xev's attempt to commiserate. "This is serious."

"I'm listening."

His brother averted his gaze. "I haven't been truthful with you."

That was also nothing new.

"Yeah, and? You've always been a bit dodgy. Nothing new with that." Shadow lived to hedge around things and never answer questions, no matter how straightforward they were. Even if he did manage to answer one, it was either vague or a half-truth.

So why would Xev be upset by his natural tendency?

"This is different, Xev."

"Okay..."

Shadow looked up from beneath his eyelashes. "I started out in this war working for Azura."

Xev felt the blood drain from his face. "What?"

"I wasn't neutral, like I told you I was. I was angry at my father and wanted to lash out at him by fighting against him. I didn't want anyone to know, especially given your true loyalties...and I want you to know that I have *never* betrayed them or you. I wouldn't do that to you."

That much Xev knew, because he was still alive. If

Shadow had betrayed him, their mother would have seen him dead.

"Where is this conversation going, Shadow?"

"I think I might have caused the death of Lil, and I feel like shit." Unshed tears shone in Shadow's eyes. "I wouldn't have hurt Caleb for anything. Or you. But I think I destroyed your brother."

Dread clenched Xev's stomach tight. "What did you do, Shadow?"

"I went to warn Caleb that I thought they might attack Lil. To try and tell him that he needed to get her to safety." Shadow drew a ragged breath. "I was there, Xev. And so was my father. I was so busy insulting him that I left without saying anything to Caleb about the ensuing attack. Why didn't I just warn him and leave? Why did I have to let my father suck me into that fight over the same bullshit we always fight about?"

Same reason they all did. It was easy to say that you wouldn't let them bait you. But they were family. They knew where to hit to set off the worst bit of temper. And for some reason, certain family members seemed to thrive on watching you bleed emotionally. "It's not your fault."

"It feels like it is."

Xev knew all about that. His own emotions kept gnawing at him. "What were you going to say to Caleb that night?"

"To watch her. I didn't have precise intel. Only that my contacts had told me they were coming for the humans."

"Same information I had."

"I guess." Shadow raked his hands through his hair

and jerked at it. "I just got so distracted when my father started insulting me."

"Easy to do." Xev had done the same thing when he'd gone to free his father.

He curled his lip. "Why do we let them get up under our skins? It's not like we're children. I'm ancient. I know what he's going to do and say. Why do I still let that bastard set me off?"

"Because no matter how old we are, there will always be a hole inside us that can only be filled by our parents. That wants their approval and love, even when we know they're rotten pieces of shit who aren't worthy of our devotion." Xev set his sword aside. "That lingering, wounded part where you keep wondering what is so wrong with me that not even my own mother could love me."

"Exactly."

Xev got up to get Shadow some water. "Look on the bright side..."

"There's a bright side?" Shadow asked.

"You don't have kids." Xev pinned his brother with a gimlet stare as he handed him a cup. "I can't explain to you the feelings I had when Jared was born. You think you hate them right now? It's nothing compared to what you feel when you see your own child and you realize just how wrong they were for what they did to you. That's the moment when you really understand that it wasn't us. We were innocent babies, and we didn't deserve them for parents. There's something wrong with them that they couldn't look at a baby and love it. Because I promise you, there is nothing on this earth I wouldn't do to keep my son safe. It wasn't you, Shadow. Azura's not capable of love. As for your father, I don't know. Maybe she bitch-slapped him one time too many when they were together."

Snorting, Shadow nodded slowly. "Jared's not mine, and I feel the same way toward him. To be such a rotten bastard yourself, you do have a good kid."

"The best."

Shadow smiled at that. "You think Caleb will ever recover?"

Xev shook his head. "I wouldn't. If anything ever happens to Myone or Jared, I'm finished. I have nothing else in this world that I care about or value, and that includes me. They're the only thing that keeps me going."

"And I have nothing at all."

"You have me and Caleb."

Shadow rudely scoffed at that. "Great. Two hemorrhoids. No wonder I can't sit still."

Laughing, Xev sheathed his sword and put it away. "So who are you fighting for now?"

"Same side you are."

"Both?"

Shadow nodded. "But when the storm comes, I'll be on the same side you really want to win."

Kalosum. Because Apollymi, Noir, and Azura would destroy Xev's son and wife if they won. Whatever he did, Xev could never allow that to happen.

"We *are* doing the right thing, aren't we?"

Shadow shrugged. "That's the worst part, brother. No one knows until it's too late."

## 32

"Myone? I need to see you in my war room. Could you follow me?"

She didn't like the ominous note in Jaden's voice, at all. He rarely spoke to her, but normally when he did, it was with a much kinder tone.

She handed her practice sword off to Jared, who had an equally concerned scowl on his face.

"Don't go, Mom," he whispered to her.

That sent a chill down her spine. "It'll be fine, baby."

But the look in his amber eyes made her heart pound.

She offered him a kind smile before she followed after Jaden.

What in the name of the Source could have happened?

As soon as she was inside the room, Jaden used his powers to shut and seal the door behind her.

That not only made her jump, it caused her stomach to cramp. "What's going on?"

"We have a situation."

She'd figured that much. "We always have a situation."

He pressed his hand to the bridge of his nose. "This one is a little more delicate than normal."

She moved to sit, as she had a feeling from his tone that it wasn't something she wanted to hear while standing. "And that is?"

"My siblings are beginning to speak of a truce."

Relief rushed through her. That was it? After all these years, could it be? Could the end finally be so close?

She wanted to turn a cartwheel!

"That's wonderful!"

He shook his head, causing her relief to die quickly.

"That's *not* wonderful," he said, drawing the words out. "Not for you."

There was that horrible tone again. Just what were they proposing? "How so?"

Jaden let out a tired sigh as he refused to meet her gaze. "When I took you as my wife, I was only trying to protect Jared and Xev. I didn't think ahead to this day."

That much she already knew. So she didn't understand where he was going with his thoughts. "And?"

"Because I married you, Noir and Azura are demanding your life."

Her breath caught in her throat. Yes, she was very grateful she'd taken a seat. "What? Why?"

"We killed Kissare over Braith. They're demanding we do the same with you."

The room tilted around her. "What about Apollymi?"

"She hasn't said a word. But the other two won't be reasoned with. They say that as long as you're alive, they won't consider a truce, as it's not fair to allow my happiness while Braith suffers."

Myone felt as if she'd vomit. "I see."

Forget Kuru. He wasn't her greatest threat after all.

Xev had been right. It all came back to the gods. They were never going to let them live in peace. No matter what, they would always strike out against them.

Trying to keep herself together, she cleared her throat. "If I were gone, would they consider a truce then?"

He hesitated. "Not exactly. They just said they'd be willing to come to the table...provided you were dead."

"So even if I die, they might not end it."

"That's my fear."

She sat there, trying to imagine what this would do to Xev. But then she knew. It would destroy him. Just as Lil had destroyed Caleb. He was barely functional these days.

But there was a bigger problem.

"If I'm gone, Xev will attack the Kalosum without restraint."

"Not with Jared in charge, he won't."

That was where Jaden was wrong. Understandable, since he didn't have a mother. He had no idea of the bond she shared with her child.

She met his gaze levelly. "My lord, listen to me. If they order my death, Jared will help him destroy your army." Like his father, he would tear down their forces and demand the gods appease his righteous fury. "I doubt if even the gods would be able to pull them back from it."

Jaden hadn't thought of that. But she made a valid point. Caleb was only controllable because he didn't have a specific enemy to go after, nor an army to control. His army was now under Kri's control.

Xev and Jared were different.

*Very* different.

Each of them commanded a considerable force. One they wouldn't hesitate to use to avenge the woman in front of him.

Jaden offered her a kind smile. "Forget I said anything. I will make sure to let Cam and Rezar know that we won't consider their terms." Leaning down, he kissed her on top of the head and left her alone.

But his mind spun with the reality he needed to convey to his siblings. That this wasn't the solution they were looking for, and if they pressed it...

It would not end the way they hoped.

Right now, he had one sibling in particular he needed to speak to.

As expected, he found Apollymi alone in her bower. Dressed in a black gown, she was the epitome of cold grace. Her white hair was held back from her face by a black diadem.

She was beauty incarnate.

And lethal beyond words.

"Why are you here?" Her voice was as brittle and icy as her heart. "Hasn't anyone bothered to inform you? We're at war."

He ignored her sarcasm. "We've been discussing a truce."

She scoffed. "You and the worthless ones have been discussing a truce. I've not even considered one."

"Then you're content to continue?"

She raked him with a bitter stare. "You know my terms. I will not allow the death of my son. I will see you all burned before one hair on his head is harmed."

Yet they wanted the death of his grandchild and expected him to offer Jared and Myone up as if they meant nothing. "You are the only reasonable one on your side, Apollymi. How do we settle this?"

She shrugged with a nonchalance that really pissed him off. "Cam and Rezar require that I put down my Malachai forces. I have agreed to that. But only if you put down your own pit vipers so that they can no longer threaten my child."

"I cannot sanction the death of Jared any more than you'll agree to killing off Monakribos."

She drummed her long fingernails against the arm of her chair. "There's only one thing our brother and sister will accept from you in trade for that."

His own freedom. He would have to agree to subjugate himself to their will.

For eternity.

Jaden wanted to scream out in violent denial. The mere thought of being enslaved by them drove him to madness. But if he didn't agree, they'd demand Jared die alongside all the Sephirii.

Myone's blood damned her son. And it damned him, too.

There was nothing he could do to save her.

"What about Xev?" he asked.

"What about him?"

"I can't let him die, either." For better or worse, Xev was his son. In spite of what the boy thought, Jaden *did* love him. And he did want to protect him.

In the end, Azura had gotten what she wanted most— A way to control Jaden because he wasn't capable of completely turning his back on his child.

*Damn me for it.*

"There's no reason Xev has to die," Apollymi said. "He's a god, not a Sephiroth."

True, but Myone was right. This would kill him. He'd go after the gods with a fury unimaginable.

And he'd never forgive him for making this pact.

*What choice do I have?*

This had dragged on for far too long. Too many lives had been lost. They'd annihilated worlds. It was time to put a stop to the waste. Time to rebuild.

The only question was...how were they going to put down their armies? How would they ever clean up this mess.

And how would he break this news to his son, who already hated him?

"Tell them I'll do it."

## 33

Dressed in his battle armor, Caleb joined Jared at the front of their forces. They were heading out for battle.

Myone was about to place her helmet on her head when she heard Cam call out to them. She turned toward the petite goddess with a frown. "My lady?"

Cam motioned to Jared. "I need your son to stay behind with me."

Myone was confused by her order. "Is something wrong?"

"We've been warned that there might be an attack here. I'm keeping a small group of Mimoroux back, just in case."

Xev hadn't mentioned that to her. And he wasn't the only spy they had. Surely one of them would have known about such an attack and warned them.

But then, it also wasn't uncommon for their enemies

to lead multiple attacks at once. Maybe they'd been unable to get word to them.

So she inclined her head to her goddess. "Jared, stay with Lady Cam."

He didn't question his orders. "Be careful, Mom."

"And you." She blew him a kiss, then put her helm on her head and led her forces toward the battlefield.

"Monakribos?"

Xev paused with his friend at Apollymi's call. Leave it to her to stop them as they were heading out to fight. She often called her son back for a quick hug and kiss.

With an irritable sigh, Kri turned to face her. "Yes, Mother?"

"Anat is leading this battle. I have another one for you."

Xev went cold at those words. Another battle? What the hell was going on?

Kri scowled in confusion. "Pardon?"

"Grab your forces and head to another site."

Shrugging, he pulled at Xev's arm. "All right. Guess we're off to—"

"He's to go with his sister."

Xev didn't move as he heard those words. Apollymi had *never* sent Kri off without Xev by his side.

What was going on?

Kri exchanged a baffled frown with him before he turned to face his mother. "Why?"

"Azura commanded it. She wants him to guard Anat's back."

Since when? And when had Apollymi ever approved such a thing?

Something wasn't right.

Xev felt it with every part of his being. Did they know he was a traitor?

Kri appeared as baffled as he felt. "This is weird, right?" he whispered.

"Little bit."

"I don't like being separated."

Neither did Xev. He had a really bad feeling about it. But he had no choice other than to obey Apollymi. She was his commander.

But in spite of his misgivings, he clapped the boy on his back. "I'm sure it'll be fine."

Kri nodded. "Meet me for drinks later."

"You got it. We'll celebrate our victories." Xev left him to return to his mother's realm so that he could meet up with Anat, who appeared as thrilled as he was at the prospect of fighting by his side.

It was made even better by the fact that she rode with her husband, Mot. Xev sneered at the death god, who sneered back.

No love lost there. They would always hate each other.

Didn't matter. Battles weren't supposed to be fun, and they weren't always fought with friends.

Xev rolled his shoulders and flew in formation behind the rest of their troops. Sooner they got this over with, the sooner he'd be able to see Myone and Jared.

At least, that was his thought until they reached the battlefield.

It'd been a long time since he'd seen numbers this large for one fight. There were demons and Sephirii lined up everywhere. The heat of the sun was scorching against his armor as sweat beaded on his forehead and back. The thunder of wings and the clashing of steel against breastplates echoed in his ears, as did the war cry of a thousand angry warriors.

War drums beat in time to the pounding of his heart. And when those drums stopped, the shout went out for them to charge.

Only it wasn't a normal charge.

When he went forward to attack, only one other flew forward from the other side.

Myone.

Recognition hit them both at the same time. As well as the fact that the rest of their armies had remained inert.

What the hell?

No sooner had that thought gone through his mind than both sides opened fire on the two of them. He saw the smile on Anat's face as she gleefully took aim at him, and then Myone.

Arrows flew at them so thick that it darkened the sky. They pierced his flesh and hers. He rushed to Myone, trying his best to protect her.

It was impossible.

As soon he had her in his arms, the others attacked. War broke out between their armies, and a full melee ensued.

They landed hard against the ground. Myone crawled over to him and held Xev against her while he, weakened by blood loss, tried to wipe the streaks from her face.

"I'm so sorry, Dary."

He laid his head down in her lap. "I failed you."

"No. Never."

Xev struggled to breathe as guilt and grief shredded him. "I love you."

"Love you more." Her grip in his hair weakened as she lay against his chest.

Suddenly, her troops seized him from her arms and dragged him away, even as life faded from her eyes.

"No!" he screamed. "No! Don't let her die alone!" It was the utmost cruelty. "She's your leader! Myone!"

They didn't care. After all she'd done for them. All the battles she'd fought and won, none of them spared her a second look.

Throwing his head back, he cried out as agony washed over him. This couldn't be the end.

His heart broken, he expected them to hand him over to his mother.

Instead, he was taken to his aunt, Cam, who sat in her temple with smug satisfaction marring her beautiful face.

They dumped him at her feet. He could barely focus his gaze through the tears and blood that blinded him.

Why couldn't he just die?

There was no pity in Cam's countenance. "Do you understand your punishment?"

Xev shook his head. How could loving someone be wrong? What had the two of them done to warrant this?

Never in his life had he hated his family more than he did right then.

He should have led his army against them and killed them all when he'd had the chance.

Now, it was too late. He had nothing left.

"Just kill me." There was no life without Myone.

And before he could move, he felt a searing pain over his body unlike anything he'd ever known. It was a binding spell for his powers. Crying out, he watched as his entire body was altered. His hair, eyebrows...everything.

Words appeared on his flesh—to make sure the binding spell lasted.

He was cursed even worse than he'd been on the day he was born.

Then his mother and father appeared. With the coldness in his father's eyes that he was used to, Jaden sheared his wings from his back.

None of it mattered.

Compared to the pain of losing Myone, it was nothing.

They had finally broken him. His body might live, but inside he was as cold and dead as his parents.

**34**

―――――

Furious and heartbroken, Jared flew to his grandfather. "What have you done?"

Jaden refused to meet his gaze. "What I had to do."

"You let them kill my mother."

"You live, boy. Be grateful."

Tears welled in Jared's eyes as he struggled not to lash out. Never in his life had he wanted to kill as much as he did then. Finally, he understood the destructive part of his father's powers. What it took for his father not to be like his grandmother.

Never had he respected Xev more.

"Where's my father?"

"Where we can't help him."

That emotionless tone only served to anger him more. After everything his father had done for them. Risked for them.

And this was how he was treated?

"How could you?"

"I had no choice. I did what I had to."

*Keep saying that, old man.* Maybe one day, someone might believe Jaden's lie.

Jared growled, and when he did, a surge went through the room, so powerful it splintered every piece of furniture and shattered the glass.

Jaden shot to his feet. "How dare you?"

"How. Dare. You! They were my parents!"

For the first time, he saw a crack in his grandfather's façade. "Xev was *my* son. I know you don't understand that. Be grateful you don't." He cleared his throat and returned to the cold, emotionless beast Jared was learning to hate. "Believe me when I say that the one thing both of them would want is for you to be safe. I've done that. It was the only gift I could give them."

Gift? Was he insane?

How was this a *gift*? He'd robbed Jared of the only thing that mattered.

"I hate you!"

Jaden laughed bitterly. "I assure you, it's a pittance compared to what I feel for myself."

His breathing ragged, Jared glared at him. "Release my father."

Jaden shook his head. "I can't do it. I'm not the one who holds him."

"Who does?"

"The Mavromino." The three dark Primals.

*Fine.*

Jared left him and immediately went to his icy, blue grandmother. He would do whatever it took to free his father from her clutches. Because of their cruelty, his mother was gone. He wasn't about to lose his father, too.

Without a second thought, he descended into Azura's shiny realm, where she was gloating with her brother, Noir.

The sight of them celebrating sickened Jared.

Their success had come at the expense of his family. It wasn't right. And he wanted justice.

No, he wanted revenge.

At least his presence succeeded in wiping the smiles off their repugnant faces.

"What are you doing here, brat?" Azura asked as soon as she saw him.

"Where's Daraxerxes?"

She didn't answer.

Instead, Noir leaned over to loudly whisper in her ear. "I thought all the Sephirii were supposed to be gone? Why's this one here?"

Azura sighed heavily. "They're not all gone. Most of them are still around."

"That's not good."

"I know, brother. Apparently, they're hard to kill." She tsked at Jared. "And you're their leader now."

A bad feeling went through him. What was her point in saying that? "I am."

"You want to save your father, you say? Then step over here, dear child. Let us chat a bit. There may be something you can do after all."

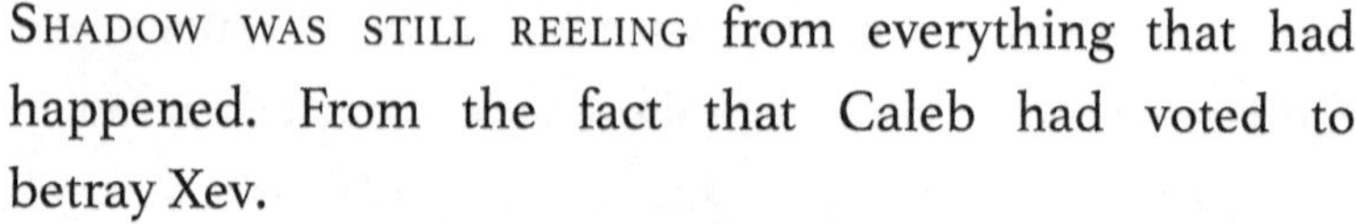

SHADOW WAS STILL REELING from everything that had happened. From the fact that Caleb had voted to betray Xev.

"What were you thinking?"

"He didn't save Lil!"

In other words, Caleb hadn't been thinking. He'd been hurting. Lashing out.

Poor Xev that he'd been caught in that crossfire of pain.

That was the worst part about grief and anger. No rational thought. All the best intentions went to hell, along with common sense.

When the dust settled, all that was left was regret.

Now Shadow was left to try to pick up the pieces. His family had been torn asunder by all their combined stupidity, and he didn't know what to do.

It just couldn't end like this.

Not after everything they'd all been through. Everything they'd all lost.

"Shadow?"

He flinched at the sound of Jared's voice. The pain there made his own chest ache. Sighing, he left Caleb and went to find Jared alone in his room, sitting in the fading light.

"Hey."

Jared offered him a tenuous smile. There was so much pain that Shadow wished he could take it away. As much as he'd lost, Jared had lost more. He'd had parents who loved him. Protected him.

Shadow had no idea what that felt like.

His parents would have thrown him to the demons and not thought twice.

"I need help, Uncle."

"Anything." There was nothing he wouldn't do for Jared, especially now.

"Azura wants me to gather up the Seraph swords for her."

Shadow burst out laughing. Until he realized the boy wasn't joking. The kid actually meant it. "You're serious?"

Jared nodded. "But I don't trust her."

He was wise beyond his years. "Good call, that. Unless it involves pain or cruelty, she's not exactly reliable."

Jared nodded in agreement. "What can I do?"

Shadow hesitated. Both sides were going to put down their soldiers. They'd already started. And there was nothing that could be done to stop it.

So much for a truce.

But those swords, they were valuable. If they went into the wrong hands...

Game over.

For all the good the Seraph swords could do, they could do an equal amount of evil. It all depended on the hand that wielded them.

"Do you trust me?"

Jared hesitated. "My father always has. I know you're a good man."

Shadow scoffed at praise he knew he didn't deserve. "No, I'm not. But I *am* loyal."

Jared wrinkled his nose. "You're not the monster you think you are."

Shadow didn't feel like arguing. Especially over something he knew wasn't true. He was as corrupt as the bitch that had birthed him. "I'll help you hide the swords from Azura. Maybe we can use them to barter for your father."

"Thank you."

Shadow followed him. He wasn't sure how they were going to get something so personal from the Sephirii. His understanding was that those swords were impossible to separate from their owners.

So he took Jared into the shadows that would give them access to the Sephirii and where they kept their weapons.

As carefully as they could, they infiltrated the private rooms of the owners.

One by one, Jared crept to the swords. Every time he touched one, it would light up. Then he'd run his hand over the sword, and it seemed to calm down. The light would dim, then go out.

Shadow stood in amazement of his nephew as Jared brought him the swords, one at a time.

Until they came down to Jared's personal weapon in his own room. He kept her on a small altar in his bedroom. Pausing in front of the sword, he glanced to Shadow. "This is Takara. She's the strongest of them."

"She's beautiful."

"Yes, she is." He caressed her as if she was the most

valuable object in existence. "Can we duplicate them so that the Primals won't know?"

Nodding, Shadow used his powers. It wasn't often he did this. Been awhile since he'd needed this skill. Caleb was actually better at it than he was. But he wasn't about to ask for *his* help. In the mood he was in lately, Caleb might stab them just for asking. Hopefully, this would be enough to pass Azura's inspection.

He handed the fake swords to Jared. "What else do you need?"

Sadness darkened the boy's eyes. He looked as if he'd be sick. "I have to betray my soldiers."

"What?"

Tears gathered in his eyes. "She said she'd kill my father if I refused. If I don't put them down, she'll send my father's head to me."

Shadow felt his stomach drop. He couldn't imagine having to make that choice, especially at the age Jared was. How would he be able to live with it?

Either way, he was damned.

The boy had no idea what would come. The guilt that would haunt him.

It seemed easy.

He loved his father. Save him.

But this...

It would scar him in ways he couldn't imagine. He would be stigmatized for eternity.

Because he loved his father and wanted to save him.

No one should have to do this.

Damn his mother for it. This cruelty was beyond the

pale. The saddest part? It wouldn't be any better if Jared sacrificed his father. Either way, he was damned. That was Azura's sick plan.

And in that moment, Shadow's fury took root deep inside. He wasn't going to let her get away with this. She'd destroyed too many of them. There was no way he'd stand by and see her loose in the world.

She had to be stopped. A cancer like her shouldn't be left to spread its disease wherever it wanted to go.

Shadow had promised Xev that he'd protect his family, and he'd failed.

The least he could do was get vengeance for his brother.

Justice for Myone.

"I'll help you, Jared. But you need to do something for me."

"What?"

He gave the boy a hard stare. "I need some of your father's blood."

"I don't understand."

"I know." Shadow smiled at him. "But you will."

And Azura would spend eternity remembering this moment, her cruelty, and, regretting that she'd ever crossed Xev and his bloodline.

## 35

Xev knew the instant the Malachai demons were put down. Because they were a part of him, he could feel it soul deep. Each death caused a physical pain to him.

Just as he knew the moment Rubati had died. Kri's sounds of anguish were as loud as the screams Xev's soul had made when he watched Myone pass away.

He also knew when the last Sephiroth died, cursing his son for his betrayal.

But at least Jared lived.

That was Xev's sole consolation. Even though he couldn't see him. He knew Jared was there. He endured.

It was enough.

At least, that was the lie Xev told himself while he lay imprisoned in darkness. This was his new existence, bleak and hopeless. He was the Šarru-Dara—the blood slave who served the last remaining Malachai. Even though he'd once commanded the largest legion of the Malachai's demonic army, he was now nothing.

And there was only one Malachai left.

Apollymi's deranged son.

All the others had been put down like rabid dogs. Because that was the brutal, hate-filled pact the Primals had made. From this day forward, there would be only one Malachai.

And one Sephiroth. Jared.

Balance.

It was a bargain Xev could live with.

Even though he would remain eternally enslaved to the Malachai, just as his father would be enslaved to his mother. No peace for any of them.

Xev would laugh, had he not lost his own sanity in the process.

No, not his sanity. His heart and soul. He no longer lived. He just existed. His only happiness came in the knowledge that Shadow had used his blood to entrap his mother and Noir in Azmodea—the one realm she despised above all others.

Maybe there was some justice in the universe.

She'd sold them all out, and in the end, she wasn't happy either.

Nor was she free.

And it was *his* blood that had damned and trapped her. He could take some comfort in that.

None of them had gotten what they wanted.

They'd all been equally screwed.

And for what?

Xev had no idea. He wanted to die, but there was no death for him. Only an existence of suffering that would never, ever end.

## 36

---

NEW ORLEANS, 2055

Xev wasn't sure why he was meeting Shadow at Sanctuary today. Other than it'd become a bit of habit for the two of them for a while now. There was just something about the shape-shifter bar and grill that had a homey feel to it.

Ever since the last Malachai, Ambrose, had freed him from his slavery while Ambrose was in high school, and had allowed him to live as a person and not an animal, Sanctuary had become a home base for many of their old comrades.

And it was a very special place for Ambrose, whose mother used to work here.

Cherise Gautier.

Xev's granddaughter.

He still couldn't get over the way things in life worked out. How life always seemed to take him to places he didn't want to go.

Sometimes the trip was absolutely abysmal, and other times, it was shockingly wonderful.

Cherise and Ambrose had been two of those amazing surprises. Jared had fathered a beautiful little girl who, in turn, had become the mother of the latest Malachai.

Ambrose Gautier.

His grandson.

The sole hope humanity had for survival.

It still boggled his mind whenever he thought about. All these centuries later, hundreds of Malachai later.

The great-great-great-great-great-great-great-times thousands of grandsons of Monakribos was his biological grandson.

Life was weird and it was messy.

And he'd never understand it. But at least he no longer dreaded living. In spite of the pain and misery of his past, he'd found a reason to keep going.

Now, he actually looked forward to life. To watching Ambrose grow and mature.

To hopefully keeping him from turning evil and destroying the world.

Xev inclined his head to Remi, who was at the door. Though not quite as tall as Xev, Remi was almost as lethal. Xev definitely wouldn't want to tangle with the WereBear. Especially given the fact that Remi didn't have much in the way of a sense of humor.

"Hey, Xev," Aimee said as soon as she saw him. "Shadow's in the booth in the corner, waiting for you." She pointed the way for him.

"Thanks." He headed for his brother.

This time of day, there weren't many patrons, which was fine by him. He didn't really like crowds. It reminded him too much of battle.

Shadow already had a soda on the table, along with pretzels, waiting for him. "You're late."

That was normal, actually.

"Sorry. Ambrose cornered me before I could get past him." Xev's grandson liked to talk. And this morning, he'd been particularly chatty. Not that Xev minded. There was nothing he loved more than spending time with him.

Well, other than spending time with Jared.

"All good." Shadow looked past Xev, toward the door. "Caleb decided not to come with you?"

Xev shook his head. "He wanted to sleep in. He was up late with Aeron, Simi, Vawn, and Kaziel last night, watching movies."

"That sounds perfectly awful."

Wasn't his party, either. Especially given the weird films they chose. "Yeah. It was something called *Killer Ninjas from Outer Space*."

"That a thing?"

"Apparently. Involved a lot of profanity...although that might have been Caleb complaining about Vawn and Kaziel talking over the actors and spilling spoilers every few minutes. Both of those make him crazy."

Shadow laughed, then sobered. "So how's Ambrose?"

"Slipping." Which was concerning for all of them. The last thing they wanted was for Ambrose to turn full Malachai and end the world they'd been trying to save all these centuries past.

A tic started in Shadow's jaw. "The signs are aligning. It's going to get ugly."

"Yeah. Been through enough nightmares. I really don't want to live through any more."

"Agreed."

Xev took a drink as he reflected on all the centuries they'd lived. All the Malachai who'd come and gone.

Mostly, he remembered the one who'd started it all so long ago. Sometimes, he saw Monakribos reflected in Ambrose. Heard his voice in the wind.

So much had changed. Jared was now friends with the Malachai he'd once been at war with. They worked together to keep the balance and peace.

War did make strange bedfellows.

*Bedfellows.*

That word conjured an image in Xev's mind that he'd spent eternity cherishing.

Myone. She'd been the only woman for him. In all this time, he'd never found anyone else. Never wanted anyone else.

Once you had perfection, it was hard to settle.

Closing his eyes, he regretted losing her most of all. If he could have one wish...

"Dary?"

Xev's breath caught at a nickname he hadn't heard in centuries. Only one person had ever used it. Mostly because he'd have killed anyone else. But from her...

He'd loved the sound of it.

"Dary?" There it was again. More insistent this time.

Were his memories really that powerful?

He felt the air stir beside him.

No. It couldn't be.

Too afraid to look, Xev opened his eyes and met Shadow's gaze. His brother's features were as pale as his had to be.

There was no way for her to be here. Not after all this time.

"Myone?" Shadow whispered.

Xev turned his head to look up.

It really was her...sort of. Maybe?

Like him, she had no wings and her skin was a deep caramel instead of gold. But everything else was identical.

Same dark hair. Blue eyes.

She looked just like his Myone.

Unable to believe it, he slid out of the booth to stand by her side. His hands shaking, he cupped her face. "Is it you?"

Biting her lip as she used to do whenever she was unsure or nervous, she nodded.

"How?"

Tears filled her eyes. "Your father pulled me off the field when I was wounded."

What? His mind went back to that time he'd relived for so many centuries that it was forever etched on his soul. To this day, he could see her there, dying. Feel the soreness in his throat as he screamed out for her. For them to kill him.

"I saw you die," he whispered.

"I got to her in time and healed her. Then I hid her to keep them from knowing she lived."

Xev looked past Myone to see his father a short distance away. "I don't understand."

"I had to wait until it was safe to wake her from the trance I had to put her in. I'm sorry it took so long. Even sorrier that I couldn't tell you or Jared before this."

Was he serious? "You bastard!" Xev started for him, but Myone caught him.

"Dary!"

She was right...and yet he wanted to gut his father where he stood. Why had Jaden put him through all of this when one word would have saved him?

*What's done is done.*

She was with him now. So he settled on what was most important—he pulled her against him and held her tight, grateful for this miracle. It didn't matter how she'd come to be here. All that mattered was that she was with him now.

She'd said it best all those centuries ago when he first saw his son. *Don't let the past screw up his future.*

This time, he was going to make sure he didn't.

"Where's Jared?" she asked.

"Mom?"

Xev turned at the hesitant voice. He barely had time to get out of the way before his son almost ran him over to get to her. Laughing, he watched as Jared lifted her clear of the floor and turned in a circle.

Then Xev met his father's gaze. "Did you really have to wait so long?"

Jaden shrugged. "I'm a bastard. No one has ever argued that. But at least I'm not as bad as Azura."

He had a point. And right now, Xev was too happy to hate. For all his faults, Jaden had saved her and kept her safe for them.

For that, Xev could forgive his father anything. Sadly, they'd all screwed up so badly trying to protect each other.

But at least they'd tried.

No one could argue that. Now they were together, and that was all that mattered. He would spend the rest of eternity making sure nothing ever divided them again.

After all, family was chaos. It was fighting. It was important.

And it was everything.

No. It was the only thing.

# ALSO BY SHERRILYN KENYON
## (LISTED IN CORRECT READING ORDER)

## NICKCHRONICLES

*Infinity*

*Invincible*

*Infamous*

*Inferno*

*Illusion*

*Instinct*

*Invision*

*Intensity*

SHADOWS OF FIRE

*Sabotage*

*Last Christmas*

NEW TITLES

Eve of Destruction

Born of Blood

Dark Places

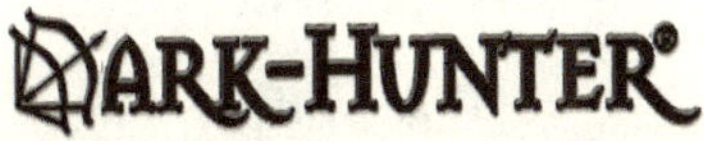

*Night Pleasures*

*Night Embrace*

*Dance with the Devil*

*Kiss of the Night*

*Night Play*

*Sword of Darkness*

*Knight of Darkness*

*Seize the Night*

*Sins of the Night*

*Unleash the Night*

*Dark Side of the Moon*

*The Dream-Hunter*

*Devil May Cry*

*Upon the Midnight Clear*

*Dream Chaser*

*Acheron*

*One Silent Night*

*Dream Warrior*

*Bad Moon Rising*

*No Mercy*

*Retribution*

*The Guardian*

*The Dark-Hunter Companion*

*Time Untime*

*Styxx*

*Dark Bites*

*Son of No One*

*Dragonbane*

*Dragonmark*

*Dragonsworn*

*Stygian*

*Deadmen Walking*

*Death Doesn't Bargain*

*At Death's Door*

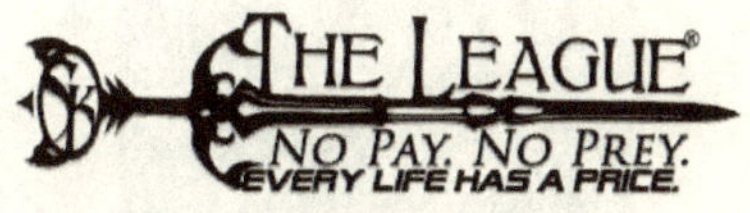

*Born of Night*

*Born of Fire*

*Born of Ice*

*Fire & Ice*

*Born of Shadows*

*Born of Silence*

*Cloak & Silence*

*Born of Fury*

*Born of Defiance*

*Born of Betrayal*

*Born of Legend*

*Born of Vengeance*

*Born of Blood*

*Born of Trouble*

*Born of Darkness*

<u>Lords of Avalon</u>

(written as Kinley MacGregor)

Sword of Darkness

Knight of Darkness

# ABOUT THE AUTHOR

Defying all odds is what #1 New York Times and international bestselling author Sherrilyn Kenyon does best. Rising from extreme poverty as a child that culminated in being a homeless mother with an infant, she has become one of the most popular and influential authors in the world (in both adult and young adult fiction), with dedicated legions of fans known as Paladins–thousands of whom proudly sport tattoos from her numerous genre-defying series.

Since her first book debuted in 1993 while she was still in college, she has placed more than 80 novels on the New York Times list in all formats and genres, including manga and graphic novels, and has more than 70 million books in print worldwide. Her current series include: Dark-Hunters®, Chronicles of Nick®, Deadman's Cross™, Black Hat Society™, Nevermore™, Silent Swans™, Lords of Avalon® and, The League®.

Over the years, her Lords of Avalon® novels have been adapted by Marvel, and her Dark-Hunters® and Chronicles of Nick® are New York Times bestselling manga and comics and are #1 bestselling adult coloring books.

Join her and her Paladins online at QueenofAllShadows.com and www.facebook.com/mysherrilyn.

www.ingramcontent.com/pod-product-compliance
Lightning Source LLC
Chambersburg PA
CBHW022036120726
47899CB00004BA/1191